Fishing with Faith

by

Gina Myers DeVries

DORRANCE PUBLISHING CO., INC.
PITTSBURGH, PENNSYLVANIA 15222

Dorrance Publishing Co., Inc.
701 Smithfield Street
Pittsburgh, PA 15222
Visit our website at www.dorrancebookstore.com

ISBN: 978-1-4809-0199-5
eISBN: 978-1-4809-0469-9

Fishing with Faith

A novel

by

Gina Myers DeVries

To my husband, Doug,
Daughter, Sarah,
Son, Andrew,
And friend, Chelsea, thank you for believing in me. To my big brother,
Chuck, thank you for teaching me it's not just all that you come to know in
your life; it's what you choose to hang on to, and what you then choose to
let go of, that will make all the differences.

Part One

One of my first memories, I am sitting in my wood highchair. At the table sat Dad, Mama, brothers' Will and Sam. They are all laughing at me because I am taking the long pieces of spaghetti and trying to make a necklace around my chubby baby neck. I keep saying, "Pretty, pretty." I am wearing a simple dress made from a red and yellow feed sack, no shoes, and a yellow bow attached to what little blonde hair I had.

The big picture window in our dining room shows the trees are full of color and raining yellow, orange, and red leaves. We lived in Michigan, so it had to be about the end of October.

I was born January 16, 1958, so I would be nine months old, and that's about the time Mama said I started talking, forming words that turned into sentences. I have a lot of memories of my childhood and they come to me easily. I have had this ability to remember events in my life by the clothes or shoes I was wearing at the time. I can close my eyes right now and see that red and yellow dress. And I know there's a yellow bow in my hair because I would pull it out, and Mama would patiently put it back in, throughout our supper of spaghetti.

Dad

L et me give some background scenery to how we, the Bakker family, got to that autumn day and beyond. First up would be my dad. Every child should have a daddy like mine. John, or Johnny, what Mama would call him, is the most kindhearted, agreeable, faithful man you could come upon. He has been, and still is, the calm of our family. You can go to Dad with anything, and he will make problems seem not so bad, or good things seem better than you thought.

John was born April 13, 1933 to Todd and Mary Bakker. Grandpa Todd owned a big dairy farm in Iowa, and John was the youngest of four boys who all wanted to be farmers like their dad, except John. My dad had a different calling. From a very young age, John was always making something out of wood. Grandpa Todd had a workshop off one of the barns, and after school and chores, that's where you would find John, fixing the wood structure of the barns, or making his mother a new kitchen chair. She would say, "Boys can be so rough with furniture." By the time John was twelve, he had made his own wooden bed, and at fourteen, he made the large dining room table that is still as solid as the first time his brothers and parents ate from it.

One day, a Bible salesman came calling to Todd and Mary's home, seeing all the fine furniture John had made. He told John his brother had a furniture factory in Grand Rapids, Michigan, that could use him. John was just seventeen, graduated high school two days before, and was praying for an adventure.

John packed a small suitcase and took the ninety dollars he had saved. His father, Todd, gave him fifty dollars, and his mother, Mary, held back the tears as she made beef sandwiches for his trip. She would make sure to put paper, pencils, envelopes, and a few stamps in his sack. His oldest brother, Joe, took him to the bus station in Des Moines, and he was hired end of the week in Grand Rapids, Michigan, in 1950 making furniture.

That Bible salesman had a good family in Michigan, and one of his sisters, Anne, and her husband, Bill, rented John a room in their home. Bill and Anne had two girls that had both married that year before, and it wasn't long before they both loved John like a son. Bill was so impressed with John's work ethics. My dad has never been shy about his faith, how grateful he was in knowing God and talking to God every day. Dad has always said, "Talk to God every day, and everything else just falls into place."

Bill would become an important person in John's life. My brother Will is named after Bill, who became "Big Bill" to us children.

John settled easily in Grand Rapids. He was likeable, and made friends around town as well as the furniture factory. He would fix furniture on the side after work, riding his bike with his tools in a knapsack on his back. He would write home every week, telling his family he loved his work, was eating well, and making enough to save. He told how Bill was helping him find a truck before winter and he had taken up fishing with his best friend, Sam.

Sam worked alongside Dad at the factory. Dad had never gone fishing in Iowa, but the first time Sam took him to a nearby lake to "drown some worms," John was hooked on fishing. My brother Sam is named after Dad's best friend who became Uncle Sam to us children.

Just before John's nineteenth birthday, he would tell Sam he was on the lookout for a "soul mate to share his life with." John would tell Sam, "If you talk to God, put your faith to work, then everything will fall into place."

Sam loved hanging out with John, and would tease him a little about his talking to God so often. But Sam also saw how everything in John's life so far was working so well, that Sam took up talking to God a little more often.

One day at work, Sam had told John about this Bible class at his mother's church that he would attend occasionally. He said, "There are these two girls who are both pretty and sweet. I was thinking on setting up something for the four of us, what do you think?" So, for John's nineteenth birthday, Sam would set the date for the four of them to go to the local A&W for root beer floats, and then catch the movies at the Civic.

Sam had told John he had his eyes on Patricia, and he sat John up with Betty, who Sam would say was just as pretty. Well, that all changed when John was introduced to Patricia, or Patty, as Dad always called her. Sam knew he better go for Betty, because Patty was just what John had prayed for. He had found himself his soul mate.

Mom

Mama was what you could say was very pretty. But ask my dad and he'd say, "She's the picture of human beauty." Patricia May was born May 11, 1934 to Allen and Rose Doyle, who also had my aunt Sara Mae, two years older than Mama. Allen was Irish descent, with bright red hair. Rose, being blonde, made both girls have strawberry blonde hair, when they were young, and sky blue eyes, with fair skin. Patricia had the same smile her mother Rose had, where if she was smiling big, her top gums would show.

She was a good girl with a lot of common sense. She had graduated high school that spring, took some nursing classes that fall, and worked as a nurse's aide at Saint Mary's hospital in Grand Rapids that winter.

Johnny and Patty pretty much spent all their spare time together from that day of sharing that root beer float. They would become best friends. Mama told me they would make plans of how they wanted their life to be. Dad was a planner, and she was the dreamer. But together, they wanted the same things in their lives: a home, family, and love for God.

Fishing and Marriage
Hand and Hand

Fishing was to become their thing to do together, Johnny, Patty, and Sam. John had the truck, Sam had the boat, Patty would make sandwiches and lemonade, and off they would go. Sam was courting Betty at the time, and they would try to get her to go fishing with them, but Mama told me Betty would say, "I wouldn't be caught dead trying to catch some stupid fish, and worms, well, they are disgusting!" Mama always teased Sam by saying, "Worms, why they are disgusting!" and Sam would laugh.

John, being his sweet self, would tell Betty, "Betty, you don't have to touch a worm, or a fish for that matter. Just come enjoy the day and the beauty of being outside in nature."

Well, that didn't work either, and Mama said, "I don't think Sam and Betty did much together, outside, that is." Johnny and Patty courted that next year, 1952, and Christmas, 1953, Johnny gave Patty a hope chest that he had made and a gold ring with a little chip of diamond in the center.

The story told was, John got down on one knee, and took Patty's hand in the living room of Allen and Rose's with both present. Holding Patty's hand, John said, "Patty May, if you marry me, I will do the best I can with the help of God to make sure we live a good life, and always have love for each new day." That would become Mama's favorite saying to us children. I can still hear her voice as she would enter my bedroom each morning saying, "God is good, and let's have love for this new day."

Sara and Patty got busy the next week and planned the wedding for March. Rose was a seamstress, and fitted Patty with the dress she wore when she married Patty's dad, Allen. She added daisy eyelets, Mama's favorite flower, and made a new veil. John had already told his parents about him going to ask Patty for her hand in marriage when he went to Iowa that summer for the wedding of his brother, Jack. Todd and Mary had made plans for coming a week early to Michigan so they could spend time getting to know Patty and her family. Bill and Anne insisted Todd and Mary stay with them that week. They so loved John, and wanted to meet the fine folks who raised such a fine young man.

Let me tell you of what I know about Bill and Anne. Us children came to call them Big Bill and Nana, thanks to Will who had started it. Bill was a businessman who always wore a suit; what business it was I couldn't tell you. All I know is Big Bill and Nana had plenty of money, and Bill always wanted Dad to work for him. I remember many of nights, Big Bill would be at our house talking to Dad in another room, while Mama and Nana would fix supper for us all, and we would share plenty of stories and laughs into the evening. Bill would always shake Dad's hand when leaving our home saying, "Think about it, John," and Dad would say, "Thanks, Bill, but I don't think so. I still like making furniture." Mama told Will once—who in turn told me—that Big Bill and Nana gave her and Dad five hundred dollars as a wedding present. That money became their down payment on the house that was our home.

Mama said they got married in a little church on the outskirts of Grand Rapids. It was the church Dad had been going to with Bill and Anne. When we went to church later, as a family, it was at Mama's church where Grandpa and Grandma Doyle went.

There was plenty of snow on the ground, but the sun was shining on March 13, 1954. Sam was Dad's best man, and Sara stood alongside Mama. They had dinner downstairs of the church, cut the cake, and talked and thanked each of the thirty-five guests who had come to share their day. The Bible salesman even came. His name was Thomas. He gave Johnny and Patty a beautiful Bible with their names and date of the marriage engraved in gold. That Bible is still with Dad to this day. Then Johnny whisked Patty away to a little cabin Dad had rented in northern Michigan, on a lake where he knew there would be some good ice fishing to go along with the honeymoon.

Johnny and Patty rented a little house in Grand Rapids that first year. Mama worked at the hospital until Will was born there December 13, 1954. Yes, Will was a honeymoon baby.

Big Bill helped Johnny and Patty find a house just outside of Grand Rapids the next summer. Dad's job was good at the furniture factory, and Dad has always been good with money. Bill, being the businessman he was, helped Dad with some investments that would pay off, then and later. Life was good for Johnny and Patty. They were a healthy, happy family of three.

As for Sam, Dad's best friend, or should I say, Uncle Sam, well, Mama would tell me things didn't start out for him as well. Sam would say, "I don't understand, John. I pray to God, try to be a good man, and things just don't work as planned." Dad's answer would be, "Sam, you've got to have faith. That is what's missing in a lot of people's lives. We can say we have it, but it's the hardest thing to believe. To have religious convictions is one thing, but to have trust in God is your faith, and a strong faith will carry you through."

While Sam was figuring out his faith, as you know, he was courting Betty. They had become engaged a few months before Dad and Mama were married. But Sam started liking Mama's sister, Sara, and likewise for Sara. The story told by Mama is that Betty found out that Sam was going to break off the engagement. So, Betty asked Sam to her parent's home while they were away out of town. Betty fixed Sam a fried chicken dinner, and poured him a glass of her Daddy's fine whiskey. Sam never drank, but maybe a beer or two after fishing. Betty then unbuttoned her blouse and pulled up her poodle skirt, and let Sam have his way with her. Nine months later, beautiful brown-eyed Lily was born.

Sam married Betty but not all was well; nine months after Lily was born, Betty moved across state to live with an aunt and uncle. Sam was really sad about everything and spent time with John, mostly fishing and praying. Sam would try to see Lily, but Betty wouldn't allow it. A weekly alimony check went to Betty after the divorce. Betty soon married, and her new husband adopted Lily.

About the time Betty moved with Lily, Mama became pregnant with little Sam. He was born August 11, 1956.

Sam and Sara moved on; while Uncle Sam was married to Betty, Aunt Sara was dating a man she had met through some friend. They became engaged, but from what I was told, Mama found out this guy (no one ever said his name) hit Aunt Sara in the face, out of anger, causing a bloody lip. Mama told her dad, and Grandpa Allen took care of it. That so-called guy was never seen in this part of the state again. Sara, not knowing what her dad did, told Mama that she had gotten a letter from the man, saying he was sorry, but he thought he needed to join the service and learn how to control his anger. Sara was fine with it. When Sam and Sara were both single, they would hang out together, and were always together at all of our family functions. But as told to me, no one knew if they so-called dated until later on.

Time for Faith

In 1957, Patty was busy with the boys, and also had a job watching an older lady in the lady's home. Mrs. Vandyke had trouble with her legs, so Mr. Vandyke would have Patty come each morning (except on Wednesday and weekends, when the daughter in law would) to help Mrs. Vandyke get clean, dressed, and ready for the day. Patty also helped with some light house cleaning, and took home their laundry to be cleaned, ironed, and back the next day.

Sometimes, Patty would take the boys with her, which the Vandyke's enjoyed, for they didn't have any grandchildren. But most days, Grandma Rose would come watch them, or Aunt Sara loved to watch the boys on her days off from the department store where she worked.

All the money Mr. Vandyke gave Patty was put away in a blue and red tin that she kept in her and Johnny's closet. Patty was saving every bit to buy John a fishing boat.

One day in June, Patty was bent over in the bathroom helping Mrs. Vandyke put her white soft leather shoes on. As she was tying the shoe, without warning, Patty threw up all over those white shoes. Of course, Patty was so embarrassed, and Mrs. Vandyke, who I am told was as sweet as can be, told Patty, "Patricia, you better make a doctor's appointment, and find out this baby's due date."

That night, when Patty told Johnny what happened, Johnny laughed, and asked Patty if she told Mrs. Vandyke, "I wouldn't want to be in your shoes."

Patty, not feeling Johnny's sense of humor, then said, "Mrs. Vandyke seems to think I am with child."

As John got serious, he then said, "Maybe, but you never got sick with the boys."

Patty said, "I know, and I had my monthly, so I don't think I am."

The next morning, and many after that, Patty would throw up. Mama told me that she was so sick when carrying me, that she would worry something was really wrong. Mama's doctor was concerned, too, because this was Patty's third pregnancy in such a short time, and told Patty working outside of the home was out of the question. Mr. Vandyke had found someone else to help with Mrs. Vandyke, but kept tabs on Mama, for they cared for her so.

John would have to reassure her all the time. He'd say, "Pray and have faith, Patty, and everything will be fine." Mama said at times she would spot blood in her panties, and would cry, pray, and put her feet up the rest of the day, which would be close to impossible with two young boys to care for. That's when Grandma Rose would come and help Patty. Grandma Rose was born domesticated; she was so devoted to home duties and family, which Mama would say in later years, "I think Grandma Rose waits by that phone for a call of help from someone. That's her pleasure in life." I tend to believe Mama was a lot like that, but would deny.

Johnny was a lot of help also. Mama said Dad would come home from work and help with the supper and give the boys their bath. Most nights you could find the four of them in Dad and Mama's wood bed reading stories from children books and the Bible with the gold engravings.

Mama said, "Grandma Mary came to stay with them that autumn before you were born. She wanted to help out, just as she did with each of the boys when they were born, and also love being with her grandsons." Grandma Mary, or Mama Mary, which everyone but us children called her, was soft-spoken and as sweet as pie. She had dark hair and hazel eyes, as a grandma, her hair became streaked with bug hunks of gray that glistened in the different degrees of light. She had a thin build, and it wasn't that she was so tall that she stood and walked tall. Grandma Mary just had these looks and demeanor that when she would enter a room with her big smile, everyone would take notice and for some reason, feel better, be better.

My dad has the same features except for his brown eyes like his dad. Dad has the same smile, and he too would have the hunks of gray flow through his dark hair later. I would say Dad was most like Mama Mary of all his brothers, but knowing them all, they all got their love for God and strong faith from their Mama Mary.

Patty so loved her mother-in-law, and the two of them got along so well. Mama had said she could tell Mama Mary anything, and Grandma never judged or found fault, unlike—Mama said—her mother, Rose, often did. When Mama Mary left before Thanksgiving that year, she told John, "You are a good son, husband, and father. Your dad and I are so blessed to have you, please take care of Patty, I am a little worried about her health." John would say, "Don't you worry, Mama Mary, Patty and I are having faith, and with that everything will be fine."

That Christmas in 1957, Patty took her blue and red tin from the closet, and bought Johnny a new fishing pole, some tackle, and a fishing hat. She got Will and little Sam new toy trucks, hats, and fishing poles made just for kids. Johnny surprised Patty with new garden tools, and a pretty blue sweater to match her eyes. Johnny would say, "Things in our life keep getting better and better, because of our faith in God, love of family, and doing the best we can with what is given, and being grateful for our freedoms."

January can be one of the worst months for snow in Michigan. Just before I was born, Mama said it had been snowing every day for weeks. Aunt Sara started staying with them in the guest room so someone would be there for the boys.

It was three in the morning on January sixteenth that Patty woke up Johnny saying, "Johnny, you need to get me to the hospital, because I am having faith that this baby is coming soon, very soon," as she grabbed at her swollen belly. Patty had heard that, most of the time, one's third baby can come fast.

The side roads were snow-covered and slippery. Dad said, "It wasn't until our truck made it to the main road that I was able to breathe again." That's when Mama's water broke, and she no more got to the hospital and they sent her to delivery and Dad to the waiting room.

In the days when I was born, Mama said, "Dads were sent to a room to wait until the doctor would come after everything was done, and tell the dad if they had a boy or girl. Then the dad would go to see his new baby for the first time through a nursery window, where the baby would be all cleaned up and wrapped tightly in a blue or pink blanket and placed in a nursery bassinet." The hospital stay would be five days for a normal delivery. I was born on a Thursday, and came home early Tuesday morning.

Mama said she was just so happy that I was fine, that it took her a few days for it to sink in, that Johnny and she had themselves a healthy little girl. I was only five pounds at birth, and didn't look at all like the boys. All the pictures prove that. I had lighter features with very little hair. Both Will and Sam had Dad's dark hair and eyes. Also, they both came into the world weighing a whooping eight pounds each.

When Patty and Johnny talked about names for their new baby, they had picked out John junior for a boy and Dad wanted Grace May for a girl. Mama told Dad after she held me for the first time that she really wanted to name me Faith. Because it was Dad always saying, "Have faith, everything will be fine," so Faith May Bakker was put in place.

We were a family of five in a time where things were pretty good. The president of the United States was Dwight Eisenhower. The average income was around five thousand dollars, and gasoline was twenty-four cents per gallon. One of the number one hits played on the radio was *All I Have to Do Is Dream* by the Everly Brothers.

God, Family, and Grandmas

Mama had her hands full taking care of us all. But I am here to say, motherhood came easily to Patty. That summer Dad became a foreman at the furniture factory and life was very busy. In late August, 1958, John was called home to Iowa for two weeks. Dad's second oldest brother, Uncle Jim, had a farming accident, which took off his right leg at the knee. Uncle Jim was married to Aunt Sylvia. They had two young sons. Uncle Jim grew corn, but had at the time acres and acres of hay to be cut and bailed.

Dad's whole family came together, got the hay cut and bailed, and Uncle Jim was back on his foot in no time. I really liked my Uncle Jim; he was the friendliest of all of Dad's brothers. I will always remember him with his Mama Mary's big smile, and a wooden leg that he would let all of us kids poke at with our forks at the yearly family reunion.

Dad's oldest brother, Uncle Joe, and his wife, Aunt Sally, who also had two boys, owned a house on Grandpa Todd's land, and helped run the big dairy farm. Uncle Joe eventually took over the family dairy business. I never really got to know Uncle Joe too well. I only saw him at the family reunions, weddings, and funerals. I believe he and Aunt Sally never made it to Michigan for a visit. I heard it said that he never understood why my dad would move so far away.

Uncle Jack was Todd and Mary's third son. Uncle Jack grew soy and married Aunt Marion, a heavy-set woman, very friendly, and pretty. But I do remember when we were young, her big breasts scared us kids. Whenever she saw us, she would pick us up to her big bosoms, and we would scream until she put us back to earth. I know now she only loved us all so much because she and Uncle Jack couldn't have children of their own. Uncle Jack and Aunt Marion came to Michigan the most of Dad's brothers. Maybe because they didn't have children, or that Uncle Jack liked fishing just like Uncle Sam and Dad.

Each year the Bakker's held the family reunion on Todd and Mary's farm. It was usually the last week in August. Dad was already in Iowa helping Uncle

Jim, so Aunt Sara traveled with Mama and us children by train to spend a few days with the entire Bakker family before the reunion. It was the first time everyone would meet me and Mama said I was passed around like some kind of precious jewel.

Then we would all take the train back to Michigan. I was just about eight months old, but I remember Aunt Sara holding me on the train. I was wearing a blue romper, and I remember a little of Will and Sam making me laugh. Big belly laughs, that is.

When I was two years old, Grandma Rose gave me Dolly. Dolly was handmade by Grandma. She was stuffed just right with a plastic head, arms, and feet. That birthday I received Dolly, I wore a purple dress, fancy white lacy socks, and shiny black patent leather shoes. The strap went on top of my foot, and I remember Mama putting them on me that morning as we were singing *Mary Had a Little Lamb*. Mama would always sing to me while she dressed me. Then she would hold a mirror to my face and would say, "God loves you, Faith May."

Maybe that's why I could remember events by what clothes I was wearing. The holding of the mirror went on for years. Both Dad and Mama would tell us about God and his love that it's a reflection of who we are.

Grandma Rose was a seamstress and a darn good one. When Rose married Allen in 1930, things were hard and making a living was harder still. Rose would make children clothes and sell them in the local Five and Dime. Allen worked for a feed store for years, until he got a job at General Motors. He retired from there in 1970. Rose would make clothes from the feed sacks, which is a sack where chicken feed would come in. Allen would bring them home from the store. I had worn many dresses made from those sacks and even Dolly had a few.

Grandma Rose did everything just so. Her whole life was getting up early and working around the clock cleaning, sewing, washing, cooking, and baking. Everything had to be just so, and when her and Grandpa's home was perfect, she would be at ours going over what Mama did, tasting Mama's soup and telling her the season it needed, or what to leave out next time. Mama didn't seem to mind Grandma cleaning her already clean home or testing her already delicious soup. She would just smile and say, "That will be fine, Mother; I'll just play with the children." Rose always had her dark blonde hair, and later white, in a tight bun on the back of her head. She wore plain simple dresses that she made herself all week. Then for church, she would wear mostly store-bought dresses with white gloves, and she always carried a small purse with a fancy lace handkerchief and some pink peppermints inside. But of course, us children would ask nicely for one each time we would see her. Please and thank you were some of our first words spoken, and still come to us easily. Grandma Rose was a thin-built woman, but as the years went on, she did become quite plump.

Patty wasn't as close to Grandma Rose as I was to Mama. Although Grandma did spend a lot of time around our home, I don't remember Grandma Rose or Mama saying bad things to each other. Rose would tell Mama things like, "Patricia, don't you think Will and Sam need haircuts?" or

"Patricia, Faith should be potty trained by now." Mama would just roll her eyes. Rose thought, and dreamed, her girls would take up fashion, maybe become famous. But Patty didn't like sewing one bit. Rose would be showing Sara how to put a dart in a skirt, and Patty would be outside tending to her flowers she planted, or the family garden. Mama would have trouble sewing buttons on Dad's work shirts. As for Aunt Sara, she did her share of sewing, and could make dresses for her and Mama that would make anyone think they came from a fancy department store.

Rose didn't like that Patricia and John didn't go to church every Sunday. It wasn't that Mama and Dad didn't go to church, but sometimes, Dad would say, "I am sure God wouldn't mind if one gets up early on Sunday to go fishing and have a picnic with one's family." Dad always said having fellowship at church is good for the soul, but talking to God every day is what is important; don't ever be someone who only thinks of God on Sunday. If Rose didn't see Patricia, John and us children in church on Sunday, you could bet she wouldn't talk to Mama for a few days.

Grandma Rose was nice, and we loved when she and Grandpa Allen would visit. But you could tell Mama and Dad didn't feel as comfortable as when we spent time with Grandpa Todd and Grandma Mary. My very first memory of Grandma Mary had to be when I was three years old. That's when Mama said all of us children got chicken pox, one after the other; first Will and then two days later, Sam, and a few days after that, I was to get them. Mama said I ran a high fever, and looked a mess. Grandma Mary was here in Michigan for a visit. I can remember I had Sam's hand-me-down cowboy pajamas on with the feet worn so that my big toe stuck out of one. Grandma Mary was rocking me in the rocker in our living room. I can close my eyes and see her smiling face. I had fallen in a very deep love with this human that held a cool washcloth to my head, singing, smiling, and holding my soul in her arms just so. I always felt love from all the adults in my young life, and was lucky to have so many. But Grandma Mary rocking me that night, I felt a different love, and the only way I can explain it is, I felt that God was looking through her eyes at me.

Summer, Lady, and Fishing

The great memories continued. Will and Sam remember the same June week I do in 1962. I was just over four years old when Grandpa Todd and Grandma Mary came for a week's visit, and along with them came a new puppy. Grandpa Todd has always had border collies on the farm in Iowa, and asked Dad and Mama if we children could have one of the pups. "As long as it's a female," Mama would say. "We have to even it up around here." So, that week not only did we enjoy the company of Grandpa and Grandma, we were busy with the cutest puppy ever.

If I was ever to have an opportunity to live a week over, it would have been this week. I wouldn't change a thing, not one thing. Dad would have the week off from work. We would all get up early, eat a big breakfast together, and plan the day from there.

Dad took the boys and Grandpa fishing in Uncle Sam's boat a few mornings that week, and we girls would do things around the house. Mostly, we would be outside digging in Mama's flower garden. That was the week Grandma Mary got Mama a hummingbird feeder to hang by our big kitchen window. Every year we enjoy these small unique birds as they would drink from the feeders and visit Mama's flowers.

When the boys and men were not fishing, we packed a lunch and went to the lake to have a picnic, and our puppy went also. We ate bluegills and perch on the days they fished, and Dad put hamburgers on the charcoal grill out back and we would eat at the picnic table that Dad and Uncle Sam had made the summer before. Grandpa Todd would say, "These are the best hamburgers ever; you have mighty tasty cows here in Michigan."

It was also Grandma Mary's birthday that week, so I helped Mama make a birthday cake. Mama bought her some knitted dishtowels, and talked Aunt Sara into making a yellow dress for Mama Mary, which was Sara's pleasure for she loved Grandma Mary also.

At night, we would all sit around the living room after supper, laughing at the puppy, eating homemade ice cream, and trying different names out to call our new pup. Dad would tell us all the names of the dogs they had on the farm all the years he was growing up. The dogs would herd the cows to the barns at night to be milked. They were working dogs, but always came in the house at night to sleep at the foot of someone's bed. Grandpa said, "Your Dad and his brothers spoiled those dogs." We spoiled Lady, too; she was a good dog who was always with us kids. When we played outside, she stayed right by us, watched over us, and she slept in my bedroom on a red rug by my bed all those years.

The day Grandpa Todd and Grandma Mary were to go home was a Sunday. We all went to church, which made Grandma Rose smile so big her top gums showed. Grandma Mary wore her new yellow dress, and I wore a light-blue and white checkered dress, one of Grandma Rose's creations. That Sunday, at dinner, both sets of grandparents were at the table, along with Uncle Sam and Aunt Sara. I remember thinking what a happy, lucky girl I was to have so many people around that cared for one another and a new puppy, too!

That summer, my dad took me fishing for the first time. I had on a simple summer dress, pink, that tied in a bow in back. I had to wear shoes in the boat, one of Dad's rules until he would say we were big enough to watch out for fish hooks. We would fish on Gun Lake where Dad knew I would be able to catch some bluegills, which would make fishing fun. Dad said, "I'll put the worm on the hook, but watch me, because someday you will do it." I didn't take my blue eyes off that worm as it tried so hard to squirm its way away from the sharp hook. I said, "Daddy, does it hurt the worm terribly?" He said, "Why yes, it does, Faith, but that worm now has a job to do, and that is to catch a fish. So it goes into the water on a mission, and it wiggles with happiness." Dad handed me the fishing pole and said, "When you feel that worm dancing, and a fish tugging, pull up and then hold tight and start reeling." I laughed thinking about the worm dancing. Dad then got his fishing pole in the water, and I remember him winking at me and saying, "Faith May, you are about to catch your first fish."

About that time, I felt a tugging on the fishing pole that went right up my arms like I believe baby lightning would feel. I pulled up my little arms, held tight, and started reeling. There it was, a baby bluegill on the end of my pole, and now it lay on the bottom of the boat. I know I smiled so big my top gums showed. "It's just a baby gill," Dad would say, as he released the wiggling fish from the sharp hook. Then he said," We will throw it back, and catch it next year." I was so glad that it was to go back in to the water, and it got to eat the dancing worm; when I caught the next three keeper gills, I was hooked on fishing.

When we came home that afternoon from fishing, Dad would clean the fish out back at a table he made just for the job, with a hose to wash the blood away. At four years old, it was still hard for me to watch the cleaning of the catch, but I had found if I didn't look them in the eye, I would be fine. I don't know what Mama would fry, bake, or grill those fish with, but they sure tasted great!

Dad would tell Will and Sam that day, "Watch out, boys, little Faith knows how to fish, and does quite well." Then he would turn to Mama saying, "Patty, I think it's time we get a boat big enough for all of us to fish from." Mama said, "Yes, Johnny, I think that's a great idea, I would love to take the children fishing up north as we did when we were first married." I saw Dad wink at Mama.

I spent a lot of time with my dad in a boat fishing, and I have all good memories of not only pulling fish in, but watching nature, seeing deer with their babies, drinking alongside the river or lake's edge. Birds, minks, foxes, even coyotes. Then there was the weather, from the morning cool, to the afternoon hot, and back again to evening chill. We watched storms come in, and storms leave, the beauty of the sun rising, and the wonder of it setting. We had our best talks, tears, laughs, lemonade, and sandwiches. Coffee came later for me, but Dad always had his thermos by his side.

We fished as a family, with friends, grandparents, uncles, and aunts. But my dad was always at the hull. If we didn't catch a fish that day, or if we were catching and releasing, it was all good. It was our family thing to do; it made us strong, and kept us in love.

Our Home

That autumn and winter came with no surprises. Will and Sam went off to school in the mornings, and Dad to work. Mama would do the chores around the house, and I would play with Dolly and Lady, or color. I remember a few television shows Mama would let me watch. One was *Captain Kangaroo*, another was *Romper Room*. I found it was quite peaceful around our home with just us girls.

Mama kept a clean house, just like Grandma Rose. She had rules, and one was we were not allowed toys or food in our bedrooms. She'd say, "Bedrooms are for sleeping, and resting for God's new day." We were allowed books, and of course, Dolly slept with me. Later in our teen years, we each had a desk and chair for homework, and things would, and did, start to collect, so Dad built shelves to hold it off the floors.

Our house sat a good ways from the road. It wasn't a farm house; all the rooms were on the same floor. But it was a big house with plenty of room. I was told that it was specially built years ago by a builder who only lived there a few years, when told by my dad, that builder built a bigger home further down the road. Mama would say that we sure did benefit from someone else being unsatisfied. Dad would say our home is just what he prayed for.

My bedroom, after the crib was put in the attic, had a twin bed with a red quilt—made by Aunt Sally from Iowa—nightstand, dresser, and a picture of a little girl, praying on the side of her bed with a collie dog hung on my off-white walls. Mama had said, "Your Aunt Sara got your dad and me that picture the Christmas before you were born. She was so sure you were going to be a girl." I loved my bedroom; it was my own. Mama, Dad, even my brothers, would not invade without knocking first. And I was taught to do the same at their doors.

Will and Sam shared the big bedroom. They each had blue quilts (made by Aunt Sally), nightstands, lamps, one big dresser, and pictures of boys fishing on a river hung on their sky-blue walls.

Mama and Dad's bedroom was cheery yellow, with a big, wood poster bed that came from the furniture factory where Dad worked. I remember there would be nights that I would make my way to that bed when the thunder or howling wind would wake me up. Mama would scoop me up and cover me up with the blanket and her arms. I would always find myself back in my own bed come sunrise, and never remembering getting there.

Then, there was the guest room. When Johnny and Patty went looking for a house, they knew it had to have a guest room and extra bathrooms. Because of Dad's family being in Iowa, they wanted them to know there would always be room for them when they would visit. The guest room was my favorite place to go if I just wanted to be alone. Mostly because I could go and lie on the bed and feel the presence of the people that had slept there, and remember their visits. Mama had that room fixed just so; she would put fresh flowers from her garden in vases on the nightstands when guests would come. If flowers weren't available, she had some kind of trinket that was in season. It had the full-size wooden bed that Dad made for him and Mama when they first got married. The bedspread was off-white chiffon, which was a wedding present from Grandpa Allen's sister, Aunt Peg. Even if no one visited, the room was always clean and inviting.

The dining room, kitchen, and living room all had big picture windows, which would let the outside come in our home. Mama explained it was important to have shelter, but never be completely disconnected from our physical universe, your environment, nature.

I loved our home. I think it was just like the home Johnny and Patty talked about when they courted. They both wanted a place where their children would feel safe and loved. That is just what it did for us.

I remember my pink birthday cake with five blue candles. It matched my pink dress with blue stripes. Mama sang the "Happy Birthday" song as I dressed myself that morning, and put the handheld mirror to my own face saying, "God loves me." We celebrated on a Sunday, and Grandpa Allen and Grandma Rose, Aunt Sara, and Uncle Sam came to dinner after church. Grandma Rose made some doll clothes for Dolly, Aunt Sara made me a green dress, and I got a red bike with training wheels from Mama and Dad. But the present I remember most, and still have, was from Uncle Sam. He gave me my very own fishing pole with my name painted on the side in front of the reel: "Faith May."

When June came that year in 1963, Grandma Mary came for a long visit, and Grandpa Todd stayed on the farm in Iowa because of work. Grandma came by train. When Dad and my brothers went to pick her up from the train station in Grand Rapids, Mama and I were home making sure everything was just right. I, Faith May, got to pick the flowers from Mama's garden to place in the guest room. They were large blossom pink peonies. That was one of the flowers in bloom. There was such excitement in the air; even Lady was dancing about, doing her many tricks.

We had just over three wonderful weeks with Grandma Mary, and I remember wishing Will and Sam were still in school so I could have her all to myself. Dolly and I got to sleep with her in the guest room most nights. She would tell me stories of Dad when he was little like me, and read my Dr. Seuss books. Grandma Mary fell asleep before me one night and I can still, to this day, remember staring at her face in the light of a full moon coming in the bedroom window. She was so beautiful to me. How the streaks of gray that ran through her hair glisten in the moon light. I felt in the moment that she would never leave me.

Dad took Mama Mary fishing one night that first week after work, just the two of them. I gave Grandma my "Faith May" fishing pole for luck. They came home after sunset with no fish, just talking and laughing like children. I knew then, they were just enjoying each other's company, in the presence of God and nature.

Mama had her time with Grandma Mary also. They put more hooks up for two more hummingbird feeders, and I can picture them with their big straw hats outside in the gardens that would spring up each year outside in our backyard.

On the nights I didn't sleep with Grandma, Mama and she would be at the kitchen table drinking tea, talking and laughing until the wee hours. I heard Mama tell Grandma Mary one of those nights, "Mama Mary, I couldn't be happier. I just love my life with Johnny, and the children, and let me tell you, God surely has blessed us. They are each so amazing! I am thankful, very thankful!"

Then Grandma would say, "I know just what you mean. I too have had this most incredible journey called life, and have enjoyed and treasured each moment. As I have told my boys since they were very small, as you take in nourishment to grow big and strong each day, you must also take in the love from God so your heart will grow emotionally and morally strong. I have told them your body will carry you through life, but it's a good heart that will let you have the life God intended his children to have."

I think Grandma Mary was saying the same thing my dad would tell us children, only Dad would say, "Each and every one of us is born with a heart. God puts a little round empty space for love to grow, and as we take in that love, we feel good, and when we release or give the love after the round space is full, well that's when your heart is doing just what God intended. Pumping your blood for circulation, and receiving and releasing of love."

When Grandma Mary went to leave with Dad to the train station, I found Mama crying in a chair in her bedroom. I said, "What's wrong, Mama? Why are you so sad?" Mama said, "I don't know, Faith, I guess I am just going to miss having Mama Mary around here." "Me, too," I said, and I hugged Mama.

When Mama hugged Grandma Mary before she left that June day, I saw a sadness in Mama's face that I would see in her face a few more times through the years, and it wasn't good.

That summer would bring more fishing, and a family vacation in August, to Northern Michigan. Dad bought a good-size fishing boat from someone Big Bill knew. He would hitch it to our family station wagon, and off we went. Lady would bark with happiness as she would jump in the backseat with me.

We stayed in a little cottage on the shores of Little Glen Lake, next to Sleeping Bear Dunes. Big Bill and Nana visited us for a few days while we were there. I remember running around barefoot the whole time. Mama even said, "Why did we even bring shoes, except for church?" But her shoes would come off as we would run up the big sand dune and walk down the shoreline hunting and collecting shells and pretty rocks. Mama would put the rocks in her flower gardens back home.

There was plenty of fishing, swimming, camp fires in the evening, with hot melted marshmallows, and a few thunderstorms that would send me to jump in bed with Mama and Dad. Dad would say vacations are good for the soul; he would say they are important. I think Dad just liked spending time with his family.

Back home again, Dad had called Grandpa and Grandma Bakker saying we wouldn't be able to make the family reunion that year in Iowa. He said something about being busy at the furniture factory, and school starting a little early that year. Faith May was starting school, too.

School, Molly, and Heaven

That September, on my very first day of school, I met and fell in love with my best friend, Molly June Warner. I wore a blue dress that day. The teacher, Mrs. Plank, sat Molly and I at the same table, and from that moment on, we started telling each other everything we knew about one another we could possibly say or know from our five short years of life. I think—well, I know—I did most of the talking and Molly looked me right in the eyes and listened, just like my dad.

Molly was pretty. She had big brown eyes, short brown hair, and freckles from the summer sun across her nose, same as me. When I found out Molly only lived a few country blocks from my house, I knew we would be best friends forever.

School was fun, and I liked it just as Will and Sam did. But I also learned that not everyone was as nice as Molly, and not everyone wanted to be Faith May's friend. I remember a boy named Curtis James. He told me, "Faith, your gums show when you smile, and it makes you look dumb." When I told Dad at the supper table that night about what Curtis James said to me, he said, "Faith May, your smile is just like your mama's, and that smile is what makes her shine." Mama smiled, and her gums showed; Dad winked at her.

That next day, I went right up to Curtis James with my arms crossed in front. I said loud and clear, "Curtis James, when I smile, I shine!" Then I gave him my biggest smile, and Molly stood right beside me.

Dad always seemed to make things better. But, no one, not even my dad, could take away the pain of a phone call we received from Uncle Joe the morning of October 13, 1963.

We were all sitting at the breakfast table before getting ready for church when the telephone rang. Mama answered and listened, and then I saw the same look in her face that she had the day when Grandma Mary left. Mama handed Dad the phone and said, "Its Joe, something's wrong." Dad took the receiver and walked as far away from the table as the cord would allow him. When he hung up the telephone, and returned to the kitchen table, I had just finished my toast and put the crust on my plate to give to Lady later.

As Dad sat down at the table, he put his hands over his face and said, "Grandma Mary went to heaven this morning." Both Will and Sam started crying along with Mama. At first, I didn't get it. From what I was told, in my church classroom, "heaven was a great place to be." Then, Sam said something that made my toast want to come back up: "Grandma is dead."

That was the moment I learned that life wasn't always going to be as fun and wonderful, as I thought in my first five years. I knew about death, but only in nature. A bird dies when it flies into a window; a fish, chicken, or cow will die to bring us nourishment. A flower dies after what Mama says was "its season." But grandmas don't die. That can't be.

When our family traveled to Iowa for the funeral, Aunt Sara stayed at our house with Lady, and we took our first plane trip together.

It was a time of many tears and hugging, but also because of Dad's family faith, there were many stories and laughter. I remember overhearing Mama tell Aunt Sylvia that she had a bad feeling when Mama Mary left that June. "Sylvia," Mama said, "I just got this sick, sad feeling that I wasn't going to see her again." That's when Mama broke down and Dad carried her off to bed.

The day of the funeral, I wore the blue dress that Grandma Mary sent me for my first day of school that year. I held Grandpa Todd's hand the whole time. When he cried after the prayer, I said, "Grandpa, it will be okay. From what I have heard about Heaven, Grandma is in the best place in the whole wide world." Well, that made him cry even more.

Grandma Mary was only fifty-eight years old, but what she left us all was what my dad said in front of everyone at the cemetery that day. "Mama Mary was a beautiful soul that God gave each and every one of us to love in our own way. To show us that we were made good, and with faith, love will always be there, as God's love is, until all is made good again." Then Dad looked into the big blue sky that October afternoon and said, "I love you, Mama Mary."

It wasn't until years later that I learned Grandma Mary had died of a brain aneurism. It took her in the night of a full moon as she lay next to Grandpa Todd. Their Border collie, Max, lay on the rug on her side of the bed. Funny thing was, Max never went into Grandpa and Grandma's bedroom to sleep, but that night Grandpa Todd said Max whined and whined until he was let into the bedroom where he laid there watching Grandma Mary as she slept. Watching still, later into the night, when she fell into her maker's arms.

November 22, 1963 came, the assassination of President Kennedy. I watched the funeral on television, thinking how sad that little boy and girl must be to have their daddy go to Heaven. From what I understood then, the President was killed with a bullet from a bad man's gun. What I didn't understand was why. I was learning so much, so fast, about the way the world was, that I remember being scared for the first time, of not just thunder or wind howling, but of the whole big wide world.

That winter was when I started waking up in the night, and Dolly, Lady, and I would sneak into the guest room and lay on the big wooden bed Dad made. I would think about how I loved each new day, and wishing that bad man with the gun had had a Grandma Mary and all the other people in my life, to love him enough, that his round empty space in his heart would have been full enough to work properly. I would lie in that bed and look out the window where you could always see the moon. Then I would talk to God. Even at such a young age, I was told to talk to God, and that I could trust God with all my feelings. I would let God have it, so to speak. Sometimes, I would ask God to let Grandma Mary leave Heaven, and come for a visit, because everything was so much better when she was on earth.

Spring Comes June

With spring came better spirits around the Bakker home. Mama started her flower garden, and hung the hummingbird feeders. Dad got the boat and tackle ready for fishing, and we kids were outside in the neighborhood with our friends, planning the summer when school would release us.

Molly and I were inseparable that summer. We lived less than a mile from each other. My house was on a hill down the road from where she lived in what they called a subdivision. Our school was in the same subdivision, only a few blocks from Molly's house. We would play mostly at my house. I had been to Molly's house a few times to play and told Mama, "My head races when I am at Molly's house. There is so much stuff, and Molly's mom yells at us to keep quiet because Molly's dad is sleeping. I guess he works when we sleep."

Mama would say, "It's fine if Molly comes here to our home, I like having you girls around."

One warm day that spring, Mama made a cake and called Molly's mom. Her name was June Warner. Mama asked if she could drop by to meet her. So Mama and I went with the cake that day after school.

June answered the door with a lit cigarette in her hand, and what looked to be a glass with some ice and a caramel-colored liquid in the other. "Come in, come in," June said. June then put her cigarette out in the full ash tray that sat on the coffee table in front of the green couch, and cleared a chair of some paper clutter for Mama to sit. She then took the cake from Mama's hand saying, "How nice to meet you, and thank you for the cake," as she walked the cake into the kitchen.

I could see Mama's eyes move about the living area that was really messy, dirty glasses, full ash trays, and a few empty beer cans. Molly turned off the television that was announcing how to keep your floors clean with *Spick and Span*.

"Pat," June called from the kitchen, "would you care for a drink?"

Mama said, "Why yes, thanks, water would be fine, thank you." June then came back with Mama's water and more ice in her drink. She sat down on the couch next to Molly and lit another cigarette. I was in a chair next to Mama, staring at Miss June. I always called Molly's mom Miss June and Molly called my mama Miss Patty.

I was staring because first I had never seen a woman smoking in person, only on television. I was thinking about when Grandpa Allen will smoke his pipe after dinner that I kind of liked the smell. But the smell of that cigarette, well, it was disgusting.

Miss June was much more stylish than, say, my mama. She would wear her dark hair all done up in what I think they would call a beehive, with bobby pins stuck everywhere. She wore tight, bright sweaters with pants just as tight. Her makeup was on all the time. I even asked Molly if her mom's eyes woke up that colorful each morning.

Mama said to June, "Molly tells me her daddy works the night shift. That has to be hard to sleep when the sun is shining."

June said, "Paul has been doing it so long, we don't know any other way," June finished saying.

"What does your husband do?" That's when mama said.

"He works in Grand Rapids at a furniture factory." She took a drink of water, and said, "Days, he works the morning shift."

At that moment, the front door opened and in came Molly's big brother, Paul Jr. Molly called him Pauly most of the time. The door slammed as it shut, and June raised her voice, "Can't you get it through your thick head, Paul Jr., that your father is sleeping?"

We stayed a little longer, but Mama would say something about getting supper on the table, and when we were saying our good-byes, Mama said, "I'm sure John would like to meet Paul sometime. Maybe Paul would like to go fishing with him this summer?"

June said loud enough, but with her head looking at their bedroom door, "Paul don't do shit." Both Molly and I laughed, because she said "shit." Mama took my hand sternly and we started walking home.

On our walk home, you could tell Mama was thinking. I said, "Mama, I told you Molly's house was really messy! And isn't Molly's mom a hoot?" Mama said, "Why yes, Faith dear, she is what I might call a hoot. But as for their home being messy, Faith, that is not our business, and we don't judge people on how they keep their home."

That night at the supper table, Dad asked how our day was. Mama said little, and didn't even tell Dad about the cigarettes, or messy house. But she did ask Will if he knew Paul Jr. Will said, "Yes, Mom, but I don't care for him. He likes to shove you, to get you to fight, and sometimes says bad words."

I said, without thinking, "Does he say the word 'shit' like his mom did?"

Sam started laughing and Mama said, "That's enough, eat your supper."

Dad said, "Will, sometimes people are hurting on the inside, so that's when they want to hurt others, as to make themselves feel better, fit in better."

Then he said, "Maybe you could try to be extra nice to—I'm sorry, what's his name, Paul Jr.?"

"Molly calls him Pauly," I said.

Will said, "I guess it won't hurt to try."

That's when Dad asked, "Ask if Pauly would like to go fishing sometime."

I said, "Daddy, can you please take Molly and me fishing this summer? That would be a hoot!"

Mama said, "What's with you and the word hoot. Are you an owl now?"

Sam started laughing, and this time we all joined in.

Summer Fun and Paul

That summer, all of the kids in the neighborhood were outside playing, from early morning to supper. We wore a dirt path from our house to the subdivision. It went right through the fields, and more paths would spring up each year from our bikes and mini bikes. Our parents didn't mind because it kept us away, and safe, from the road and cars.

Molly and I would be to my house for lunch, where Mama would be there to fix us a sandwich of peanut butter and jelly, and sometimes, grilled cheese. My favorite!

Will and Sam would be off playing somewhere in the neighborhood. We all got watches for Christmas the year before, and Mama would say, "Be home at noon for lunch. I might be a nice mom, but I am not running a restaurant." We always had to be home at five for supper. Mama kept more watch over me those first years. I didn't wonder too far; also, Lady didn't leave my side. Sometimes, Mama would pack the boys sandwiches in a brown paper bag and lemonade in a glass jar, because they wanted to stay all day in the woods behind our home. The boys all had a fort of some sort. It even went up into a big tree. I remember Dad checking it out a few times after work; he said he wanted to make sure it was safe. Mama would say dads can be just like boys who never grow old. I got to go with Dad a few times when he carried some extra pieces of wood from the furniture factory, but I wasn't allowed to go there on my own.

After supper, we were all to stay close to home, mostly because we did family things like fishing.

Molly and I went fishing together that summer. The first time was a Saturday. Mama went with us; I think to put the worms on Molly's hook. Even though I could put my own worms on my hook at six years old, Dad put mine on that day. I think it was to make Molly not feel bad about not knowing how. We had so much fun in our matching green and blue pullover sleeveless shirts and blue shorts that hit just above our sun-brown knees. I was the first one to pull in a bluegill. Molly caught a bass, and almost let go of the fishing pole. Mama would help her pull it into the boat. She took it off the hook and went to throw it back in the water.

Molly screamed, "Hey, what are you doing, Miss Patty?"

Mama said, "Well, Molly, this fish is called a bass, a large mouth bass. They are fun to catch, but not to eat. So we get them safely back into the water right away so they can go on living."

We all pulled in enough fish for a supper, and Molly did end up catching a few keeper gills. We went back to shore, cleaned up, and had lunch. I remember cold fried chicken and potato salad. That afternoon, we asked Molly's parents, June and Paul, and brother, Paul Jr., to come over to our home for a fish-fry supper. They said yes. Molly and I were so excited; we helped Mama get everything ready. We snapped green beans and set the dining room table. Dad and Will cleaned the fish, and Sam brushed Lady. Molly and I changed our clothes. I let her wear my green dress that Aunt Sara made me. Molly always looked good in green. I wore a red-and-blue plaid dress, one of Mama's favorites.

Supper was to be at six o'clock that night. The Warners came knocking at the side door at six-thirty. "Come in and welcome," Dad greeted them. Paul had a six pack of beer in one hand, and shook Dad's hand with the other. Dad then said, "John here, nice to meet you."

Paul said, "Paul here, right back at you," and smiled.

Then Dad shook June's hand lightly and said, "Nice to finally meet Molly's parents and brother Paul Jr.," as he took Paul Jr.'s hand for a shake.

Miss June handed Mama a brown paper bag from the local A&P store that contained the store-bought brownies. "Thank you, June, please come in and sit down in the living room," Mama said.

Will said, "Hi, Pauly," and they headed to the den where the television was on.

Paul pulled a beer off the six pack, one for him and handed my dad one. Then Dad took the other four and put them in our refrigerator. Mama said from the kitchen, as Paul and Miss June walked into the living room, "Would you like a glass for your beer, Paul?"

He replied, "No, no I'll be fine, thanks." I watched Dad put his glass back into the cupboard, and with his can of beer, took a seat with Paul in the living room. The ladies sat on the couch together, and the men in our two wingback chairs that came from the furniture factory where Dad worked. Their talking seemed kind of boring, so Molly, Lady, and I took off to bug the boys watching TV, until we would be called to supper.

At the table, when my dad said a short prayer of thanks, I peeked and saw that Mr. Paul didn't close his eyes or bow his head. Then Molly told how much fun fishing was. She said, "If ever I was to be a fish, I would want to be a loudmouth bass because they don't get eaten." Everyone laughed.

Sam said, "Molly, it's called a large mouth bass."

Molly turned a little red, and Mama said, "That's okay, Molly, I still call sunfish starfish sometimes." Molly smiled. Then the boys said it was their turn to go fishing next.

Mr. Paul got up from the table and got another beer from the refrigerator. He said, "John, are you ready for another beer?"

Dad said, "No thanks, Paul, one's enough for me."

"Suit yourself," Paul said.

There was plenty to eat besides fish. Mama always put a ham loaf or meatloaf on the table when we had company over, and fish was served. She would say, "Not everyone likes fish." It was a good thing, because Miss June didn't want anything to do with eating fish.

It was a good evening and Molly and I agreed that it went well. Paul drank all of the beer, one after another. Dad and he went to look at the boat after supper. That's when Mr. Paul smoked his cigarettes. The only thing bad that was said was when Mama served the brownies Miss June got from the store. Sam, oh silly Sam, who will always say just what's on his mind, took one bite of his brownie and said, "This brownie is really bad, who made them?"

Mama said, "The store, Sam. What have I told you, if you can't say anything nice, maybe you should keep it to yourself?"

June said, "I just don't take the time to bake like I used to."

Sam then said, "That's all right, Miss June, I bet if you did make your own brownies, they would be real good."

Mama smiled and said, "Nicely said, Sam."

That night, after the Warners left for home, I helped Mama clean up. I was really tired and just wanted to crawl into bed, but I knew I should say my prayers. Dad always says, "You need to talk to God each day."

So my prayers were short and sweet that night. "Dear God, thank you for this most wonderful day, for my family, Lady, and most of all, thank you for my best friend, Molly, who you made a little girl and not a loudmouth bass. Amen." I smiled big and I knew my top gums showed. Then I said out loud, "Faith May, sometimes you say the funniest things." I gave Lady a kiss, because she was always by my side when I went to bed. Then as I fell asleep, thoughts of Grandma Mary came to me, very happy thoughts.

Families Grow and Sleepovers

The last week in August 1964, we went to the Bakker reunion in Iowa. As I have told, I am the only girl born to the Bakker boys. So when we all lined up for pictures, there I was amongst six boys. I told Mama on the train ride back that I was going to talk to God and ask if next year he will bless us Bakkers with a little girl. Mama just smiled.

September brought school again and the best thing was Molly and I were in the same first grade, with the prettiest, nicest teacher ever, Miss Donna. Miss Donna let Molly and I have our desks right next to each other. Even when we were always talking to each other, Miss Donna never got mad. She would say, "Okay girls, let's open our lesson book." We would open the wooden desk's top and retrieve our lesson books and yellow pencils that were always sharpened with the crank pencil sharpener mounted on the wall next to the door of our classroom.

Molly would tell me, "Miss Donna is my favorite teacher ever!"

Then I would say, "Molly, you don't know that for sure. You haven't had but two teachers so far."

Molly would come back and say, "She still is my favorite!" Molly, sweet Molly.

School was easy for me. I was just one of those kids who loved to learn. I would come home from school each day and tell Mama everything I had been taught that day. Then at the supper table that evening, I would tell Dad everything again. My dad was the best listener; he would always look me right in the eyes, just like Molly did. It made me feel so important to each of them. Not that my mama was a bad listener, it's just that she would always be doing something else while listening. Mama was just that way, always in motion. Maybe that's why she was always so thin.

October would bring the sadness of one year from Grandma Mary's passing. Then on a Friday in October, Mama would say at the breakfast table before school, "Your grandparents, Aunt Sara, and Uncle Sam will be here for supper tonight."

I said right away, "Mama, can Molly eat with us also?" Mama said, "Yes, if it's all right with her parents. Also, ask her parents if she can spend the night because it may be a late supper."

I couldn't wait to get going to school. I always walked to Molly's house first, using the dirt path through the field, and as the Michigan snow and cold would come, Mama would drive us, picking up Molly and Pauly on the way. I knew Miss June would let Molly eat with us, because she did it often and Molly really liked my Aunt Sara. Then to be able to have her sleep over, I was so excited!

At Molly's front door that morning, Miss June would kiss Molly good-bye, and I would ask, "Can Molly eat supper with my family, then stay the night for our very first sleepover?"

Miss June said, "But of course, as long as you mind your manners, Molly."

I said, "Molly has lots of manners."

Miss June then said, "Stop here after school and I will have Molly's things ready."

I said, "Thank you, Miss June, will do," then as Molly hugged her mom, she said, "Don't forget my Barbie dolls. I love you, good-bye," and off to school we went.

That evening as everyone gathered in our home, I notice that Uncle Sam and Aunt Sara came in the same car together, Uncle Sam's car. They had never done that before. Maybe, I thought, Aunt Sara's car was broken again.

Mama baked a cake that day, and I knew that Aunt Sara's birthday was at the end of October, so I figured that was what we were going to celebrate. I even asked Mama, "What did you get Aunt Sara for her birthday?"

She said, "It's not Aunt Sara's birthday cake; it's a surprise cake."

I gave Uncle Sam a big hug when he entered the kitchen. We hadn't seen him much lately. Grandpa Allen got him a job at the GM plant where he worked. Not even Dad would see Sam like when they worked together at the furniture factory. I think I remember just a few times that Dad and Uncle Sam went fishing that summer.

At the dining room table that evening, Mama had her good china out and wine glasses for everyone. Uncle Sam poured from a bottle of red wine that he had brought with him into each of the adults' glasses. Aunt Sara poured a sparkling lemon lime drink into us kids' glasses, and Grandma Rose's glass. I remember the adults drinking red wine at dinner one other time, at Easter dinner I believe. So I was confused. Then, my brother Sam, oh sweet Sam, who is not shy, said, "What's the occasion? And why can't I try the red stuff?"

Grandma Rose said, "Sammy, not for many years, and as Sammy said, what's the special occasion?"

That's when Uncle Sam said, as he stood up from the table with his wine glass in his hand, "I have gathered you all here to tell you I have asked Sara for her hand in marriage, and she has accepted."

Dad said, as he lifted his wine glass, "I'll toast to that," and then we all took our glasses and lightly tapped each others'. I was so happy and surprised, but my Grandma Rose seemed to be really happy and surprised. She even had tears of joy, as she would say. She always liked Uncle Sam, even if he didn't go to church that often.

Who couldn't like Uncle Sam? He was good-looking with his dark hair and big brown eyes. He was funny, sweet, and always smelled good, like Old Spice cologne, only better. "Now you are really going to be our Uncle Sam!"

Will would say, and Grandpa Allen said with a big smile, "It's about time."

After supper, Mama brought out the cake that had "Congratulations, Sam and Sara" written in pink icing on top of the chocolate frosting. Grandma Rose said, "You knew about this Patricia, didn't you?"

Mama said, "Of course, Mom. Sisters never keep secrets from each other," as she winked at Sara.

They said they would plan for a spring wedding, and then Aunt Sara said the best thing ever. "Faith and Molly, Sam and I would love it if you two girls would be our flower girls in our wedding."

We both jumped up from our chairs saying, "Yes! Yes! Yes!" Lady was jumping, too.

That's when Grandma Rose said, "I better get busy making all these dresses."

Sara said, "Don't worry, Mom, I'll help."

Mama said, "I'll have to help in another way, why, I can't even sew a button properly on Johnny's work shirts." We all laughed.

That night Molly and I got to sleep in the guest bedroom. Mama had even put a mix of her late blooms from her flower garden; there was a vase on each of the night tables. We got into our pajamas, said our prayers, and as we were climbing into bed, Molly picked up the picture off the nightstand on her side of the bed and said, "Who are these people?"

I gently took it from her small hand and said, "This here is a picture of my Grandpa Todd holding a fish he caught with his son, my dad, and the beautiful lady next to him was my Grandma Mary." Then, I said, "She lives in Heaven now, where it is beautiful every day, and nothing bad ever happens, only good."

As she took the picture back, and carefully set it next to the vase on the nightstand, Molly said, "I would love to go to Heaven. I have a grandpa who lives there, too. But I would only go for a visit because I would miss everyone who lives here on earth."

I said, "Don't be silly, Molly. Everyone knows when you go to Heaven, you don't get to come back. But don't worry, Molly, I have faith like my dad, that someday, we will all live in Heaven, and my dad says until then, we can see Heaven on earth. You just have to look around and be aware."

Molly said, "Faith May, I learn something from you every day."

I said, "I learn from you, too, Molly. Now let's talk about the dresses Aunt Sara is going to make us for the wedding. Did I tell you Aunt Sara made that pretty yellow dress that my grandma is wearing in the picture?"

Molly said, "Wow! We are going to look fabulous, just fabulous!" We both giggled, and talked until the sandman came.

Isn't She Beautiful?

While Mama, Aunt Sara, and Grandma Rose planned, sewed, and prepared for the wedding, Molly and I spent every day at school and after school together. We would do all we could to spend time together until we would have to separate for supper, and later, bed.

We were just seven years old and we thought then that we were going to conquer the world. Molly wanted to be a teacher, and I was going to be a nurse. Only thing was, Molly would tell me, she was scared that she wouldn't be as good as a teacher as Miss Donna. I would watch Molly in our classroom each day as she took in everything Miss Donna said and did. When Molly got a red star on her paper, she would tell me, "Isn't it beautiful? Miss Donna makes the nicest stars."

I would just smile and say, "Yes, Molly, Miss Donna's stars are just dandy." I would tell Molly, "I want to be a nurse, but I don't think I could take care of people as good as my mama takes care of me. She's the best at taking care of people"

Molly would reassure me and say, "Faith, you are good at caring of people who are hurt. Every time someone gets a skinned knee or a bump, you are right there telling them it will be okay, and you know just what to do." I told Molly that when someone gets hurt or doesn't feel well, it makes me happy if I can make them feel a little better.

Molly and I liked all the same foods. We both would say, "If we could only have one meal to eat, and only one, it would be macaroni and cheese." We also both like fish, perch fried just right in the bread crumbs that my mama would make herself, and we both hated lima beans. Our favorite color was blue; mine was sky blue and Molly's being more royal blue. Molly was good at math and I did better at reading, but we would help each other and Miss Donna liked that.

Sometimes I would tell God, as I would talk to him at night before going to sleep, "Thank you God for Molly, she is my best friend, besides Lady. Each new day is so fun; I am the luckiest little girl alive because my hole in my heart is full and pumping just right." Once I told God that I thought Molly was really my sister because we got along like Mama and Aunt Sara, and they were sisters.

Then came April 1965, and with it came the wedding. Aunt Sara wore a simple, yet beautiful, very light pink long dress. Aunt Sara designed it herself and Grandma and she sewed it together, along with Mama's dress, Molly's, and mine. We all wore a shorter version of Aunt Sara's dress. We would have different hues of pink, which I found out was Aunt Sara's favorite color.

Aunt Sara's bouquet was daises and purple hyacinths, which smelled so good. Mama's bouquet was all daisies. Molly and I would walk down the center aisle of the church and lightly toss daisies from small purple baskets that we carried. We followed the white cloth that led to the front of the church where Uncle Sam was standing. Uncle Sam winked at us girls as we reached the front and said, "Great job, you girls look divine." We both giggled.

My dad was standing next to Uncle Sam, and I watched him watch as Mama came walking down the aisle. He just stared at her with such a loving smile, like he was falling in love all over again, or maybe thinking of their wedding day. That's when I looked at Mama as she reached the end of the white cloth. She was so beautiful, with her dark blonde hair all done up and baby breaths tucked in just so, makeup just right. Then she smiled at Dad with her top gums showing. I could only think Dad saw her as shining. Then Aunt Sara would come down the aisle with Grandpa Allen's arm around hers. The wedding music got loud as it played *Here Comes the Bride*. Aunt Sara was just as beautiful as my mama. When Grandpa Allen gave Sara's hand to Uncle Sam, I saw water in both Grandpa and Uncle Sam's eyes.

After the ceremony, we went to a reception hall, where we ate, a band played, and people danced. Then they cut the three-layered fancy cake, which I am proud to say my mama baked, with the help of Miss June. I would find out later that she worked in a bakery before Molly was born and was quite good at baking. She even knew how to make delicious brownies as my brother Sam would say. Molly and I had so much fun. I remember we fell asleep on the ride home. Molly slept at our house, but I was so tired that I could hardly get ready for bed. I know I didn't say my prayers, but the next morning I woke up and told God, "Thank you for marrying Aunt Sara and Uncle Sam, and also thank you for having my dad marry my mama. Amen." Then I woke up Molly and said, "Lady and I smell bacon. Come on, let's get moving on this new day." Molly smiled.

The Bringing of Bad News

Spring brought summer, which meant all of us children were looking forward to the fun with school letting out. We Bakkers planned our family vacation over a few suppers, one in which Big Bill and Nana were present. The hummingbirds had returned, and fishing began. You would find Mama out back in her gardens and Molly and I on our bikes. I was looking forward to starting my swimming lessons at the high school, just like Will and Sam had when they were seven. Everything was just fine until one evening towards the end of June 1965.

After our family had finished our supper of beef stroganoff, we gathered on our front porch, which we often did in the summer. Dad was playing catch with Sam when Pauly came riding up on his blue bike. He said loud and clear, "Guess what? We are going to be moving. A man just put a for sale sign on our front lawn." I played with Molly that day and she had said nothing about moving.

Will said, "Are you pulling our leg, Pauly?"

My dad came and sat in his chair on the porch and Paul Jr. continued, "No, my mom said that we have fallen on hard times and we are going to move back to the city."

I looked at Dad and said, "Dad, can you tell the Warners that they can't move away?"

He said, "No, Faith that is not the answer."

Paul Jr. then said, as he got off his blue bike and sat on the edge of our porch, "My mom and dad have been fighting a lot lately. Mom keeps telling Dad if he didn't drink so much we could keep the house, and Dad yells at Mom to get off her butt and clean the house." Mama looked at Dad like maybe they shouldn't be hearing what is said. Paul Jr. continued, "I hate my dad. He's a bum and because of him losing his job, we have to move."

Mama said, "Pauly, please don't be so hard on your dad, I am sure he is hurting also." Then Mama turned to Dad and said, "John, is there anything we can do to help?"

Dad said, "Let me think on this. I will call Paul and talk to him."

Then I said, "I am so mad! This is not fair. If Molly moves away, I will just die!"

Mama snapped at me and said, "Faith May! I know this is sad news, but don't say you will die. That isn't nice."

Will then said, "Come on, Pauly, let's go for a bike ride. I want to see the for sale sign."

Sam said, "Me, too!"

As the boys went to gather their bikes, I said, "I want to go see Molly."

Mama said, "You stay put, you will see her in the new day. Things will look better then."

The boys took off on their bikes with Dad saying, "You two boys be back at dusk."

I knew Mama and Dad would discuss what was just said, but not in front of me. So I said, "Come on, Lady, let's you and I go inside and watch some TV." After the front screen of the porch door squeaked shut, I stood back and put my forefinger to my lips to let Lady know to sit and be quiet. I was just inside enough to hear Mama and Dad's discussion.

Mama would say first, "John, I didn't think this would happen. June and I talk, but she never mentioned Paul losing his job. And his drinking, well, remember the time we dropped Molly off after fishing one evening, and Paul was just leaving for work? He greeted us with the strong smell of alcohol on his breath."

Dad said, "I do. Maybe I can get him a job at the factory, but it sounds like he needs to get his drinking under control or why he drinks. That's his biggest demon now. Unless you fix why this has happened, you can't just put a bandage on an open wound."

Mama said, "I don't know what to think or do. Things are always good for us; we have so much to be grateful for. I guess its things like this that make you stop and realized that life can be hard, and without God, I would think it would be harder still."

Dad said, "Yes, Patty, we will have to pray and have faith that things the Warners are going through will be all right and get better."

I heard Mama get up from her chair, and I jumped back from the door. Then I realized that she got up to sit on Dad's lap for a hug. I heard her say softly, "I love you, Johnny." I know my dad would wink at Mama.

I then said, "Come on, Lady, let's go watch TV."

That night when I said my prayers, they were like this: "Dear God, please don't let Molly and her family move away. And please don't have Paul Jr. hate his dad. No one should hate someone and I really don't want to die just yet. Even if I would get to be with Grandma, it won't solve Molly having to move. Oh and God, thank you for my family and Lady. Amen."

In the morning, I couldn't get dressed or eat breakfast fast enough and I was on my bike to Molly's house. I looked at the red, black, and white square sign with phone numbers on the front lawn of Molly's house as I knocked on the side door. After a few minutes, Molly answered saying, "Come in Faith, but be quiet, everyone is still sleeping."

As I walked into the small kitchen, all around me was stuff. Messy dishes piled up, food left out, beer cans everywhere, and it smelled of cigarette smoke as I looked at the full ash tray on the kitchen table. I thought to myself, *I don't think I have to worry about anyone wanting to buy this house.* As I touched Molly's arm, I said, "Molly, what's going on? You can't move away! What are your mom and dad thinking?" Before Molly could open her mouth, I kept talking, "My dad and mama have always said that one can't outrun one's problems, and that they always catch up sooner or later. They say just face them head on. Has your family tried talking to God?"

Molly was rubbing her eyes to get the sleepy stuff out and said, "I know, Faith. I have been crying all night, and you know my mom and dad don't talk to God."

I said, "Maybe that's why they are in this mess, but don't worry, my dad can fix it, and what he don't fix, God will!" Then I said, as I stood in my not-so-matching outfit, "Now get dressed, Molly, we have a new day to enjoy. Come on, come on!"

Molly turned to go to her room and said, "Do I have to wear stripes and polka dots like you?"

Then she giggled and I said, "You're funny, just maybe this is just what is in style."

As she left the kitchen, I got a little nosy. I went into the living room to have a look, where there was more stuff piled up. One thing is, Molly and Pauly had a lot of toys. Molly had every Barbie doll and accessory there was, an easy-bake oven, and a mini kitchen set with its own dirty dishes that were piled up just like the family's kitchen.

I remember telling Mama before, "Molly is so lucky, she has so many toys and gets things all the time, even if it's not her birthday or Christmas."

Mama would just say, "That's nice, and you should be happy for her. But we stay on a budget and it doesn't allow for that kind of stuff." For the first time since I have known Molly, I was happy I didn't have all that stuff. But I was still going to ask for an easy-bake oven for Christmas this year.

Molly came out of her bedroom dressed in striped shorts and a checkered shirt that looked goofy together. We both laughed, and I know we were thinking, *that's what friends do.* Molly said, "I haven't eaten yet, can you wait until I eat a bowl of cereal?"

I said, "Of course."

She turned the television on low and I cleared a spot for us on the green couch. I knew she would bring her bowl of cereal out and eat while watching TV. Only once in a while were we Bakker children allowed to eat in the den with the TV on and TV trays. But that was okay. I liked that we ate our meals as a family at the table, and talked about our day.

Just then Miss June emerged from her and Mr. Paul's bedroom, with a fancy robe over her fancy nightgown. I knew what her nightgowns looked like, because most of the time Miss June wasn't dressed at the door when she would kiss Molly good-bye for school. Miss June sat down next to Molly and me on the couch. She lit up a cigarette that she took from the red and white box, and she took a deep puff. Then as the smoke came from her nose, she said, "What's up, kid? What brings you here this early?" First of all, I thought, it wasn't early; it had to be at least eight-thirty in the morning. Then I decided to just lay the cards on the table, which I had heard my Uncle Sam say before, and I knew it meant to get it out.

As soon as I waved the cigarette smoke from the air, I said, "Miss June, you can't move away and take my best friend. It's just not fair!"

Miss June was playing with her dark hair, which wasn't pinned back but laid over her shoulders. She said, "Oh, moving away will be fine. We will miss this neighborhood, and you folks have been very nice, but that's life. Things happen, kid." Then she looked at Molly and brushed her hand through Molly's short dark hair, "Besides, I told Molly here, when we move, she can have a kitten. You like that, don't you, Molly?"

Molly said, "Yes, Mom."

I said, "Why can't she have a kitten right here in this house?"

I could tell Miss June didn't like what I said, and her voice went up a little and she said, "Because I said she can have one when we move, Faith. That being said, don't make this any harder on Molly. Now you two go outside and play. I have a house to clean."

At that moment, I didn't like Molly's mom, and I even had a bad thought that maybe I didn't care if Miss June and her stinking cigarettes moved away as long as Molly could stay. We got up and went outside; we headed to the school playground on our bikes. Playing took our minds off the move and we didn't mention it the whole day.

How Could You?
Fishing Always Helps

Days turned into weeks and I was still not happy about seeing the "for sale" sign on the Warners front lawn each time I knocked on Molly's side door. My dad would tell me, "Worry won't get you anywhere, Faith May; just talk to God." Dad had talked to Mr. Paul, but from what I could gather, it didn't go so well, and Dad would tell me, "You can't help someone if they don't want it, Faith May. The Warners have been told that if they need anything, your mom and I are here."

About the middle of July, Mama went to the Warners to help Miss June with the cleaning. I was a little mad at her and said, "Mama, why would you clean Molly's house? Do you want her to move away?"

Mama said, "Faith, Miss June asked for my help and as a friend, that's what you do. Of course, I don't want Molly and her family to move, but we have to support their decision. I am sure this is hard on them all." When Mama planted some flowers in the flower boxes of Molly's house, I didn't talk to her for the whole day.

That night when Mama came to give me a hug and kiss goodnight, I said the meanest thing I had said to her in my first seven years of life. "Mama, if Molly moves, I blame you for helping make the Warner's house sell!"

Mama said as she hugged me, "I'm sorry you feel that way. I love you and Molly so much and this is very hard on all of us, but things happen and now we have to make the best of it."

With tears forming, I said, "Mama, I love you, too, but I have this bad feeling like you did when Grandma Mary left that summer day. I feel like if Molly moves away, I will never see her again."

Mama hugged me tighter with tears coming down her face, and wetting my face, she said, "Oh honey, I am so sorry you have these feelings. They are the worst. But I promise right now, if and when Molly has to move, we will do our very best to make sure you two girls see each other. Miss June and I have talked and our plans are getting you girls together often. Grand Rapids is not that far away at all, Faith, just a hop, skip, and a jump." We both smiled.

I went to sleep feeling a little better, but still didn't know why I was feeling something bad could happen. Also, I was thinking about the kitten Miss June was going to let Molly have. I would look down at Lady, lying on the red rug beside my bed, and I said, "What do you think, Lady? Should we ask Mama and Dad for a kitten?" Lady just wagged her tail, put her head down, and sighed.

A few days later, Dad said at the supper table that he was taking us Bakker children on a camping and fishing trip. He said, "Your mom won't be able to come because she is going to be helping her friend Mrs. Vandyke. As you all know, we told you about Mr. Vandyke's passing, and now Mom's going to help the family with her move into a place where she will get the care she needs." I remembered a few weeks ago that Dad and Mama went to the funeral for Mr. Vandyke. Mama had said it was a heart attack that took him. I thought to myself then that it was God that took him home, and the heart attack had just sealed the deal.

I wanted Molly to come on our trip, but Dad said, "Not this time." I was okay with it because just being with my dad and brothers fishing was going to be great. I know Dad had taken the boys camping before with the tent. Mama and I stayed behind, so this was my first time camping. I was excited!

Dad and Mama packed the boat with all the fishing supplies and camping gear, and the station wagon seemed full in back with food, clothes, and what-nots. After a big breakfast with Mama and Lady Friday morning, we would kiss them and wave good-bye as we headed to Ludington, Michigan.

After arriving and setting up camp on what the weatherman would say was going to be an overcast but warm weekend, we would pile back into the car to ride around and scope out the area, as Dad would say. I think Dad just liked to look around at nature, so we would drive down dirt roads looking for deer, wildlife, and take in the scenery. Then we stopped, and got ice cream cones. I laughed and said, "Boy oh boy, Dad, if Mama could see us now, she would say, 'what are you doing eating ice cream before supper?'"

Dad said, "Faith, you know your mother well, but sometimes you've got to mix things up just a little." He winked at me.

At a campfire before turning in for the night, we would talk about forgiveness. Sam was having trouble forgiving his friend Billy for breaking his bike chain, "on purpose" as Sam would say. Dad would tell Sam that it was fixed, and he did hear that Billy said he was sorry.

Sam said, "But he wasn't really sorry. He just said it because his dad told him to. If I forgive him, he will just think it was okay to try to wreck my bike."

I was thinking how important our bikes were to us when Dad would say, "Don't hold on to resentment, Sam, it will only hurt you, not the person that it's aimed towards." Dad continued and said, "Forgiveness seems to be one of the hardest things God wants us to acquire while we live on this earth. I believe it's the most important ability one can pursue. If you live your life holding on to all the wrongs, you won't have room to let what's right in, and as you grow old you, will have regrets that could turn you cold and bitter."

Sam said, "You're right, Dad, I have to let it go. I feel better. Thanks, Dad. Besides, tomorrow is a new day."

Will said, as he started to get ready for bed, "Can I sleep out here, Dad, with the stars?"

Dad said, "Sure."

I said, "Will, aren't you afraid of bears?"

Will laughed and said, "No, Faith, I think I will be just fine, but you better get some sleep. As soon as that sun starts waking up, I want to be on the lake." And with that, it wasn't long before I fell asleep on the cot in the tent, away from any bears.

The next morning we were up early. Dad fixed breakfast and Will packed the coolers, and Sam loaded the boat, and we were off. Dad and Will wanted to try to catch some walleyes in Hamlin Lake. I had eaten walleye before, the ones that Uncle Sam and Dad had caught over the years. They taste even better than perch, but from what I was to find out, not as easy to catch.

Once on the lake, we would get our poles in the water. Dad said the walleyes will hang around on the bottom. Our night crawlers were put on a crawler harness and we trolled. I loved that I was learning a new way to fish, and even if all we were catching and releasing that morning were pike, we were having fun.

We went ashore around ten to relieve ourselves, clean up, eat, and then all agreed to go back out again. The sun was shining, but Will said it would last night because of all the stars out. Dad said it would be better if it was cloudy for walleye.

Back in the boat, Sam would ask Dad, "Why do some people drink beer and smoke cigarettes?" I was thinking he was referring to Molly's dad, Mr. Paul, but I wasn't sure.

Dad said, "Well, I guess it's because God gave man and woman," as he looked at me, "free will, that means we all have choices on what we do, bad or good, you are the one who, if of sound mind, make those choices."

Then Will asked, "If you drink alcohol, are you a bad person, Dad?"

Dad said, "Of course not. Drinking doesn't make one bad, but if you consume too much, it does change your mind into not making a clear decision. It's the same with any kind of drug. They can become addictive, and then the drug itself will make your choices."

I could hardly wait to ask a question. I even raised my hand and my brothers both laughed. Dad said, "Yes, Faith, what's on your mind?"

I asked, "Dad, why don't God just make everything better and take away all the bad things in the world?"

Dad reeled in his fishing pole to look at his night crawler, and I knew he was thinking on what to say. Then he said, as he put his line back into the water, "Well, Faith, that is a very good question, and a question that could be answered by so many, in so many different ways. But, I think only God knows the right answer. With that being said, I shall tell you what I think, and then you children will have the choice to agree or disagree."

Sam interrupted, "We will have free will?"

Dad smiled, "Yes, Sam, that's right." Dad continued, "I believe God takes away bad things every day with our prayers, if when you pray you have the faith that God will answer your earnest request. The thing is, not all prayers get the answer that we want, and in the timely matter that we expect. But that's when we must really have faith that God still hears our prayers, and the right answer will come." Then Dad would say, "I think too many of us wait until something bad happens before we pray to God to fix it. I think God wants us to grow up with the sense that if we know, and talk to God all the time, then a shield of faith surrounds you and protects you. I have faith in that belief."

Sam said, "Dad, tell us again why you talk to God?"

Dad said, "I would love to!" He continued, "As a very young child, I was told about God. That God was my creator and ruler of the universe, the one who put breath in me upon birth. I was told to talk to God every day and as much as I wanted. To thank God for all I have and will have, to ask God for what I needed, to cry to God when I was sad, and tell God what made me happy. I was told not to let one day go by without talking to God. I was told I must talk to God no matter how sick I felt or even if everything was going just great! I still needed to talk to God. Just as I have told you children to pray or talk to God each day, and the reason is I have been told this and have passed it down to you children." We all knew the answer, but wanted to hear it again. Just as Dad started to speak, a fish took his bait, and he started reeling in what looked to be a walleye.

"Get the net, Will," Dad said, as the fish got closer to the boat. It would put up a really good fight; when it surfaced near the boat, Will said with such excitement, "It's a walleye, Dad! A nice-sized one!"

Dad said, "Net it, Will!" Sam and I stood back as the fish was netted in and put in the boat.

We all were amazed and happy with Dad's catch. Then Will said, "Because of your strong faith, you believe that God listens to each and every one of us all the time. God wants to hear from us. God wants us to tell of what we need, and wants us to be grateful for what we have, and to know with God, all things are possible, and the most important is God loves each and every one of us the same."

"Well said, Will," Dad said, as he put the walleye in the cooler of ice. Then Dad said, "I just want my children, as well as every child, to know of God. Please read all you can on God, hear all there is said about God, and then make your own choice on your own faith, and never think your faith is better than someone else's. For that's their faith, our faith belongs to us, and I think just as God made each and every one a little different, that our faith can be different, but for those who have the trust of God, then it's a powerful faith."

Then I said, "All I can say is I am praying to God that Molly doesn't have to move away."

Dad said, "I know, honey, I hope God will make that so. Now, we best get our poles in and call it a day. We have a nice fish to clean for supper."

Will said, "Yea, let's try again early tomorrow morning. Thanks, Dad, for the fishing lesson, and a life lesson."

Dad said, "You are welcome."

Sam said, "Amen to that," and we all laughed and was soon at the dock.

Back at camp, Dad went to clean the fish, and Will and Sam were wrestling a little in the grass by camp. I think being in a boat all day made them need to move their growing limbs. One thing about my brothers, they were never mean to each other, or me. It was how we were taught. I remember one day that spring, after school, on the way home, two boys of Will's age started a fight. We all circled around them because they were really swinging their arms hitting each other. I watched my brother Will, then ten years old, stand back and assess the situation. I said, "Will! Do something. They are really hurting each other!" But Will was so much like Dad; he would never jump into something unless it was an emergency. After the one boy was held down by the other, and he started to punch him, Will walked over and grabbed the boy off the other. Will said in a deep, loud voice, "That's enough!" The boy looked like he was going to hit Will, but I am not sure what it was, but Will looked so big and tall at that moment. Both boys brushed themselves off, gathered their books, and went in opposite directions. I believed that Will talked to God at that moment and asked God what to do. Maybe God made Will look really big and tall, or just maybe, Will knew with God he could help.

We were taught to respect each other, not to let anger or bad emotions get the best of us. Yes, we were normal, there were times where feathers would fly, and we misbehaved. We had plenty of talking to and corners to look at from a chair. But never once, not once, did our dad or mom call us a bad name. They would praise us often and listen to us always. We were not to call each other names. Stupid, ugly, retarded were words never said in our home. We were to carry what we were taught outside of home also. Dad would say, "You are no better than anyone you will ever come to meet. You may look different, act different, but in God's eyes, you are the same."

Hitting was not allowed, and spanking, well, that just didn't happen. We were so blessed to have parents who really worked hard every day at making our family feel good. Maybe it was because I know for sure Dad and Mama talked to God each day. Just maybe, Dad was getting answers from God on how to love and raise children, because he sure had it down right.

Home. Bad Dreams.
And Welcome Little One

We got home the next evening with no fish in the cooler, but good memories in our head. Right away Will was telling Mama how hard it is to catch walleyes, but sleeping under the stars was the best. Mama said, "I sure did miss you all." Then, I saw her turn and hug Dad, and then she had that look of sadness in her eyes.

The next day was Monday, and Mama was up early with Dad. I could hear them in the kitchen, the smell of coffee and bacon in the air. In the summer months, most mornings we kids slept until eight o'clock. Dad would have already gone to work when we would rise. But Mama always got up with Dad, and made his lunch, and drank coffee with him. They would listen to the news from a radio in the kitchen.

Because my bedroom was the closest to the kitchen, I could hear some of their conversation as I lay in my bed. Lady had already left my bedroom to sit by Dad for her daily handout of maybe a bit of bacon. I heard Mama say, "Oh, John, I so don't want to tell her. I guess God is going to answer this prayer in a different way." Then it hit me, Mama's look of sadness the night before, it could only mean Molly was moving away! I wanted to get up right then and there, but my legs were frozen. I couldn't move, and then sleep consumed me, and I fell into a bad dream.

I dreamt that Molly was calling for me in the distance. It was cloudy, and I couldn't find her. I was running but not moving. "Molly, where are you?!" I woke up suddenly and heard the hard rain. I believed the thunder was what woke me. I was thinking maybe it was a bad dream, and maybe what Mama said was the beginning of the bad dream.

I went into the kitchen and the table only had my place setting. *Will and Sam must already be up*, I thought. I heard the television in the den, looked in, and saw only the boys and Lady in there. I found Mama in her bedroom chair reading. She put her book down as I walked in, and she said, "Good morning, sunshine, it's late. I guess camping made you tired for your own bed."

I said, "Hi, Mama," as I climbed up into her lap for a hug.

Mama said, "You are warm. Are you hungry?"

I said, "No, just thirsty," then I said, "Mama, I had a bad dream that Molly was moving."

Mama's soft hand brushed the hair from my eyes and said, "Faith, I'm so sorry to tell you, but the Warner's home was sold last weekend, and Miss June has told me they will be moving in a few weeks. They have found a house to rent in the city, not far from a school for Molly and Paul Jr."

I pushed away from Mama and stood my bare feet on the wood floor, and I took a few steps back. I knew I should think before I speak, but at that moment, thinking wasn't important to me and I said, "How could God do this? I prayed often that Molly wouldn't have to move. This isn't the answer I wanted for my prayers! This is not fair! I am not talking to God ever again!" I left the room and went to my bedroom. I grabbed Dolly off of my dresser and lay back in my bed and cried myself to sleep.

It rained the whole day, and when I did get up, I felt really sick. Mama felt my head, and took my temperature with the stick with the red ball on the end. As a rash appeared on my neck and chest, she called the doctor.

By late afternoon, I was to the doctor's and back. I was told I had scarlet fever and was to stay in bed and take this pink syrupy stuff until the bottle was empty. My throat was real sore and I was so tired. The worst part was, I couldn't see Molly.

By the time I was better, Molly and Paul Jr. were staying with their grandmother a few days before the move. Molly and I got to talk on the phone a few times, but I needed her close to me so she could look me in my eyes while we talked. I started talking to God again after a few days of not. Dad had come and sat by my bed when I was sick. He said, "Faith May, I know you are mad at God, but God really isn't the reason the Warners are moving. I think the reasons are what we talked about on the boat. Maybe it was Mr. Paul and Miss June's free will and the choices that came that lead to this path. I know it doesn't seem fair to Molly and you, but now you have to have faith that everything will work out just fine. Maybe it wasn't God's choice, but pray and have faith God will bring them through it." I decided then and there that I wasn't going to ever stop talking to God, because all and all, I felt so much better when I did.

Before the move, Molly got to stay at our home for a few days. Mama and Dad took us fishing, and then they took us for a day to the Ionia Free Fair. We would ride the Ferris wheel, and when our Ferris car stopped at the top, we both made a promise to be best friends forever, no matter how far our parents moved us away from each other. We said that when we got married, we would move into houses right next to each other so our children could play together.

I said, "We will teach our children how to catch fish."

Molly said, "As long as you hook the worms for them!"

We laughed and hugged.

The last week of August, we Bakkers took a plane trip to Iowa for the reunion. I was wearing one of my favorite dresses of all time. I think it was because it was yellow, and of course, Aunt Sara had made it.

Uncle Jack and Aunt Marion picked us all up at the airport. Aunt Marion sat next to me in the backseat. She kept looking at me and smiling. She looked like a cat that just swallowed the canary, so to speak. I got the feeling she wanted to tell me something real bad, but made a promise not to.

As we drove up Grandpa Todd's long gravel driveway to the big farmhouse, everyone seemed to be there by the look of all the cars. After gathering our luggage and coming in through the kitchen to the dining room, which still held the big wood table Dad made, my Uncle Jim, with his big smile and wooden leg, came to me and said, "Oh! Faith May, I'm so happy to see you! Come, come! Sit in the other room on Grandpa's couch." As I sat down, everyone seemed to gather around me in the living room. I was looking for where Uncle Jim disappeared to when he emerged from a bedroom with Aunt Sylvia. In Aunt Sylvia's arms was a wiggling pink blanket. Uncle Jim then took the bundle of pink, and as he preceded to hand it to me, he said, "Faith May Bakker, I am proud to introduce you to our youngest Bakker, Mary Hope Bakker!" And into my arms was the prettiest little baby girl I had ever laid eyes on.

I said, "Wow! Can this be? Look at her, Mama!" she was sitting next to me on the couch. Then I said, "She is so pretty, why didn't you tell me?"

Mama said, "We all agreed you needed to be surprised."

I said, "That I am. Aunt Sylvia and Uncle Jim, I just love her name."

Aunt Sylvia said, "Faith, when I told your mother I was expecting last fall, she told me you were going to ask God for a little girl to bless us Bakkers, and we thank you, because we couldn't be happier."

I said, as I looked from Mama to Dad, "I was thinking on a baby sister, but I guess God answers prayers sometimes in a different way." Everyone laughed, and I added. "But at least I know now that God does answer prayers."

When at the reunion, all we Bakker children lined up to get our pictures taken. I held Mary Hope. She was smiling up at me, and I was thinking even if I won't be able to see her that often, she will grow up being part of my life. Just like Molly moving away doesn't mean she's still not part of my life. After pictures, everyone passed Mary Hope around like a precious jewel.

Before we left for home, as Mama was holding Mary Hope, I took a beaded necklace from around my neck and put it around Mary Hope's. I said, "This is a necklace that our Grandma Mary gave me when I was little like you. She gave me two of these, so she must have wanted you to have one someday. Grandma Mary would love to have held you. I am lucky to have had some time with her, and can remember her. But don't you worry, Mary Hope, because I have faith, like my dad does, that someday, many, many years from now, you will meet our Grandma Mary."

Mama said, with a tear coming down her cheek, "Faith May, you are such a good soul. I know Grandma Mary is so happy right now."

On the plane trip back to Michigan, I told Mama what a stinker she was not to tell me about Mary Hope, and how I couldn't wait to tell Molly all about her. My brother Sam, on the other hand, was so happy about being in the air above the fluffy white clouds in the plane. That very day he decided he was going to be an airplane pilot.

Dad said, "That's great, Sam, I personally like both feet grounded."

Will said, "I'm with you, Dad. My feet like the earth, and the bottom of a boat."

The Rented House and Ice Cream

The next school year was about to begin, and I had to think who I would walk to school with. Molly and I had played with a girl named Tina. She only lived a few houses down from where Molly lived. Tina was a grade ahead of us, but I had heard that she got held back. So as faith would have it, she would be in the same second grade as me. I liked Tina, but the only thing was, she talked more than me, if anyone can believe it.

I knocked on Tina's side door two days before school began. Tina answered, "Hi, Faith. I bet I know what you want, but do tell."

I said, "Hi, Tina, I was wondering if I could walk to school with you this year? I can be here at seven thirty-five, and that should bring us to school at seven fifty-five when the first bell rings."

Tina said, "Yes, Faith that will be fine. I heard Molly moved, and was thinking on you wanting to walk with me. I got held back this year, not because I'm dumb, like my sister Pam says, but because my mother says I have a learning disability, and that's the reason I have to do second grade over." Without taking a breath, she continued, "My Uncle Don said that some of the smartest people he knows had to do second grade over, and he sees no reason it will do any harm, and do you want to play now? Because I have to help Pam with the dishes but . . ."

I quickly said, "Tina! Please slow down, I have to be getting on home. I'll see you in two days at seven thirty-five."

Tina said, "Okay, Faith, what are you going to wear the first day of school? Because I just went . . ."

I interrupted as I stood my red bike up to climb on, "Wait a minute, Tina, I think I'm supposed to walk with my brother Sam. I'll get back to you."

As I started to pedal my bike, I heard Tina say loud so I could hear, "Well then, I'll just see you, Faith, in two days, at—did you say seven thirty-five?

51

I will be wearing a new purple dress, and white knee socks and what color shoes do you think, black or brown?"

"Good-bye, Tina, see you later," I said. I know I could still hear her as I rounded the corner.

When I got home, I plumped on a kitchen chair where Mama was making sandwiches for Dad and Will to go fishing with that afternoon. I said, "I can't do this without Molly. I just feel so bad, I miss her so."

Mama said, "I was just on the phone with June; we have planned a play date. I guess that's what you call it, for next Saturday. You and I will spend the day at the Warner's new home."

I said, "Thanks, Mama, I am going to need it after a week of walking to school with Tina."

When Mama and I arrived at the Warner's home in the city, I couldn't believe how different city living was. All the houses were right next to each other. Why, I bet you could almost reach out from one house and touch another. We drove up Molly's short driveway, and Molly was sitting on the front porch waiting. She was wearing blue seersucker pants, the same as me, and we both had cotton blouses. Molly's was pink and mine was white. I jumped out of our station wagon as it came to a stop, and ran up to her.

I said, "My goodness, Molly, I sure have missed you. Do you like school? Did you meet anyone like me?"

Molly said, "Don't be silly, Faith May, there is no one like you," as she smiled.

As we walked in Molly's house, it was full of stuff, just like her old house. I thought to myself, *some things never change*. Molly led me to her bedroom, where she had all her Barbie dolls, and our moms sat at the kitchen table talking. I knew Miss June lit a cigarette; I could smell the smoke as it made its way into Molly's bedroom. Then I would tell Molly about walking to school with Tina and how she talks and talks. Molly laughed, "Faith, that's funny. Remember when we played with Tina, and we both counted all her words she said. We got to something like three hundred, and you said, "I'm exhausted.""

I laughed, "Yes, I do!"

Molly then said, as she brushed the Barbie's long blonde hair, "Faith, I hate it here. My mom and dad fight even more than they did at our old house, and Pauly is not even nice anymore. He tells me to go away all the time and he's supposed to walk to and from school with me. But, after the second day, he said, "Grow up kid you're on your own." Molly sighed, "I hardly know my way yet, because everything looks the same."

I said, "I am sorry. I guess this move would be harder for you than me. At least I don't have so many different things to learn. Did you tell your mom about Paul Jr. being mean?"

Molly said, "No, she's always getting ready for work. She started this new job working nights at some restaurant where Mom brings people food and drinks. Pauly said it's called a bar. All I know is, Dad doesn't like it, and when he gets home at night from his job at the used car lot, he says he's going to start sitting in the restaurant to watch Mom."

Then, I said, "Let's go ask our moms if we can play outside. I think some fresh air will do us both some good." When we went to the kitchen and asked, Miss June suggested we all walk a few blocks to the *Dairy Queen* for ice cream cones. I said, "Who could turn down ice cream?"

On our walk, we would pass a candy store, a food market, a church, and a gas station. I said, "Wow, Molly, you have everything so close to your new house."

Miss June said, "Yea, I already send Paul Jr. to get milk for us, and Molly can go to the candy store anytime she wants." Mama looked a little dismayed, but said nothing.

We all got vanilla and chocolate twists, and the three picnic tables were full of people licking their cones. At the fourth picnic table sat a man who stood up as we passed and said, "Ladies, girls, please sit down here, I will be leaving shortly," as he sat back down with his big cup of ice cream.

At first my Mama said, "That's okay, we can walk with our cones."

But Miss June said, "Don't be silly, Pat, let's sit. There is plenty of room."

As we all sat down, the man looked at me funny as if his eyes hurt my body, but I would look the other way. Then the man said, "So are you lovely ladies from around here?"

Molly said, "Yes, I just moved in a rented house a few blocks away."

The man said, "What are your names?"

Miss June said, "Oh, sorry about our manners," she held out her hand and the man shook it gently. "My name is June and this is Pat," as she nodded toward Mama. Then she said, "And of course, my lovely daughter, Molly, and her friend, Faith."

The man said, "Nice to meet you all. Such a nice day for ice cream." Then the man turned and looked the other way as to not interfere with our time together. I was thinking, he never did tell us his name.

As we were licking our cones, Molly said, "Mom, when am I going to get my kitten that you promised me?"

Miss June, shooting a glare at Molly, said, "Molly, I have told you, just a day ago, that there are no kittens this time of year. Besides, your dad said no cats in the house."

Molly whined a little and said, "But Mom, you promised."

Miss June said, "Don't be a baby. I swear sometimes you can be a brat, Molly." I could tell Mama wanted to say something like, "a promise is a promise," or maybe she just wanted to tell Miss June that you shouldn't call your children bad names.

Mama looked at Molly and said, "So Molly, do you like your new school? What's your teacher's name?"

Molly said, "Mrs. White, and the classroom is big and the school is much bigger. I have to walk to school and home by myself and I am afraid of getting lost."

Mama said, "It will get easier as time goes on, Molly." Then she leaned over and gave Molly a hug, and I heard her say in Molly's ear, "Just remember, Molly, God is with you. Talk to God, tell God how you feel. I can promise God can help."

Molly said, "Thanks, Miss Patty, I sure do miss you."

When we started to get up from the picnic table, the man stood up, too. He said, "You young ladies have a lovely afternoon," and then he looked right at Molly and said, "I hope you get that kitten you want, Molly."

Molly smiled and said, "Thanks, mister. Me, too." Miss June shot the man a dirty look and as we walked away, I watched the man look at Molly in a strange way, and I didn't like it, not one bit.

Before we left the Warners that Saturday, we planned another play date for the second Saturday in October. That was only four weeks away. Mama said Paul Jr. could come, too. Then Molly said, "Maybe Faith can come and stay overnight on Halloween night, because with all these houses around here, we could have our treat bags full in no time."

Miss June said, "Sure, but I will have to check and see if I have to work that night."

Mama said, "I am not sure; I will have to talk to John."

I said, "Just no matter what, our moms promised to keep us together, and a promise is a promise!" Then I watched Miss June give me a look, and I kind of got the impression Mama didn't like the tone of my voice when I said it. But I was kind of mad at Molly's parents for not letting her have the kitten they had promised. Molly told me she was lonely.

My Uncle Jack and Aunt Marion came for a visit the next week. I liked having Aunt Marion around. She would help me pick out clothes for school the night before and be up early to brush my hair before leaving. When I came home from school, she would help my brothers and me with our homework. She was always so cheerful; just being around her made you think of how funny life could be.

She would tell me stories of when she was a little girl my age. She said she had a best friend named Elise, and they were always together playing on the farm where she lived. Then one day Elise didn't come to school, and when Aunt Marion went to her house after school, it was empty, everything gone. She told me how she was heartbroken, and that her family never did find out where Elise and her family went. They just moved away in the night.

Aunt Marion said, "That's when food became my best friend. It's always there to comfort me. It fills the empty hole in my stomach that was there when Elise left." I would think I was lucky to know where Molly moved to, and that Molly moving away didn't make me hungry.

Dad and his brother Jack would go fishing after Dad came home from work. Will and Sam went, too, but for some reason, I didn't get to go. I knew Dad would be putting the boat away before the cold came. I would miss fishing and always felt sad when the boat was cleaned and winterized. But I had faith that just like the hummingbirds would come back in the spring, so would the boat come out for fishing.

When we said our good-byes to Uncle Jack and Aunt Marion, they asked if maybe next summer I could come stay for a few weeks with them in Iowa. Mama would say, "We will see." I was thinking how much fun it would be to play with Mary Hope, but I was happy I had time to think about it.

The Man and the White Car

It had started to turn cold outside that first Friday in October. I left Tina at her door, and was walking the rest of the way home from school, when Molly entered my thoughts. Because it was a chilly, cloudy day, and the sun was nowhere to be found, an afternoon where you would think that at any minute the dark sky would open up and dampen everything. I was thinking, *I hope Molly has her umbrella with her, because I didn't want her to get sick from getting wet.* She was going to spend the night at my house the next week on Saturday.

Molly left school at 2:45 in the afternoon, just like she did every school day. She buttoned her pink sweater all the way, wishing she had her jacket because of all the damp chill in the air. She crossed the street with the crossing guard's help, walked a block down Lincoln Street, and then cut through the yard of the little green house. That would bring her to Grant Street. That meant she only had one more street before she was home safe.

The man in the white car pulled over to the curb, and with his passenger window rolled down, he said, "Good afternoon, Molly."

Molly smiled and said, "Hi, mister." She walked from the safety of the sidewalk to the curb. The man had befriended Molly since that day of sitting together on the picnic table at the *Dairy Queen*. He started showing up after school, and after Molly crossed the busy intersection, he would walk with her until she got to her street. The man was even at the candy store one day, and when Paul Jr. would ditch Molly for one of his friends. The man told her it was okay, he would never do that. He even gave her an extra seventy-five cents to spend in the candy store. That night when Pauly saw all the extra candy Molly had, he said, "Hey, Mom only gave us each twenty-five cents, how come you have so much more candy?"

Molly was going to tell Pauly about the man, but the man said, "Molly, lets you and I be secret friends, and I bet I can find you that kitten you have been wanting. It's best we don't tell anyone about us being friends; they wouldn't understand."

The man would show Molly how to cut through the yard of the little green house, because no one was living there. He would always hold her hand when cutting through the overgrown bushes and grass, letting go of her hand when they reached the street. Molly started to like the man. He seemed nice, but each night as she would go to sleep, she would have this feeling that something wasn't right in her life. Like a bad energy had encircled her, and she wasn't sure why, but she was thinking it was their secret.

Back at the curb, the man in the white car said, "So Molly, what do you think, should we go look at them kittens I found?"

Molly smiled big and said, "You found kittens? Where?"

The man said, "On a farm in the country, not too far from here." Then the man produced a picture with four baby kittens. Molly moved closer to the car to have a look.

"Aw, they are so cute," she said.

The man then said, "Come on, Molly, let's go see them."

Molly said lightly, and shaking her head, "I better not. My mom doesn't want me to ride in cars without her permission."

That's when the man said with excitement in his voice, "Oh, but Molly, I did talk to your mom. Just this morning, she said it would be fine for me to take you to the farm to hold the kittens. She even said you could pick one out." Then the man reached over and opened the white car's passenger door and said, "Come on, Molly, we won't be long. Your mom really wants you to have a kitten; she was so happy that I found some."

Molly had thoughts of yesterday afternoon. Her mom was putting on her heavy makeup for work, and Molly asked about a kitten again. Her mom got mad and said, "Molly, I wish you could have a kitten, but there are none to be found. Now leave me alone!" Then Molly thought, *Maybe the man did talk to Mom.*

The man broke into Molly's thoughts and said, "So, come on, Molly, those kittens are growing by the minute."

Molly smiled, "Okay, mister, I guess it won't hurt to look." And Molly left the safety of the curb and climbed in the front seat of the white car. The man was happy as he reached over and shut the car door.

The young man that was parked behind the man in the white car looked on as the white car pulled alongside the curb, and with the window down, watched as the man talked to the little girl, with short brown hair, a tan and red print dress with a pink sweater on top. He had just gotten into his car with his paperwork in hand. The young man was feeling good about selling a vacuum cleaner, just that he wasn't sure if the sweet old lady he just sold it to could really afford it.

The young man had a sense that maybe that wasn't the little girl's dad, but he was thinking, *what do I know, I don't have any kids. How old do you have to look to have a little girl that age? Maybe it was her uncle giving her a ride home from school.*

As the little girl climbed into the front seat, the young man's eyes were drawn to the white car's license plate. He smiled and said out loud, "Look at that, the plates have my wedding date, and they are Indiana plates, the state where my beautiful wife is from. Gosh, going on two years married, I better not forget to buy flowers soon." After the white car pulled out, so did the young man in his red car, with one less vacuum in his trunk.

Back in the white car, Molly was holding the picture of the four little fluffy kittens. She noticed that the picture looked old, like a lot of people had held it before. Then she said to the man, "I really like the fluffy orange kitten with the pretty blue eyes."

The man said, "I think that would be my choice also." Molly looked out her window. They were out of the city and going down a road with trees on both sides, and every so often would come a field with cows, and maybe a farmhouse sitting back off the road.

Then Molly said, "Mister, are we going to be there soon? I think my mom would like me home before long."

The man reached over and pushed the knob down on the door where Molly was leaning against. He said, "We don't want you falling out." Then he pulled Molly closer to him.

Molly was feeling a little fear not knowing where she was and within a few minutes said, "Mister, I want to go home."

The man, starting to feel his nerves get to him said, "Why, Molly, we are almost there."

Molly said again, "I want to go home." That's when the man turned the white car down the two tracks with trees on both sides. He only drove about fifty feet in from the country road, because he didn't know where the road led and he just figured the trees would hide the white car.

Miss June started pacing back and forth in the little rented house. Molly was now a little over an hour late from school. She was feeling bad as it was because she was short with Molly the afternoon before. Then that morning, when she got up to get Molly and Paul Jr. up for school, she went back to bed, because not only did she work late at the bar the night before, she also stayed there and had a few drinks before going home, and her head ached. She then realized she didn't even get up to kiss Molly good-bye before school. The guilt started to get the best of her, and then she dialed the police department.

"Ma'am, calm down!" said the police officer. "Little kids come home every day late from school." Then the officer said, "She probably went to the candy store."

Miss June shouted, "You don't understand! Molly is a good girl, she is never late! She wouldn't go to the stupid candy store without telling me!" Miss June then pleaded, "Please, officer, look for her. Molly is only seven years old for God's sake! I don't dare leave the house in case she comes home."

The police officer said, "I'll send someone over to your house right now. Give me your address, and have a picture of Molly when they arrive." When June got off the phone, she called Paul's workplace.

Back in the white car, the man reached over and put his hand on Molly's brown hair, and as he started stroking her head, he said, "Molly, I love you and want to bring you home with me to live. It will be okay."

Molly looked into the man's eyes that had turned black. Her body started to shake with fear, like she was just put in a freezer, and the door was slammed shut. Molly closed her eyes, and the thought of Miss Patty saying, "Molly, talk to God, God will help, I promise." Molly then said to herself, *God, please help me, what do I do?*

Molly opened her eyes as the man unzipped his pants. Molly tried to get out the door, but it was locked, and when the man pulled her hair saying, "Hey! You aren't going nowhere!"

Molly got an answer, *Fight Molly Fight! You are strong!* Molly hit the man's face with all her might, screaming, "Stop it! Stop it!" Somehow she hit the man's face hard enough to make the man stop. She had angered the man; he no longer wanted Molly sexually, or he no longer loved her. He wanted the little girl with brown hair dead.

The man reached in the white car's backseat where he took a club from the seat. That man not only hit little Molly's head once, twice, but five times. As blood poured from Molly's brown hair, the man unlocked the passenger side door and pushed Molly's limp body to the grassy ground. He unrolled his car window, and threw the club as far as he could. He reached over and slammed the car door shut, put the white car in reverse, and stepped on the gas. The dust would rise as the car made its way back to the country road. The man was sure he had left the little girl dead, and needed to get back to Indiana, where he lived.

George and Helen always went early to the town hall for the meetings they had the first Friday of each month. They had lived down the road in the same farmhouse where they had lived their whole married life. They had raised their family there and now they enjoyed retirement. George had been a farmer and Helen a retired nurse who had worked in a hospital for many years. That afternoon they passed the two tracks where the white car was parked with Molly trapped inside.

Down the road a mile or so, Helen said, "George, we need to go back home, I forgot the umbrella, and it looks like rain will be upon us soon." George never argued with Helen. And knowing that she had just gotten her silver hair all done up pretty that morning, he knew she wasn't going to get it wet. George pulled up into a driveway to turn around. As he was just pulling out onto the road, the white car with the man behind the wheel sped past him going very fast. George said, "That crazy driver, he almost hit us. I wish people wouldn't drive so fast down these country roads."

Molly laid on the ground and felt her head. It already felt very big and was so wet with blood. Molly heard a voice as the man drove backwards towards the road. It said, "Molly, get up and go towards the sound of the man's white car. You need to get to the road. Now, Molly! Now!" She didn't know where the voice was coming from, but it was persistent. Although her eyes felt very heavy and wanted to shut, she started to stumble towards the road, holding her head as it felt like it could come off at any minute. Then Molly told the voice, "I can't walk anymore. It hurts so badly!" The voice said, "Crawl, Molly, crawl. You must make it to the road." Molly crawled the last ten feet towards the road. When she felt the gravel and tar against her hands and knees, she closed her blood-wet eyes, the rest of the way, and then it all went dark.

When George pulled to the side of the road, Helen said, "What now? Don't tell me we have a flat tire." Then Helen saw what George saw. The little body, with the then red sweater, and she said, "Oh my God!"

Helen wasn't a young woman, or George a young man, but the speed in which they got Molly safely into the backseat of their car was incredible. As faith would have it, Helen knew just what to do, and as she sat with the little girl in the backseat, she knew how to stop the bleeding, and to keep her flat and warm, as to not cause further injuries. And George, well, George became Mario Andretti as he drove as fast as he safely could, thinking the white car had nothing on him.

The police officers had already been to the candy store, Molly's school, and around the block a few times with Molly's picture in hand. No one had seen Molly that afternoon. Just then, the officers got the call that a little girl was brought to the hospital with a severe head wound.

Paul was home with Miss June when the police officers stopped back at Molly's house. They told Mr. and Mrs. Warner that they needed to come to the hospital. They might have found their little girl.

When June and Paul met with the doctors that had just gotten Molly stable, they said, "Please be aware, that if this is your little girl, she has been hurt terribly, and the sight of her is worse. We have done all we can. She is comatose as of now, and the next forty-eight to seventy-two hours will tell us more. We would suggest you call on your priest or clergy for prayers."

As they led the Warners into the room where Molly lay, Miss June screamed, "That's our little girl, Molly!" Paul held June up from falling as they both cried with fear. Soon after that, Mama got the phone call, and I will never forget what happened after that call.

Molly, I'm Here, So Is God

We had just finished supper, and it was Sam's turn to help with dishes. So, while Dad and Will sat at the dining room table discussing a homework assignment of Will's, I took Lady outside one more time before it got dark. I was wearing my navy blue leggings with a navy and light-blue-striped pullover sweater. It was chilly and I wished I had grabbed my jacket.

After walking the yard a few times, I said, "Come on, Lady, I am getting cold." Lady always went to the field to do her duty, and when she got back in the yard, I was already at the door to go in. I said, "That a girl, let's get you a treat." I opened the kitchen door just as the phone rang.

Mama answered the phone that was in the kitchen. I could hear her say something like, "We'll be right there, honey, please calm down. I am going to hang up and John and I will be on our way."

Mama hung up the receiver of the phone when Dad came in and said, "What's wrong, Patty?"

Mama looked at Sam and me standing in the kitchen waiting for her answer, then she said, "You children, gather Will and your jackets, and meet Dad and me back here," she snapped. "Now, go now!"

Sam and I left the room and told Will about Mama being so upset from the phone call. Will said, "Maybe the world is going to end. They have been talking about it at school. I told Dad we needed to build a bomb shelter."

Just then Dad walked into the dining room. He said, "Come on, children, let's get in the car. Faith, why don't you grab Dolly to take with you?"

Sam said, "What's going on, Dad?"

Dad replied, "I will explain in the car."

I went to my room, and picked Dolly up off my bed and thought, *Dad knows I don't play that much with Dolly anymore, why would I bring her?* And then I remember when Dad came to sit by my bed when I was sick, and Dolly was by my side. I had told Dad that whenever I feel sad, Dolly feels good to hold. She makes me strong.

As we all got into the car and started down the driveway, Mama started to cry and pray, "Please God, be with her, take care of her, please let it be okay!"

I said, "Mama, you are scaring me, what's wrong?"

Mama looked to Dad to speak. Dad said, "Miss June called and told Mama that Molly has been hurt, and we are going to the hospital to be with the Warners."

I said, "Mama, did Molly fall? Did she get hit by a car? There are so many cars in the city." Mama looked at Dad again to answer.

Dad said, "All we know is that someone has hurt Molly. We don't know all the details yet."

Sam said, "How could anyone hurt, Molly? She is just a little girl."

Will said, "Mama, is Molly going to be all right?"

Mama said, "I hope so."

I didn't say any more, and as we entered the hospital parking lot, I felt Molly. She was right with me, like she had been looking for me. I knew Molly needed me. As we entered the big doorway of the hospital, I held Dolly real tight, and was glad that Dad had me take her.

The young man and his beautiful wife, as he would call her, were curled up on their couch watching the six-o'clock news with their TV dinners when the newsman told of the little girl that was hospitalized with severe head trauma. After Molly's picture went up in the background, the newsman said the person, or persons, who had left her on the side of a country road was still at large. The young man didn't waste any time. He picked up the black phone and dialed the police station. He told them what he had witnessed earlier that day. He was able to tell the police the make and model of the white car, and of course, the license plate, the state and number, how could he forget that.

I know little of hospitals. I had only been to one once when Mama went to visit a friend of Grandma Rose. All I know is, that time, we kids had to stay in the lobby of the hospital and wait for Mama's return. But, to my surprise, when the lady at the big desk told Dad what room and floor Molly was at, Mama held my hand tightly, and we all marched right on the elevator together. The lady got up from her big desk chair and walked towards us saying, "Miss, Mister, the children will have to stay here in the lobby." But as the door to the elevator shut, I knew Mama wanted her children close.

On the fifth floor, we walked off the elevator. Mama found the waiting room right away. She led us children inside and said, "I want you children to stay put. Your dad and I will be back as soon as we can. Don't leave this room, you hear me?"

My brothers both said yes and went and turned on the television in the small room. I held the door open and watched my parents enter a room only a few doors away. I said to myself that must be where Molly is. I need to go see her.

Down from the room where Mama and Dad had entered was a nurse at a desk talking to a police officer with his back turned toward me. I watched as the hallway had people with white coats and clipboards pass me. The smell of rubbing alcohol and disinfectant made me rub my nose. Will came up behind me and said, "Faith, you better get inside and shut that door. You heard what Mom said."

I said, "It's okay, Will, I'm just looking." Will turned and just then, Dad and Mr. Paul came out of the room.

They walked right by me standing in the door of the waiting room. Dad didn't even look at me. Paul was holding an unlit cigarette in his right hand, and when he saw me, he tried to smile through his tears, but held both hands to his face and bawled. My dad put his hand on Paul's back, and led him to the elevator. Dad pushed the down arrow as they got in the elevator, and the door shut. I was thinking Mr. Paul needed to smoke. I looked again towards the room, and my mama and Miss June emerged. They went towards the nurse at the desk and I saw the nurse point down the other hall. I was thinking maybe it was to the ladies room that they were headed. Ladies always go to the ladies room together. I told Dolly, "Here's our chance, we need to see Molly." I looked back at Will and Sam who both were engrossed in television, and let the door shut behind me.

I walked two doors down the hall and pushed open the heavy door to where Molly was. The sight of Molly made my tears well up, and as I walked closer to the big bed that held little Molly, I held Dolly so tight that her plastic head hurt my chest.

Molly's head was misshaped, like a big football. It was wrapped in white bandages. Her eyes looked like the pink marshmallow cookies I had liked so much, but would never eat again. She had a tube in her little nose and one hand had what looked to be needles poked in. They were held with white tape. The tubing from her hand led to a bag with clear liquid that hung above her bed. There were machines behind her that made beeping sounds and showed green lines that would bump up and down. As I got closer to her, I felt fear well up inside of me. I tried to speak, and at first no words would form. I could only taste the salty tears that fell into my open mouth.

I reached for her hand without the needles and tape. As I touched it, I was shocked on how cold it felt. "Molly," I said. I put Dolly down beside Molly and held her hand with both of mine as to bring warmth onto it. I said, "Molly, I am so sorry this has happened, but I am here now, right next to you. Please talk to me. Molly, come back!" I pleaded, "Molly, its Faith!" The sight of Molly's puffed eyes was what scared me the most. I needed her to look me in the eyes. Molly without eyes was the worst.

Then, I started to talk to God. I said, "God, please don't take Molly to Heaven. Not now, she's just a little girl who loves to play, and fish, and learns new things each new day. Molly is my very best friend and I love her so much. We all need Molly here. Please God, make Molly better." At that very moment, I felt a calm enter the room. As my fear left me, the bright sunshine came from the darkened clouds. It entered the dark room from the window, but only for what seemed to be seconds, but enough for Molly and me to know that God had answered back. I looked at Molly's face, and although it was red and swollen, I saw a hint of a smile from it, like Molly had just come back from far away.

I let go of Molly's now warm hand, and said as I tucked Dolly up under her arm, "God said it's going to be all right, Molly, and I believe it. Rest, Molly, and I will be back soon." Then I turned and opened the big door to leave the room. The door felt very light, or was I just stronger knowing I had faith.

The same time the sunshine entered the room where Molly lay was the same time the darkened clouds let loose on the white car with the man inside. The APB had already been out for more than an hour, and as the white car passed the black and white police car at the Michigan, Indiana, border, the police checked the plates, pulled out, and turned the flashing lights on. The man in the white car saw the red and blue lights behind him and said, "Oh hell, how can this be. I have been driving the right speed." Then, as the man pushed the gas pedal down to the floorboard, he said to himself, "This is the way it has always been. My father was always telling me I was a no-good kid, a son of a bitch. Then, making me do all those bad things with him. I hate him, I hate myself."

The rain came hard, and as the white car left the road, it hit the only tree on the road for miles; a very big tree.

I went back to the waiting room where my brothers were watching a western on the television. As I sat down on the hard plastic couch next to the window, Will looked up and said to me, "It's about time you came away from that door." I thought he didn't even know I was gone. I looked out the window, and it was dark out. The streetlights and car lights were on as they passed below. I wondered what happened to the sun.

When Mama and Dad came back in the waiting room, I was just about asleep. Dad came over and scooped me up into his arms and said, "Faith, are you okay?"

I said, "Yes, Dad, just sleepy."

Sam asked "Is Molly okay? Can we go see her?"

Dad said, "Well, the doctor was just back in to see Molly and said she is already making progress, but the next few days will be important. She is in what they call a coma."

Will interrupted, "That's a deep sleep."

Dad said, "That's right, Will."

I said, "I know Molly will be just fine."

Sam said, "How do you know, Faith? You're not a doctor."

I said, "God told me."

Dad gave me a hug and got up from the plastic couch and said, "Well, that's all I need to hear. God is in charge."

As we drove away from the hospital, my family said a prayer for Molly and her family. Then we stopped at Molly's rented house on Washington Street. My dad and brothers went inside. I said to Mama, "What's going on?"

She said, "Paul Jr. is going to stay at our house for a few days so Miss June and Mr. Paul don't have to worry. They have enough to take care of right now."

When Pauly got in the backseat of our car with my brothers, he had a small bag of clothes and school books. As he shut the car door, he didn't stop talking. As my dad pulled away from Molly's house, he said, "I've been watching the news and Molly's picture has been on the screen. They were saying she has head injuries, that she was hurt real bad. Then later they said they were looking for a man in a white Ford." Then Pauly added, "I'll kill that man for hurting my sister. He better hope my dad don't get a hold of him before the police. I know my dad will tear him from limb to limb. I can't believe this is happening. I sure am happy, Mr. and Mrs. Bakker, you came to get me. I started to get a little scared when my mom called and told me to lock all the doors until you came." Then he asked, "Did you see Molly? Is she going to be okay?"

As my dad turned the car on the road that would take us away from the city, he said, "Miss Patty and I did see Molly, and the doctors say she is improving. I know you are scared, and mad, Pauly, and that's normal, but anger won't solve anything. Try to think with a clear head. Molly needs only good thoughts right now."

As the rain started to hit the windshield, I fell asleep leaning on my mama's side with her arms around me tight.

Heal, Faith, and Angels

Two days went by and Molly still laid in her coma. I felt that a deep sleep is just what Molly needed as to help her heal. I still knew she would wake up and be fine.

I heard Mama and Dad, as they sat with Uncle Sam and Aunt Sara at the kitchen table, tell the events of what happened that day Molly was hurt. I sat with Lady on the floor in the dining area just within hearing distance. They told about the white car with the man inside had crashed, and how the police officer said he tried to get the man out of the white car, but the doors wouldn't budge. When the ambulance arrived, the white car released the man, but it was too late. The man had bled to death, and crumbled tight in his hand was the picture of kittens. Then they talked about the angels that they believed had been put in place that day to help Molly. The young vacuum cleaner salesman, who was behind the white car, and how he was drawn to look at the plates, and later to see Molly on the news. Molly's first angel.

Then when Helen forgot her umbrella, and at the right moment was told to go back home for it. George and Helen were two very special angels.

At the hospital that day was one of the best neurologists in the country. He had been training others there all week, and was to leave late that morning. He told the Warners something kept nagging him to stick around, and then Molly came in—another angel.

Then Dad told how he and Mr. Paul went outside the hospital that night. That Paul had a lot of anger, which Dad said was understandable. Paul would tell Dad, "I really have never been told much about God as a child. And, to tell you the truth, I don't think I believe in all the holy God stuff." Paul lit his cigarette and said, "Really, John, how can there be a God? How would a good God let someone hurt Molly so badly? And how come everything in mine and June's life had turned upside down? Where is this God? And why should I talk to him? God has never been there for me."

Dad told Paul, "Paul, God has always been with you since your first breath of life. God gave you many good things. Two healthy legs, arms, eyes, and the list goes on and on. How about the first time you held Paul Jr. and little Molly? You had to have thoughts of the miracles that had been given to you. Paul, God didn't make you drink too much, God hasn't made the choices throughout your life, and most importantly, God didn't hurt Molly. Someone very disturbed and troubled hurt Molly. Paul, don't blame God for all the bad things that happen. Praise God for all the good! Just the fact that Molly has had the best of care, and she is in a safe place, Paul, talk to God, tell God how you feel, and thank God for Molly! God is listening to you, Paul."

Dad then told how Paul went to his knees, and talked to God. He said, "God, thank you for being with Molly. Please, please don't take her from us. Please heal Molly! God, forgive me and help me to heal as well. I want to do better. I am just so scared. I love my family so much, make this better, God. Please let me have faith!" Paul had cried until there was no fluid left inside to make more tears. He got up off his knees and told John, "I don't know how to explain this, John, but right now, I feel I have been healed. Like, for the first time in my entire life, I have found a feeling that I have been longing for, and it feels so good. I have this new faith that everything is going to be okay. Thank you, John."

Dad just smiled and said, "Don't thank me, thank God. And yes, no matter what, Paul, it will be okay."

Mama took her turn and told about her and Miss June in the hospital ladies room that evening. How Miss June broke down and told Patty how bad things were. That two days earlier, she had asked Paul for a divorce. She was sick of his drinking. She said that she herself had a dark moment where she wanted to just take all the sleeping pills her doctor had given her.

June said, "Pat, I have prayed to God many times. I believe God doesn't hear me. I believe in God, but I give up on prayers. Now this, not my Molly, I couldn't live without my Molly, I won't live without her."

Mama would tell June, "June, God had heard all your prayers, it's you not believing God. That could be what's troubling you. You have to have faith Molly will be okay no matter what. Maybe right now, believing God has been working on all those prayers you have been asking for is your answer. June, all I can say is taking your life is not the answer. Believing a better life is God's answer, God loves you and Molly no matter what happens."

June closed her eyes and prayed, "God, I believe you are with our Molly, helping her head to heal. That she will be okay, and thank you for the prayers you have already answered. I know you love us. I have faith that nothing but good could come from this."

June wiped her wet, blackened eyes on the tissues Mama gave her, and then said, "Pat, I feel better. And right now, I need to be with Molly and find Paul. He needs to know how much I love him and that I am going to stop blaming and be responsible for my actions. I know this is going to sound really weird, but I feel really strong right now, like I could carry my whole family out of a burning house."

As I sat in the other room with Lady, and listened to my parents tell of all that had happened, my thoughts were that I was glad Mr. Paul and Miss June believed God would help Molly, and that they had talked to God. Also, I thought about the man that hurt my Molly. How I remembered the man who sat with us at the *Dairy Queen*. How when Mama and I were leaving the Warner's rented house that day, that man with the white car drove by, and as he passed Molly's driveway, I was getting into our car, our eyes would meet, and I didn't like him. How now, I wished I had told Mama.

It was Thursday morning. It had been almost a week from when Molly got hurt that she opened her eyes. Mama told us children when Paul Jr. arrived home with Aunt Sara from the city school. Mama had been taking Pauly to his school in the morning, and Aunt Sara would finish work at the department store downtown in time to pick Pauly up from school and bring him to our house for the night. Mama said, "I have good news! Miss June called this morning. Molly is awake, and although she is very weak, she seems to be okay."

All of us kids were jumping up and down saying, "Yea! Yeah! Yea!" Lady would bark with excitement. I said, "When can I go see her? When will she come home?"

Mama said, smiling, "Hold your britches, Faith May, one day at a time." Then we all stopped, and watched Pauly. He was sitting in the wing-back chair in our living room with his hands to his face, crying. Mama walked over and put her hand upon his back, "What's wrong, Pauly? This is good news," she said.

Paul Jr. stood up and hugged Mama, and said, "I know, Miss Patty. I am happy Molly is awake. I just wish she wouldn't have gotten hurt. It's all my fault! I should have been walking her home from school. If I had been doing what I was told, she wouldn't have gotten hurt that day."

Mama kept hugging Paul Jr. and said, "Pauly, it's not your fault, no one has blamed you. You didn't hurt Molly, and please forgive that thought. Don't let the devil steal this happy news from you. God loves you so much, Pauly, and he's showing us with this good news."

I watched from the kitchen as Mama comforted Pauly, and then I looked at my Aunt Sara. She looked different, like a glow surrounded her. She looked like she was taking notes on what Mama was doing. I went over to her and asked, "Do you need a hug, Aunt Sara?"

She said, "Why yes, Faith, how did you know?" She reached for me from the kitchen chair where she sat and we gave each other a big hug. I was thinking Molly getting hurt was hurting everyone that loved her, and it wasn't anyone's fault but that man's.

After my embrace with Aunt Sara, I said, "Aunt Sara, are you gaining weight?"

Aunt Sara laughed, "Why, Faith, you sure are inquisitive. I guess I might as well tell you now. Your Uncle Sam and I are expecting a baby in early May."

I know my gums were showing as I hugged Aunt Sara again and said, "Aunt Sara, I just love when good news comes in bunches!"

Thanksgiving and Forgiving

Within the next couple of days, Molly—with Dolly—would get out of bed to go to the bathroom. Then Molly would ask if she could have ice cream and peanut butter sandwiches. Miss June would tell her daughter, "We believe Faith had come into your room that night you got hurt, and she put Dolly up under your arms."

Molly said, "I know, Mom. She and God were both in my room together, along with the pretty light, and then the beautiful angel with glistering streaks of silver in her dark hair told me to hold onto Dolly real tight. She said everything would be okay." Miss June didn't doubt what Molly told her one bit; she knew miracles had happened that night.

The next two weeks, Molly healed in the hospital. When I finally got to see her for a short visit, I was so relieved that she was able to look me in the eyes. Although her eyes were still darkened by the bruising and her head held a smaller white bandage, she was herself again. My sweet, loving Molly. Molly would tell the nurse and police officer about how the man in the white car said he was going to bring her to pick out a kitten. Then he got mad, so she talked to God and was told to fight. That's when the man hit her on the head. Molly then said, "I remember the car got real loud, and a nice voice told me to get to the road just like the car did." Another angel?

Molly asked her dad about the man in the white car. "Daddy, that man, why did he hurt me? And is he in jail? I don't want him to hurt anyone else."

Her dad decided to tell her the truth as he knew it to be. "Molly, sweetheart," he said as he sat in the hospital bed holding her in his arms, "that man hurt you because he had been hurting deep inside so long, and so bad. I believe it came out, and hurt you. It was nothing that you did wrong, and we won't know all the answers until our life is done. The man's life has ended on earth. That man had a car accident and was killed. He can't hurt anyone anymore, and I'm sure he is not hurting anymore either."

Molly looked at her dad and could tell that he had changed. She could feel his happiness, contentment, and that his breath didn't have the smell of old beer. Molly also noticed her mom looked pretty again. The mad dark face was gone. No more heavy makeup, and when she smiled, Molly saw her mom's pretty white teeth that had disappeared under her once sad frown. Molly didn't know what had all happened while she was asleep healing, but whatever it was, it felt good.

When Molly saw Pauly, he said how sorry he was for not walking home with her from school. Molly said, "Oh Pauly, don't be silly. I just had a bad day and a bad bump to my head. It's not your fault." Then she asked the nurse if her brother could have ice cream, too.

The day Molly was to come home from the hospital, her doctor sat Molly on his lap and said, "Molly, I am going to miss you around here. I am so happy to tell your parents here that you are doing great! Your mom needs to give you this little yellow pill each morning, no matter what."

The doctor looked at June and handed her the bottle of yellow pills, and stressed, "That pill must be given to Molly so as not to have her have a seizure because of her head injuries. Also, Molly needs lots of proteins—hamburger is good—and also beans, and I know you like peanut butter." As he looked back at Molly, he said, "I would love to sit here and tell you that, that day Molly came in hurt that I knew in a few weeks she would walk home. I didn't know and I am going to tell you that not just the doctors and nurses healed little Molly. I believe it was something more, something much, much more."

Molly wiped the one tear coming down the doctor's clean, shaved cheek and said, "Don't cry, I will come see you again, Doctor Neal, if you want?" The doctor hugged Molly as he lifted her from his lap and put her in front of him, her feet on the floor, and said, "I would like that, Molly sweetheart, you are one of the reasons I love my job."

It snowed the first time of the season in Michigan that early November day that Molly came home. The pure blanket of white covered the trees and ground. I remember my dad saying, "How wonderful of nature to greet Molly and show her how anything can become new, fresh, and strong again with the help of God."

A lot of activity seemed to be happening around my house the next few weeks. Big Bill had come over a few times along with Mr. Paul. My dad, Big Bill, and Paul would talk in the den with the door closed. After one meeting I heard Paul as he shook Big Bill's hand when they were leaving. Paul said, "Thanks, Bill. I don't know how to thank you. This is such good news, I can't wait to start."

Mr. Paul had not touched a drop of alcohol since the day of Molly getting hurt. He told Dad he had found something so much better. Mr. Warner would also become an active member of the neighborhood watch program, and he and Miss June founded a small organization called Every Child Home Safe. It didn't become a big program, but the Warners believe in it, and parents felt better knowing that there were neighbors watching over each other, encouraging children to walk together to and from school.

Molly told me on the phone that her mom was taking her and Pauly to school and home again. Her mom quit her bar job and was going to start working in a bakery in a few weeks, but she told them she could only work while her kids were in school. Molly then told me her family was eating at the kitchen table together and said, "Faith, I just love eating supper with Mom, Dad and Pauly; we laugh so much now." All I could think is I didn't know much about the other way, and then I would have the thoughts that I was happy that all Miss June's prayers were being answered. My best friend was happy. Life was good.

Thanksgiving Day that year, 1965, was truly a big day of thanks. We had a lot of people at our table, or, I should say, tables. Mama and Dad would fix it so that we had three tables together to hold our family, the Warners, Grandpa and Grandma Doyle, Molly's grandma, Mrs. Smith, Uncle Sam, Aunt Sara, Big Bill, and Nana. Of course, Lady was to take a seat by my feet. The turkey just fit into our oven, and the whole house had the aroma of so much food, that I couldn't help that I was bugging Mama for little bits of stuffing when she would baste the big turkey. Miss June baked cinnamon bread that my brother Sam said, "Smells like heaven."

Molly brought Dolly to me that day. As she handed her back to me, she said, "Thanks, Faith, for letting me hold Dolly while my head healed. I know she helped."

I said, "You are so welcome. It was my dad that helped that day; he somehow knew we would need her." Molly and I decided to wear our dresses that we wore to Aunt Sara and Uncle Sam's wedding. Aunt Sara made sure to let out the hems, for we had both grown some.

As we all sat at the tables, Uncle Sam suggested that we go around the tables and tell of what we were thankful for that year. Most everyone said things like, Molly being better, their family. Uncle Sam said the new baby that would be here in the spring; Will said something to do with fishing, family, friends, and food. Sam said, "Molly being better, and the snow that I am going to play in after dinner."

Then Mr. Paul asked if he could say grace. His words flowed so smoothly and articulately, "Dear God, although I have really just got to know you in this short time, I give witness that with God all things are possible. Like giving up what holds you back from having your best life, the life God wants us to have. I learned with the help of people God has placed in our lives, we can fight the demons that prey upon us. I have learned that talking to God each day can help you to find the next path through. I know now that I have a lot to be thankful for. I have prayed to you in my darkest hour, and you have answered. Now, I would like to give something to you God, as you once taught us about forgiveness. I truly forgive the man that hurt Molly, as I hope all at this table can, too. That day you gave me back my child, my life, and you took the hurt child of yours. I know forgiving is easier to do, knowing I have my healthy child here with me. But not forgiving would be like not being thankful for what you have done. Thank you, God, may the man rest in peace. Amen." As I opened my eyes, I watched as all the grownups wiped the tears of God's love from their faces.

I learned that day to forgive all the bad stuff that can come into your life each day. It was like giving God little thank-you notes for your life. The little stuff is easy for me to forgive, but for the man that hurt Molly, that had been a little harder. It felt good when I did. When Molly and I talked about the man once, she told me, "Faith, I forgive the man. I know he was hurting more than my head, and I am better. I can forgive, but my dad said I shouldn't forget that there are people who hurt, and who can hurt, and ask God for their healing."

I know my parents had forgiven the man because Mama would always say things like, "You can't change what already happened. Live from the moment on. If you didn't like it, think on it, pray on it, but always forgive it. People who can't forgive hurt deep inside."

Dad would say, "Forgiving and forgetting go hand in hand. Forgiving doesn't mean you have to forget the hurt; it just means you have accepted the hurt so you can move forward." Dad always said, "People who live on the bad from their past never seem to have much good in their future."

As the chatter from the room picked up that Thanksgiving Day, Dad started to carve the big turkey. My brother Sam, oh sweet Sam, who always pays attention, said in a loud voice, "Hey, wait a minute everyone! Molly didn't get to tell what she was thankful for!" Everyone looked at Molly, who was ready to put the first spoon of mashed potatoes in her mouth.

She said with a big smile, "Oh, that's easy. I am thankful I feel great! And next spring, I will be able to go fishing with Faith!"

Part Two

Good News, Baby, and Summer Dreams

That Christmas, 1965, I didn't get the easy-bake oven I asked for. What I did get was one hundred times better. Molly handed me a pretty-wrapped gift box with a card. Of course, I opened the box first and in it was a hat and mittens in my favorite color of blue. As I opened the handmade card, and everyone gathered around me, Molly said, "Faith, read the card out loud, please."

I said, "Sure, here goes." Then I said, loud and clear, "Merry Christmas, Faith! We, the Warners, are going to be your neighbors again! We are moving into the brick house up the street. Love, Molly."

Happy, yes, happy was the word of the day. I know Big Bill had something to do with the Warners being able to move back. I still believe to this day that I must have talked to God a million times about wanting Molly back as a neighbor, and maybe it just had to be.

On January 16, 1966, my eighth birthday, we all went to church in what was turning out to be a blizzard. After church, we plowed our way to the Warner's brick house where Miss June insisted we come for dinner, and have a piece of the beautiful birthday cake she had baked and decorated. Molly and I wore matching green sweaters and navy blue leggings, and we had plans of unpacking the boxes that were piled in her new bedroom. Molly told me that she and her mom had taken most of her and Pauly's toys to a mission where they could be enjoyed by children less fortunate.

Molly said, "Mom said she never realized how much stuff she would buy to cover up the pain she was feeling. My mom said with less stuff around our new house, the devil can't hide."

As Miss June placed the cake with eight glowing green candles in front of me, Molly said, "Make a wish, Faith May!" I looked around the table that day, and did something different. Because Molly was back, and everyone I loved was around me, I couldn't think of anything I really wanted, so I didn't make a wish that year for my eighth birthday. I just said to myself, "Thank you, God, for answering our prayers."

That spring came the birth of Uncle Sam and Aunt Sara's baby. Molly and I were sure the baby was going to be a girl. But on May 2, 1966, little John Walter Emerson was born. The first time I held him, I knew he was going to be just like his daddy. Uncle Sam was on "cloud nine," I heard Grandma Rose say. Uncle Sam would tell us all how he was going to teach him hunting and fishing. Dad said he would help with the fishing, and he liked his name.

I knew why Uncle Sam was my dad's best friend; they were a lot alike. But also, somewhat different, just like Molly and me. Uncle Sam and my dad shared the love of fishing and the outdoors. But Uncle Sam also liked to hunt. My dad didn't. Dad had told us children that Uncle Sam would take him deer hunting when he first came to Michigan, and when a deer came into range, Uncle Sam would look at him to take aim and shoot. Dad said he would just freeze; he just couldn't kill. He said the same was true with rabbit and pheasant hunting with his brothers in Iowa. So, when it came to Uncle Sam wanting to teach Will and Sam to hunt, Dad just told his boys it was their choice. He even said maybe I would like to learn to hunt someday. I would say, "No way!"

Dad said not everyone should hunt, or fish for that matter. But to keep nature in balance there has to be people willing to hunt so deer herds don't grow too big to where they aren't as healthy. If everyone hunted, then you could wipe out a species. "Balance" what Dad and Uncle Sam would say. "Just the right amount of everything, how can you go wrong?"

In the years ahead, my brother, Will, would hunt with Uncle Sam, and venison would be at our table. My brother Sam was like Dad; he didn't enjoy hunting, just fishing.

The next few years would be pretty normal for the Bakker family. The school months we would be trapped in the big, red-brick building learning all that was offered. Then the weekends would come, where we could have a break from all the energy good, and bad that was shut up in a classroom of children, with the confusion of what may happen next.

The summers, to me, were the best. We would enjoy fishing, picnics, vacations up north in Michigan, beautiful Michigan, and then there were the Bakker reunions in Iowa. Iowa was becoming a beautiful state to visit. I loved looking out the window of the car at the miles and miles of corn, soy, cows, and the blue skies were my favorite color.

In the summers, we children were able to run around the neighborhood free of fear. It was still a time when a lot of mothers didn't work outside of the home. They would look out the windows on the children playing. They would call each other on a phone that was located in their kitchen, where they would be baking cookies, and planning the dinner for that evening when their husbands would come home from working all day. I'm not saying everything was perfect. I just look back and remember it just worked. But things change, and I watched as new neighborhoods grew around us, new houses being squeezed into spaces between other houses. The building that would go up making our town bigger, and roads that were once gravel, now were black tar.

One thing that didn't change was the curiosities of us children. We would get up each morning wanting to get outside, and learn and see, and feel what we could do to make our life fun and meaningful. Molly and I would go to the creek and catch tadpoles, and watch as they would grow into frogs in a container off the back porch. Then we would set them free back into the creek. We played jump rope, hopscotch, and wore out the tires on our bikes. The boys would build stuff, cut grass, and their bikes would grow motors and be called mini bikes. Lady didn't like the noise, and would bark at them, chasing them away.

My dad would have bonfires in our backyard and invite the neighbors to sit around, and we would roast hotdogs and marshmallows. Everyone would marvel at Mama's flower gardens, and she would send them home bouquets of fresh flowers to be enjoyed at their tables.

Winter was fun also. We would go sledding and build snow forts, snow angels, snowmen, and snowballs. Uncle Sam would bring over his snowmobiles and tie on our metal snow saucers. We would ride them holding on tight as we would go through the snow, laughing all the way. I do remember, my brother Sam broke his arm sledding when he was eleven, but other than that, I remember we were pretty happy and healthy. Big on the happy.

Growing Up, Growing Old

The summer that I was twelve was when I didn't call her "Mama" anymore. It started slowly with "Mom, I'm home" and "I'm going to Molly's, Mom." I was becoming a butterfly. Not only was my body forming, my mind was causing me to change. I wanted to sleep more, and I was moody. Mom would come in my room all cheery, and open the shades saying, "Time to get up, Faith. God has given us a new day, let's enjoy it!" And even if it was going on ten in the morning, I would put my pillow over my head and wish her away.

Mom had started working at a greenhouse a few days a week that spring and into the summer. With us kids growing up, she didn't feel as needed, and Mom had to keep herself busy. "And what better way than to put your hands in the dirt," she would say. We were a family that was growing up, we children were spreading our wings and Mom and Dad were thinking on the next phase that would bring them through. Will and Sam were like small men. Their voices had changed, and their bodies had become strong with muscles. They always seem to be proving their strength.

Will had a summer job at the local library and was taking drivers training. Sam would cut grass for the elderly in the neighborhood, and although he was only fourteen, he was prince charming to all of the girls. Some would befriend me so they could stare at good-looking Sam. My dad was smart; he knew how important it was to stay a family, to grow apart, but always stay connected. What better to do just that was to have a family vacation? He worked it out that we would have two weeks together. So right after Will's last day of drivers training, we were packed up with the boat in tow.

The trip to Drummond Island was long. With two growing teenage boys, Lady and I piled in the backseats of our station wagon along with boxes of things we would need. Mom and Dad both tried to make traveling down the road fun, like when we were all young, playing games like calling colors of

Volkswagen bugs and singing were just not cutting it anymore. Will and Sam would argue about who had more space, and Sam and I would give each other dirty looks. I loved my family, but being in the car made it hard for us to flap our wings. Dad would tell Mom, "Riding in the car makes the children restless, but put them in the boat, and they become restful."

It wasn't until Dad drove the car and boat onto the ferry for the ride to the island that we started to get excited. When we arrived at the cottage that Dad rented on the shore of Lake Huron, called Potagannissing Bay, we were in bliss.

I remember so many things on that trip I could go on forever. My dresses didn't come with me, and I remember being in shorts that Aunt Sara made me for the summer months. There were pockets, and a zipper just like the shorts you would buy at the mall, and although one of the girls that had befriended me so she could get to know my brother Sam told me, "Homemade clothes are so stupid," I took it as she was jealous that she didn't have a talented Aunt Sara.

The fishing was great, and we would all catch walleyes. Even Mom would pull one in, and with her top gums showing with such excitement, we would all laugh at how happy she was to net her fish.

On days when the waters were too rough for fishing, our family would take the station wagon back into the deep woods on the island and find wild red raspberries to pick for a delicious pie Mom would bake. Mom always seemed to find the perfect mix of wildflowers for us to enjoy from the vases on the tables of the cottage. We would be this family of five, with of course, Lady, who wouldn't wander too far from me. Out where there was nothing but blue skies and waters surrounding the earth under our feet. An earth that no matter how you believed it was made or who made it, you had to take some air in and be grateful for the life that it held.

Dad would tell us there were bears on the island, but that we made too much noise for them to come close. Making noise was just fine with me. At night, after a busy day of fishing and exploring, we would sit at the shore as a family, watching the sunset and the stars and moon come forth. We talked about things we wanted to do in our lives. We talked about God, and each of us telling of what we thought Heaven would be like, and our reasons for that we were born.

The best thing was each of us felt we could be right, that maybe we all had the right answers, and maybe life was just about searching for answers. Maybe it was the love that we felt as a family that would make it easier to separate in the years to come. Because we knew no matter what, we would always be together in spirit. I didn't know it then, but that cottage we stayed at was for sale, and before we left the island that year, Dad put a down payment on it. We would take more family trips to our cottage on the island throughout the years. But there was something very special about the first time.

Back home again, Molly couldn't wait to tell me she had become a woman while I was gone. She told of the cramps and the pads you put in your panties to catch the "you know what." We girls were shown a movie about what Molly had told me the spring before in school, during a gym class. Mom had talked to me about it, and gave me the same book to look at as she gave my brothers years earlier.

As much as I wanted to do everything Molly would do, I thought to myself that part of growing up didn't seem so appealing. I would page through the book at night before I would fall asleep. I remember looking at my body under the covers with a flashlight and seeing things that were happening, just like the book said would happen. The little girl in me was somehow disappearing.

It started with her limping as she would get up each morning, and at night she would cry in what seemed to be pain, as she would turn and turn around to lie down. My sweet Lady was getting old. The vet had us give Lady an aspirin at night to relieve some of the pain, and that seemed to help for a while. All in all, it was a real hard winter for her. Molly would bring her cat Toby over for Lady to play with, but that winter, most of the time, they would just nap together. Molly received Toby the spring that she moved into the brick house.

Helen and George came to visit her, and asked if she could have one of the barn kittens that had been born that year. Molly loved Toby like a dog. Molly would bring the black puffball everywhere. In the summer she would put Toby in the pink basket of her bike and ride the cat to my house, and Lady and Toby would chase each other around the yard like two dogs. Toby even knew how to fetch, and would bring back the little aluminum foil ball to whoever threw it. We dressed Toby in Dolly's clothes when he was a kitten. But I really think Toby thought he was a dog, and the Warners never had a litter box in the brick house. Toby would cry at the door to go outside to relieve himself, something I think Lady taught Toby. The cat would eat whatever was left over from the Warner's meals.

Toby would be outside most nights. I remember him showing up outside my bedroom window, probably looking for Lady. Mom would say just as long as you don't feed him, he will go back home, and he would. Molly would even walk Toby on a leash. Funny but true.

That January 1971, I turned thirteen, and in the same week I would get the cramps that would turn me into a woman. I missed a day of school, and when I went back, I became really shy when it came to undressing in gym class that first day. One of the girls noticed and said out loud, "Faith has got her period! Ha Ha Ha!" Her name was Debbie, and I forget what I was wearing because it didn't matter. I will never forget how hurt I felt that moment. All these new emotions were getting the best of me, and it made me want to stay home where I felt safe and no one judged. I didn't like that my peers would treat each other with hostility, maybe because we were all full of crazy emotions.

When I told my mom, she would say, "Faith, being a teenager is like being a bird that is learning to fly from the safety of its nest. They are scared that the air might not catch them, and they would fall painfully to the hard ground. The parents of those birds chirp with encouragement, and the teenage birds chirp at the other birds to go first, but not with encouragement, but frustration because of the little bit of fear nature has given. But just like the birds, you have to have faith, a leap of faith in order to move forward. Don't stay back in the nest and cry, enjoy the new adventure, make it an exciting experience." Mom's talks always helped and Dad would give me a hug and say, "Stay positive, Faith May; don't fight nature, she will win every time."

Three weeks of becoming a woman, Lady would pass away. I was a mess. I cried so hard, as Lady wouldn't get up; she closed her eyes, and turned hard and cold. My dad had to pry me away from her. The whole family took Lady's death hard. The ground was frozen, so Dad said we couldn't burry her on the property, and as I cried harder. Dad said he would take care of it.

For three days, the snow fell and Lady laid wrapped in a blanket in the wood shed. Dad would come home after work, and he and Will dug a hole big enough for Lady to have a proper burial.

I would go to sleep at night looking at the empty red rug beside my bed, thinking life could be so unfair. Then, I would think about when she was just a puppy and Grandma Mary was here. All the joy that Lady was to bring in my childhood, and how she got me to the new phase in life. How could I think that was unfair?

Visits, Fast Cars, and the Past

The summer of '71 came a visit from Uncle Jim, Aunt Sylvia, little Mary Hope, and Grandpa Todd. Grandpa had retired from the farm in Iowa, with Uncle Joe taking over. Uncle Jim and Aunt Sylvia's two boys didn't travel with them for the visit. Their names were Roger and Jim Jr. They both graduated high school and had jobs to attend. Aunt Sylvia was saying how Roger, then twenty years old, was dating a girl, and that it was becoming serious. She thought a wedding might happen soon enough. Uncle Joe and Aunt Sally's oldest boy had gotten married last summer, and they were going to be a grandpa and grandma soon. I guess you could say the whole big Bakker family was growing up.

It was a great week with Little Mary Hope following Molly and I everywhere. She was six, and small for her age, but very smart. At night, she would sleep in my room, and I would laugh on how excited she would get when I read the stories from my Dr. Seuss books. I would ask her if she talked to God. She said, "But of course, Faith, everyone talks to God." I didn't want to break her heart, and tell of what I have learned of the whole big wide world. It would come to her just like it does everyone. I was just thankful she knew of God and had great parents to guide her through.

Mom would bring out the dresses from storage that I had worn when I was five and six for Mary Hope, most being made my either Aunt Sara or Grandma Rose. As I looked them over, the memories would flood my mind. I cried as I held the blue dress that I had worn to Grandma Mary's funeral.

I went to say goodnight to Grandpa Todd in the den where Mom had fixed the hideaway couch with sheets and a pillow. She put a vase of fresh-cut flowers on the end table alongside the picture of Grandpa holding the fish and Grandma with the yellow dress. Grandpa was holding, looking at the picture with his now thin, worn hands. I sat down beside him, and he started to tell me, "Faith, your Grandma Mary sure did love you." He had watery eyes as he recalled to me how he met and fell in love with her. He said, "Mary just loved life. She was a wonderful soul to all who knew her. Mary was always positive, and when we get around people who would gossip or be negative, she would try to change the conversation to something good. If that didn't work, why she would just excuse herself and walk away. Sometimes, I would wonder what people thought. But your grandma didn't care. She would tell me later, 'Todd dear, I am sorry, but I won't live this wonderful life I have been given, fighting with the devil." Grandpa took a deep breath in and released, "She made a home that was peaceful and worked with God every day to have the peace. I miss her, and talk to her every day. It's hard when the one you love is no longer touchable."

I hugged Grandpa and told him it will be okay, and that I missed Grandma, too. Most every day I did think of Grandma, but it wasn't so much that I missed her and wanted to touch her; I just didn't want to forget the touch she gave. But I knew what Grandpa was saying because I wanted so much to touch Lady again.

When that week came to an end, our visitors went back to Iowa. Our family went fishing, and life continued.

The next spring, Grandpa Todd went to heaven. Uncle Joe called and said that Grandpa had not been feeling well, but refused to go to the doctor. That morning, he didn't come to the breakfast table, and Aunt Sally would find him in bed, the same bed that Grandma had left from years ago.

At Grandpa Todd's funeral, I held Mary Hope's hand, and she wore the same blue dress I wore to Grandma's funeral. I remember I wanted to wear yellow and had nothing, so my mom must have felt how important it was to me. She would have Dad stop at the mall on the way to the airport. While Dad and my brothers waited in the car, Mom and I would go in the clothes shop, find a yellow maxi dress, and a yellow headband, and blue and yellow poncho to go over. I smiled big.

Maybe I was thinking Grandpa would like me to wear yellow that day to let him know as he looked down from Heaven that I wanted to be like Grandma, a good soul. It rained hard the whole day, and everyone seemed to be sad. But I was somehow happy for Grandpa. I had faith that he was okay.

At fifteen, I had long, blonde hair that was parted down the middle. I wore bell bottom blue jeans and bright-colored knit sweaters. I wore bras with matching bikini underwear, necklaces shaped like peace signs, and silver hoops hung from my then pierced ear lobes.

Again, changes occurring around the Bakker home. Will had graduated high school, and was training to be a conservation officer. It was only natural that he would be dedicated to protecting our land that he loved so. Will had graduated at the top of his high school class, and everyone just seemed to like him. Will had gone from a good boy to a fine young man. My brother Sam had a little trouble with the transition into final manhood.

It was the early '70s and sex, drugs, and rock and roll was the era. Sam was a follower, not a leader, and he wanted to be good, but he also liked the attention from the girls. At seventeen, he was all about fast cars, rock and roll, and girls. At home he was all nice, and "what can I do for you Mom and Dad." At school is when he would act all tough and cool. He played high school football and was pretty good. Mom and Dad went to every one of his games to cheer him on. His coach would say he has determination. The girls would say he was so sweet and good-looking. I loved him because he was my brother, and despite some teasing, he was worthy. If he wasn't my brother, I would still want him as a friend.

Sam saved his money to buy a car. He and his friends would spend time in the garage out back that spring and early summer getting it all supped up. Fishing was still in Sam's radar, but most of the time it was Molly, Dad, and I in the boat taking in nature.

I know Dad would have talks with Sam, more so than Will. Then, one weekend Sam broke his curfew after getting his supped-up car on the road. I guess Sam said he was going to hang out with friends after he had finished work at the supermarket, where he bagged groceries. He just failed to mention they were going to race their cars down the new blacktop road just outside of town. When the police came to break up the races, Sam sped out as not to get caught. The police were smart and just paid a visit to each of the boys' homes the next morning, which was Saturday.

As the police officer talked to Dad and Sam in our kitchen, I would sneak in close to listen. It was funny how I even put my middle finger to my mouth as if Lady was still by my side. Dad didn't yell or ground him; he just said he understood, but also he wanted Sam to understand that he was not to do that again. That's when Dad would take Sam to the drag strip and watch races there.

I was sitting in our kitchen that late summer morning, telling Mom something funny that Molly had done the day before when the phone rang. Mom answered and said, "Hello," and after a long pause, she said, "Well, of course, I remember you, Betty. How are you? This is such a surprise." As the conversation proceeded, I thought I should give her some privacy and left the room. I have always been one to listen to private conversations, and as much as I wanted to know who Betty was, I was still learning that I just needed to ask Mom when she was done talking.

After Mom hung up, she found me on the front porch swing, and as she sat down next to me, she knew exactly what I would ask, "Mom, who is Betty?" That's when Mom told me the story of Uncle Sam, Betty, and the little brown-eyed girl named Lily. Mom could have left a lot of the details of the story out, but I think she felt I was not only old enough but could learn from a story of young love. She told about Uncle Sam marrying Betty not because of a deep love for her, but because she was carrying their child. They thought they were doing the right thing. But from the moment Mom and Dad stood with them in front of the Justice of Peace, there was no peace.

Of course, I wanted to know what they all wore that day, and she told me. Mom then said how sad Uncle Sam had become. "He and Betty just couldn't get along. Betty was a very jealous woman, and couldn't let Sam out of her sight. After Lily was born, things seemed to get a little better. Of course, you know how your Uncle Sam is with children; he just loved little Lily. I think Betty was jealous of even Sam loving little Lily, because before long there was such a wedge between them. It had to be unhealthy for Lily." Mom continued, "The drama went on for months. Sam wasn't allowed to go fishing or hunting. A few times I talked to Betty to come over with Lily, so Will and Lily could get to know each other, and the men could fish, but she just hated the fact that Sam wanted to do something without her."

"It was the end of October 1955 when Betty just packed up and went across the state with beautiful Lily. Your dad and I were heartbroken for Uncle Sam," Mom said. Then my mom said, with tears in her eyes, "Uncle Sam's mother was very sick at the time. Sam had lost his dad to war and doesn't have any memory of him. Sam's uncle, his dad's brother, stepped in and helped raise Sam. Uncle Walter was his name."

I said, "Is that how little Johnny Walter got his name?"

Mom said, "Yes, your Uncle Sam was very close to his Uncle Walter. He was the one who taught Sam to hunt and fish, and he was accidently killed the day Uncle Sam and Betty married. I guess his hunting gun misfired while he was cleaning it. So as you can guess, Uncle Sam was a mess."

I went inside the house to grab the box of Kleenex and sat back on the porch swing. By now Mom's tears were streaming and I said, "Mom, are you okay? Can you tell me more?"

She said, "Yes, I'll be okay." Then she said, "Uncle Sam wanted to be with Lily, and even was looking for work across state. But Betty didn't want anything to do with him, and made it so hard for him to see Lily. One of the weekends, Sam traveled to see Lily. Betty had divorce papers served and said she would do everything in her power to keep him from Lily. That same weekend, we had to call Sam and tell him his mother had passed. That's when Sam let Lily go."

I said, "This is so sad, why didn't Uncle Sam just marry Aunt Sara right then and there? They are so happy now."

Mom said, "I think Sam wanted to be with Sara, but I also think he needed to work on forgiving Betty before he could have a healthy relationship again. Your Aunt Sara, well, I think she just wanted to give Sam time to heal." Mom started to cry again and said, "It was a very hard time for all of us, your dad, Sam, Sara, and me. There was a lot to learn about forgiveness that year."

Even though Mom told a lot of the story, the way she was acting, I got the feeling some of it was left out. She was clearly upset in telling me, so I asked, "What did Betty want when she called?"

Mom's thoughts came back to me as she wiped her blue eyes and said, "Oh, you know, I think she just must be at a time in her life that she is finally learning about forgiveness, and how good it can feel. You know, Faith, forgiving something or someone makes one feel better. But what really feels good is when someone forgives you for something you might have done wrong."

I kind of felt lost, and said, "Did you do something wrong, Mom?"

Mom hugged me while sitting on our front porch swing and said, "But of course, Faith, I have done things wrong. I am human, but I try to learn from my mistakes, understanding and forgiving them."

I said, "Did Betty say how Lily was?"

Mom said, "Yes, she did. That was one of the first things I asked. You know, she graduated high school the same time as Will. Betty said she is fine, a good girl she said."

I asked, "Are you going to tell Uncle Sam she called?"

Mom replied, "Why yes, I suppose I will."

It got quiet for a couple of minutes, and then Mom said out of the blue, "You know, I'm thinking we need to get away. Your brother Sam is at a cross-road in his life, and he could use a little fun vacation. What do you think, Faith? How about a trip across state to that amusement park in Sandusky Ohio that you kids are always talking about?"

"Cedar Point!" I exclaimed. "Can Molly come too?"

"For sure!" Mom said.

Blue Skies, Ferris Wheels, and Lily

We left very early that August Friday morning in Sam's supped-up car. Sam was excited to be able to drive. Mom had told Sam before what an excellent driver he was. Molly and I sat in the backseat of his '68 blue Barracuda; Sam drove and Mom sat in the front passenger seat. She had her dark blonde hair tucked under the blue scarf and wore big sunglasses. She looked young and pretty, like a movie star.

It was hot and the windows were rolled down, no AC then, just nature's fresh air blowing our hair everywhere. Molly had long brown hair then. We both would keep our hair the exact same length, and at that time, it would hit the middle of our backs. Just below our bra straps. The only difference is that Molly parted her hair on the left side and usually wore a barrette to keep it in place.

Blue jeans cut to be shorts—where you would pull a few strings around the bottoms so they would fringe—was what we wore. We wanted to wear our halter tops, but our moms would say no belly buttons showing when you are in a busy public place. So, we wore our T-shirts with colorful prints and Ked shoes with no socks.

My brother Sam was closest to Mom when we were growing up. They both were so much alike, always pretty happy, some may say even silly. Will and Dad, Sam and Mom, they were the teams whenever we played cards or board games, and of course, Molly and I would team up. I was close to both Mom and Dad, but being a girl, it just might be easier to be close to both.

In the backseat that day, Molly and I would talk over the radio that played rock and roll. Mom would somehow know some of the words. She loved Janis Joplin's *Piece of My Heart* and would sing all of Elvis Presley's songs. My brother Sam would put in the eight tracks of Alice Cooper singing *I'm eighteen* and *School's out*. We talked about what ride we would go on first: the Ferris wheel, we heard was the biggest one, at 136 feet. Also, we would talk about boys. At fifteen, neither one of us had our first kiss, but we had both held hands with boys at the roller rink. At the school dances, sometimes boys would ask to slow dance with us, but we hadn't taken that dance step as of yet.

I liked that we were taking things slow in life, that we had parents who didn't rush or push us to grow up too fast. "There will be plenty of time to do all the things you want to do in your life if you just slow down," Mom would say. Mom was a live-in-the-moment kind of gal. Way back before it was cool, she would always say these quotes like, "Quit jumping into tomorrow, and stand here today," and "Dream it, but not so much that you don't live it." I find myself remembering a lot of things Mom had said. I don't know if she had made them up or found them in a book somewhere. I guess you could say she was a Gandhi of Moms—a free but grounded spirit, if that makes any sense.

We stopped to have sandwiches and lemonade Mom had packed at a picnic rest stop just outside of Sandusky. Mom was looking into the blue sky from the picnic table and said, "Isn't it beautiful? Just to know it goes on forever and it could hold all the answers." She had us all looking up at that point.

Just then a jet plane entered the picture and Sam said, "Now then, that's what I want to do."

I said, "What's that, Sam?"

Sam said, "Be the pilot of that there plane."

Mom said smiling, "See what I mean? That could be your answer, Sam." Funny, but wonderful how Mom knew that most of Sam's frustrations was he needing to have passion in something—fast cars was just maybe a start.

I think people who grow up knowing just what they want to do have an easier time with this phase of life, like Dad with his passion to make things out of wood; Will had a passion to protect our land; Mom's passion was plants, birds, and flowers; even Miss June found her passion for baking again after years of not caring. The brownies she sent with us that day were proof that passion did matter. I had only hope that someday I would find my answer in the big, blue sky.

When we arrived at the park, Mom went over the rules of staying close and being aware of your surroundings. We had our watches and our meeting place and time. She wanted to go to Frontier Town, and have our pictures taken at a place she had heard about that she said, "You can dress up in old-time outfits and pose for the camera." She said about three PM would be a good time. It was just about noon.

Molly and I decided we would ride the Giant Wheel as our first ride, and then when it would be all lit up in the dark, it would be our last ride. We rode in antique cars, the Midway Carousel, scrambler, and made out way to shoot the rapids that would cool us off in the warm day it had turned out to be. We had blue cotton candy and pink taffy. At 2:45 we made our way to Frontier Town where Mom and Sam sat waiting at the picture place.

The young girl had the signup sheet on the clipboard when she said to Mom, "You guys are next." Then she led us into the open shop and back to the costumes of yesteryear. A pretty girl with big, brown eyes said, "Hi, my name is Lily, and I will be taking your pictures. As you can see, there are lots of costumes to pick from. You can change right back there. Boys to the right, girls to the left," as she pointed to the back of the shop. Then she said, "How about a saloon look or maybe gun fighters?"

As she looked toward Sam, Mom said, "No, I was thinking maybe just a prairie family or early settlers."

Lily said, "Well, then there are plenty of prairie dresses, and maybe the good-looking young man can dress like he is protecting his family as they travel to unknown territory."

Sam smiled and said, "I'll need a big gun, Lily." My brother was such a flirt.

Our first picture was a group picture in our prairie clothes, and then Mom and I took one together, and Molly and Sam together. Then we talked Mom into dressing like people in an old-time saloon with Sam as a gambler sitting at the table with cards in hand and a big gun by his side. Mom sat on the other side of the table dressed like a man with her hair tucked up under a brown hat, and she even wore a fake mustache. Molly and I were dressed as barmaids with black net stockings and big pink boa feathers wrapped around our necks; although, it didn't matter about the color, because the pictures would be in black and white.

As we got ready to leave, Lily said, "Thank you for making my day. You are such a nice family. It's been fun."

Mom took Lily's hand and said, "It's been a pleasure meeting you. I hope we didn't take too much of your time; you have been so patient."

Lily said, "I enjoyed it."

Then Mom said, "Lily, do you mind if I snap a picture of you?"

She said, "Sure."

As Mom got her camera out of her shoulder bag, she said, "Here, why don't you stand next to Sam?" She snapped two, "Just in case," she would say.

Sam said, "It was nice meeting you, Lily. You have a way with this here picture thing."

Lily replied, "Thanks, Sam. Drive safe on your way home, and come back again sometime. I'll be here."

As we left with the still drying black and white pictures in our hands, I looked at Mom as she looked back at Lily one more time. Then of course, it dawned on me. That Mom of mine was such a stinker.

It was a long day, and when the lights came on the Giant Ferris Wheel, Molly and I were there. As our Ferris car stopped at the top and we took in the scenic view, I said, "This is the closest I have been to Heaven."

Molly said, "Not me, I was there when I got hurt, but only for a little bit."

I said, "Molly, I know we have talked about that day, do you ever think about it now?"

Molly said, "I have forgotten a lot of it, at least the bad stuff. But I will never forget the bright light, never."

Our Ferris car started to move, and I said, "Molly, I'm so happy we are best friends!"

Molly said, "Forever, Faith, even when we are both in Heaven."

Mom took over driving the blue Barracuda home, while Sam slept in the front seat and Molly and I slept in the back. I couldn't wait to ask Mom about if that was Uncle Sam's Lily. But it would have to wait until later. I was clearly worn out.

When Mom got the photographs back from our trip to Cedar Point, we would go over the pictures together on the same front porch swing. Lily was Uncle Sam's Lily, and Mom said she would tell Sam about her soon enough.

The next few weeks would bring a trip to Iowa for the family reunion and school starting. I was a sophomore and Sam a senior. Molly and I bugged Sam for a ride to school in his car, which most of the time he did. Molly sat in the middle. We would ride the school bus home because most of the time Sam would have to work a few hours at the grocery store, and if not, he would bring his girlfriend, Alice, home.

Will also had been dating a girl, and he started a job in Upper Michigan as a DNR officer. He thought it was time to bring Susan home to meet the family. That October Sunday, after church, Will arrived with Susan. I liked her the moment I saw her, and I could tell Mom did, too.

Susan was plain-looking, but a pretty kind of plain. Her skin was sun-kissed, but not too much, you could tell she took care to wear a hat. Her brown hair cut neatly at the shoulders, and the dress, you could tell, was home-made but a good fit as to show off her fit body. Aunt Sara and Grandma Rose would be proud of the craftsmanship.

Dinner that day was to bring Uncle Sam, Aunt Sara, and little Johnny Walter, who was now seven years old, and a handful. He was growing so fast and hyper. Aunt Sara would tell Mom, "The only time that child is still is into the night when he's resting for the new day."

At the table, Susan would tell us that she worked at the fish hatchery where she met Will, and that she and Will would go fishing on their days off. She comes from a family of four older brothers, and when she came along her mother was so happy to finally have a little girl. But as time went on, the dresses would go away and she said, "I would either be fishing or hunting with my dad and brothers," then she added, "but I also have a love for sewing, and baking, as my mother taught me well."

Aunt Sara smiled, and my dad said, "Will, I think you have a keeper."

Will responded, "Don't you know it. I'm not throwing her back!"

I said, "Men," as I shook my head, and Sam laughed.

After dinner, Dad wanted to show Susan the boat. So everyone put on their jackets to go out back. Aunt Sara told Mom she would help with dishes, but Uncle Sam interrupted and said, "I got it, Sara, little Johnny wants you to push him on the tire swing. Go enjoy the fall afternoon."

I had gone to the bathroom and when I was coming down the hall, I heard a conversation between Uncle Sam and my mother that I wish I had never heard. I stopped and bent down to tie my shoelace. I couldn't see them, but as I heard the water shut off to the kitchen sink, Mom said, "Let me grab the picture, Sam." She must have thought everyone had made their way outside, because she was talking loud enough. Then I heard the desk drawer open, and shut. I knew she had the picture of Lily and Sam in her hand. As I peeked around the corner and watched Mom give Uncle Sam the picture, I should have made myself present, but I didn't, and I just hid there listening to their secret.

Mom said, with her hands now in the hot soapy water, "I can't get over how they look alike, but it could be just the dark eyes."

Uncle Sam said, "I don't know, Sam has always looked like you, and John and I both have the brown eyes and hair." *What are they talking about?* I thought. Then Uncle Sam said, "Tell me again about Lily? Did she seem happy?"

Mom said, "Yes, I do believe she is a well-adjusted young lady, and so very sweet. I couldn't get over how bubbly and friendly she was. I hate to say this, but she didn't remind me of Betty at all. Thank you, God."

Uncle Sam smirked and said, "Except she did get her pretty hair. Betty did have pretty hair, I'll give her that."

Mom said, "We are so bad."

I watched Uncle Sam put the picture of Lily and Sam in his wallet, and as he picked up the dish towel and a plate from the dish rack to dry, he said, "What did Sam think of Lily?"

Mom put the next pile of dishes in the sink, and I was thinking, *Gosh, dishes sure make a lot of noise*, Mom said, "Well, you know Sam; he likes the girls. But I was thinking because if anything, they were just spiritually drawn to each another. I hate to think that if they are brother and sister, it could be any other way."

I almost gave myself away, because they must have heard my bottom jaw hit the floor. What the H-E-double-toothpicks were they talking about? Could my brother Sam be Uncle Sam's son, and did my dad and Aunt Sara know about this?

Then, Mom would say, as she wiped her hands on her blue checkered apron, "You know, it's hard to talk about that year. Besides, it has all worked out. I am with John, who I love so very much, and you and Sara, well, that just had to be. I know going to see Lily with Sam seem like I have doubts that Sam is maybe yours instead of John's, but it's the mother in me that wanted Sam to meet what could be a half-sister, and to see that Lily was okay for your sake. I owe you that."

Uncle Sam said, "Betty's call sure has brought up a lot of memories. I still can't believe she called. All those cards and letters Sara and I sent to Lily and every one of them coming back 'return to sender.' She must have had something life changing? As for you and I, Patty, it was just a mistake that turned out good and forgiven." Nothing more was said. The only sound was the dishes making noise.

As the kitchen door opened and the crisp cool air came in with everyone, I made my way back down the hallway to my room. I sat on my bed with the red quilt that Aunt Sally made and looked at the worn edges. I was clearly shaken, so upset that I had to stop and think what to do next. One thing that was for sure, I would never eavesdrop again. I promised myself, and God, that if I didn't listen to other people's private conversations again, that what I had heard that day could somehow be made better, but somehow, after hearing that secret, I couldn't look at my mom the same way. She noticed, and said, "What's wrong, Faith? Is something bothering you?"

I would tell her, "Nothing's wrong, quit asking."

I would talk to Dad more, and at meals, I would ask him about fishing, and his new wood projects he had started in the workshop in the garage. I would hardly say anything to Mom. Sam asked me after one meal, "Why are you being so rude to Mom? It's not very becoming; take my advice, and get over whatever it is before it turns you into a cold-hearted person . . . someone who no one cares to be around."

I wanted to tell Molly about the secret, but I knew Molly wouldn't keep it. From the day of being hurt, she told me and everyone else, "Don't tell me a secret because I can't and won't keep it. I know they can hurt you in the end."

As time went on, it was even harder to just confront Mom, so I just tried to ignore what I had heard. Although I knew it was interfering with the pumping of my heart, I was lost as to what to do. I did take Sam's advice, and was nicer to Mom, which helped.

Secrets of Poison

The June of 1974 Sam graduated high school, and Big Bill helped him get a job at Kent County Airport, where Sam was to work until he would start aviation training at Northwestern Michigan College, in the Grand Traverse area. Big Bill had retired from whatever business he was in, and he and Nana had a house built on a lake by Traverse City. They said even though Sam would live on campus, he would still have a place to go for dinner now and then. That made Dad and Mom happy. Both their boy birds would be living up North Michigan.

It was the summer I was to get a driver's license and a part-time job at the Dairy Treat. Molly would work mornings at that bakery with her mom, Miss June, and me working most afternoons, we knew our days were limited to hang out. Then Molly started dating Mark, a boy one year older than us. It seemed, at times, she would rather hang around with him.

I started hanging out with Tina and her sister, Pam. There were a few times that summer of '74 that my life could have taken some bad turns. Pam was a year older and had a car, and because she was always getting in trouble, her parents would make her take Tina everywhere she went, as if Tina would tell on her sister. Pam would tell Tina, "If you tell Mom and Dad, I'll kill you."

I told Tina, "Such strong words, don't worry, Pam won't hurt you." Then I would think if I had a sister, I surely wouldn't treat her bad.

Anyway, Pam would take us to parties at her friends' houses. Tina and I would sit back and watch Pam and about five or six of her friends, mostly boys, smoke marijuana. They would try to get us to try it, but I was going to hold out and just watch. They always seemed to have fun giggling and laughing, but I had the fear of doing something that I might regret later. I know of the paths Mom and Dad had told us kids about, that if we ever needed advice, they would try to help.

What saved me that summer was fishing with my dad. I would ask Dad one early Saturday morning while watching the sun rise over the trees and onto the lake, "Dad, I don't get why people would keep secrets."

Dad said, "I guess because of fear from the outcome in telling."

I said, "What if it makes you hurt on the inside so bad, and keeps you awake at night, but in telling it could destroy years and years of that person's life?"

Dad said, "This sounds serious. How can I help, Faith? Do you need to tell me something?"

I said, "That's just it, I don't know what to do. I feel sick about it."

He replied, "There are different degrees of secrets. The simple one of keeping Mary Hope's birth a surprise to you, then there are secrets that are like poison to your gut. You want to get it out so you can feel better, but you know that sharing the poison could make a whole lot of people sick. Is that the kind of secret you have, Faith?"

I said, "Yes, and I hate it!"

Dad looked concerned and said, "Have you talked to God about this?"

I replied, "Not really." I didn't want to tell Dad that although I pray when we go to church, I hadn't been talking to God much lately.

I had no excuse except that I guess I figured I didn't need God as much anymore. I was a big girl, and was taking care of myself. Praying was for little kids, and grown-ups, or very old people.

Dad said, "God has always helped me with all my thoughts and problems. Faith, you do know if you didn't have problems, you wouldn't need faith. Use your faith in God to help you with this secret; talk to God."

I said, "Dad, do you have secrets from Mom?"

Dad said, "Yes, I guess I do."

I said, "Oh no! What?"

He said, "Calm down, my secret is not poison, it's more like a few drops of vinegar."

I said, "Can you still tell me?"

Dad said, "Well, to tell you the truth, I have been keeping this from your mother for years and years." I bit my bottom lip thinking, *oh no, oh no, what if he knows something about Mom and Uncle Sam.*

I said, "Go on, go on!"

Dad said, "Okay, if you must know. Well, the pickle bologna your Mom makes every so often for my lunch?" I nodded. "Well, she puts mustard, not one of my favorite condiments as one of the ingredients, and it ruins the whole thing. So if I catch her getting the meat grinder out for grinding the bologna, I will hide the mustard. Her face will get all puzzled, and she will say, 'Johnny, have you seen the mustard? I swear we had some.'"

I laughed and said, "Dad, you are so bad. Mom is always looking for the mustard. What if you don't catch her in time?"

Dad said, "Well then, I take the sandwiches to work, and this man named Bob loves your Mom's pickled bologna." I laughed again.

The fish started to nibble on our worms as we must have drifted over one of their beds. We both pulled our poles in and checked our bait. Putting a fresh worm on the hook can make the difference in catching fish. With our poles back in the water, I said, "Dad, I do have something to tell you."

Dad said, "Yes, go ahead, you know you can tell me anything." I thought to myself, *No, there is poison that I can't just release so I would feel better. Besides, I was smart enough to know that I needed to talk to the source, being Mom and Uncle Sam. Why would I want to share what I heard when it could ruin everything that my family was?* There was one secret that had been weighing on my mind, so I told Dad, "Well, as you know, I've been hanging out with Tina and her big sister, Pam." Dad shook his head yes and I continued, "What is troubling is that we sometimes end up at a house or even by the river where most of Pam's friends and her smoke a joint."

Dad said, "You mean, marijuana?"

I said, "Yes, I haven't tried it and Tina hasn't tried it—that I know of—but to tell you the truth, Dad, it looks like they are having fun."

Just as I finished, Dad pulled in a rock bass. As he took the hook out from the fish's mouth, and tossed the fish back, he said, "I'm glad you have trusted me enough to share your concerns. To tell you the truth, your Mom and I have witnessed a change in your behavior, like you are keeping things inside. Faith, you are going to have decisions to make throughout your life. They will come at you left and right, good and bad. The promptness in making a decision can make all the difference. In you not trying marijuana, without thinking about it, shows me that you care about the consequences."

I pulled in a small bass, unhooked it, and threw it back. It took my worm, so I was putting another one on my hook.

Dad said, "I will tell you again, your Mom and I trust that all of our children will do their best to have a life that God intended all of us to have. I know, Faith, it's got to be hard not to take the bait of something that looks too good to be true. But remember, it's the good decisions that will make you strong, keep you grounded, and keep your faith. Bad choices are the ones we have to learn from, and if we don't learn, they can make you weak, and tear at you until you feel no hope."

As I put my fishing pole down and opened the cooler to get a ham sandwich, I said, "You're lucky, Dad, that the only secret you have is about mustard."

Dad looked at little puzzled, like telling him about the marijuana was the poison I was keeping inside. Then I think he knew there was more I was keeping and he said, "If it helps you to know, I too have had secrets of poison shared, and without God's help, I might not be here fishing with my daughter." Dad winked at me and said, "Faith May, it's the journey of life, it's how you deal with what is thrown at you, and what you toss back. Talk to God, ask for help on how to release any poison. It has helped me."

My thoughts were that I felt better about sharing with Dad about the time spent with Tina and Pam. It also helped to know that even Dad had to deal with secrets of poison, whatever they would be. I talked to God that very night. I asked for help in what to do. The next morning, I woke up with a thought. It was like, *talk to Mom when you feel the time is right; until then, forgive yourself for hearing the secret, because that is what's really bothering you.* I felt so much better.

When Tina called Monday after supper, she said, "Hi, Faith, I called to ask if you have to work Friday night. Pam said there is going to be a really cool party for us to go to."

I said, "No, Tina, I don't work Friday, but count me out. I'd rather do something else. I was going to ask Molly about going bowling; you may join us if you want."

Tina said, "I don't think Pam would not let me go with her."

I said, "I think you need to think about what you want. I'll be here if you need me."

North Michigan, Wedding

Will proposed to Susan, Christmas 1974, and the plan was an outside, small wedding in Wilderness State Park in North Michigan, just below the Mackinaw Bridge. The date was set to be July 26, 1975, rain or shine. We were all excited, and even planned on taking a week after the wedding to go to the cottage on Drummond Island. Molly was to go with us, if she could leave Mark long enough, that is.

That summer I was to own my first car. It was a 1962 red, four-door Ford. Along with the car came responsibilities that I didn't take lightly. I would be the one to drive Molly and me to work. I now worked at a local restaurant along with Molly. We would play hostess and waitress to the morning crowd of hungry men wanting something to eat before work, and the occasional family having a special breakfast out.

I seemed to work every Saturday that summer. Fishing was getting harder to plan, but Dad still went with Mom or Uncle Sam. We had visits from Iowa and even Will made it down to fish with Dad when his work allowed it.

I was seventeen the summer of '75. I had a few suitors as my dad would call them. But the boys that I went with on the few dates I did have just wasn't anybody that I wanted to spend a lot of my time with, maybe because I watched the boys that would ask me out grow up. Dave was someone that I had gone to the drive in movies with. I would want to watch the movie from the car, where you put the speaker inside the window, but Dave would take my popcorn away and try to kiss me.

I tried to like kissing, but then I would think about when we were both in the third grade, and Dave, or David as we called him back then, had this an-noying habit of wiping his nose or mouth on the sleeve of his shirts. Disgusting! It's funny that it would bother me. I would tell Molly, "I would rather read a book than to kiss." Molly would tell me it wasn't normal. I would think maybe because I had older brothers, or maybe I just needed to date some boy who I never saw go through their awkward age.

Meanwhile, Molly was still dating Mark. I liked Mark. He was kind, soft-spoken, easy-going, easy on the eyes, hard-working, and having had three younger sisters just seemed to make him respect girls in general. Mark's mother, Marge, and Father Hank, went to our church. I remember when I was around six, Marge and Hank would, each year for three years in a row, bring a new baby girl to church each spring. I would think that was an amazing feat.

Hank owned the corner gas station and repair shop in town. Everyone knew Hank as an honest, hard-working, family man. Hank could repair anything on your car, lawn mower or tractor, and Mark was learning the trade. Hank's station was always busy from seven to seven each night, and eight to noon on Saturday; it closed on Sunday.

I knew the Warners liked Mark, too. But they did watch over Molly like a loyal dog would watch over its home. The only thing wrong was, while the Warners watched over Molly, Paul Jr. was getting lost in a world of confusion. Pauly was just over twenty years old and had some run-ins with the law. Molly had told me besides getting tickets for speeding, Pauly had gotten caught doing some petty theft, like stealing cigarettes. Then the big news was Molly had just found out Pauly's girlfriend, Janet, was pregnant.

I told Mom what Molly told me right away because I didn't want Mom to think I would keep secrets from her. But Mom had already heard from Miss June. Mom would say, "It's sad when something you might have done in haste becomes something that will change your life forever. Now hopefully, Paul Jr. and Janet can come together and make the right choices on what to do next."

I almost said, *did you ever have a moment of haste? Is that why I have a brother Sam?* But something told me it wasn't time. With Will and Susan's wedding coming, I knew I wanted a happy family.

Susan had asked me to stand beside her as a bridesmaid, and she would come with Will on a visit to take my measurement to make me a dress to wear for the wedding. She would show me the pattern and the flower material. It was going to be a sleeveless long dress. Susan would tell me, "Don't worry, Faith, about how it will look. You could look good in anything." I wasn't worried, and just seeing some of the dresses Susan had made, I knew mine would be divine, and besides, I liked homemade clothes. It must be because I had worn homemade clothes most of my childhood.

The day of the wedding, our families would leave in two cars. Dad, Mom, Molly, and I in our car, along with our things; we would take to our cottage on Drummond Island. Uncle Sam, Aunt Sara, John Walter, and my grandparents would follow us. The plan was, John Walter would then come with us Bakkers to the cottage for the week. We left very early in the morning and drove to Susan's family home in Mackinaw City to meet and freshen up before the ceremony. My brother Sam and his girlfriend Tiffany would travel with Big Bill and Nana from Traverse City. Sam would be Will's best man.

I loved the dress Susan made for me. I felt pretty that day and what confirmed how I felt was when Susan's youngest brother, and the only one who was not married, said as we were introduced, "So nice to meet you, Faith. Your brother Will failed to mention how pretty his sister was."

I said, as he took my hand, "Thank you, likewise. It's nice to meet you, Doug." I was thinking now, here's a boy I didn't watch go through any awkward stage, and he kind of gave me a chill . . . a good chill.

That day, Will and Susan pledged their love in front of God, family, and friends. It was a beautiful summer day, nothing but blue skies, Lake Michigan and her bridge in the background. Will looked so handsome and grown-up. He even had a mustache. Susan looked so pretty. Whenever I think of Susan, I think of wholesome. The white dress Susan's mother made her was just perfect, and crown of wildflowers she wore around her head with lilac ribbons coming down through her hair was superb, especially when the breeze from Lake Michigan would move them about.

After the ceremony, we would travel back to Mackinaw City, where Susan's parents owned a hotel and restaurant. The food was abundant and the sense of family was ample. We were to stay at the hotel that night, which was great, because I know I was tired. I could only imagine how tired Grandpa Allen and Grandma Rose felt.

Sam's girlfriend stayed in the same room as Molly and I that night. Tiffany was what I have been known to call people "a hoot." She was full of herself, and I think she had herself a few drinks before she made it back to the room that night. So of course, Molly and I would grill her intensely on everything from, "What are your plans with my brother Sam? Do you dye your hair red? Do you believe in God? Why do you take your clothes off for a living, and is that how you met Sam?"

One thing I will say for Tiffany is she was honest. She would tell Molly and me straight out, "I like Sam. He's good-looking, sweet, so smart, and he's going to be a pilot someday. How cool is that? Yes, I put Miss Clairol red dye in my hair, but I was told I was born with a red tint and men just love a red head! No, for Heaven sakes, I don't believe in God. That's just something people made up many years ago to make them feel better about death. I believe we will all be reincarnated, and I plan to come back as an ally cat. Yes, I was a stripper in Detroit for one year. That's where I met Sam; he was there with his flight buddies and we got to talking. He said he was going to school in Traverse and I was like 'WOW! That's where I am from and where my family lives.' Sam said, 'If you ever come home, look me up.' I don't remember exactly what Sam said that night, but it left me wanting to come and try to get along with my family once more. And, so here I am." As Tiffany put her hands in the air, she would add, "Don't tell your parents, Faith, about the stripping. I don't think they would like me much then."

I told Tiffany, "Mom and Dad wouldn't say much about it except Sam is big enough to make his own choices, and we are not to judge." Then I said, as I hugged my bed pillow sitting on the edge of one of the double beds,

"Tiffany, I do think it's sad that you don't believe in God, but as long as you know of God, then it's your choice. I still believe everyone is loved by God no matter what they think." Tiffany then went into the bathroom, and held her long red hair back from her face as she threw up into the toilet. I said to Molly, "Was it something I said?"

Molly said, smiling, "No, I think it was something she drank."

The next morning, we would all meet in the hotel restaurant for a big breakfast. I really liked Susan's family, and having Susan as a sister-in-law was going to be great. Just as I was having that thought about Susan, I watched my brother Sam make his way over to me. I started thinking, *oh please, Sam, don't ask me about what I think of him and Daffy Duck—I mean, Tiffany.* Sam sat down next to me as people were getting up from their seats and moving about. The sounds of informal talking were all around us, and you really couldn't make out what anyone was saying unless you were part of their conversation.

Sam looked me in the eyes, and said, "So what's up, Faith? How have you been? I don't get to talk to my little sis much anymore."

I said, smiling, "I'm fine. Have you flown an airplane yet?"

Sam said, "I have had a small plane up, and I love it. It won't be long before you can call me captain." Sam smiled big and it looked just like Dad's smile, and I thought to myself, *Thank you, God.* Then Sam said, "Faith, I still feel some tension between you and Mom. Do you need to talk about it?"

I swallowed the last of my orange juice and said, "No, everything will be fine. Just seeing you smile makes it better."

Then he said, "Well, you know you can always talk to me." Just then Molly sat back down on my other side, and Sam said it, "So what did you two think of Tiffany?"

Oh, how I wished he wouldn't ask, but Molly piped right in and said, "Sam, woo, she sure is bubbly, and pretty, and she knows how to dress, I'll give her that." As Molly rolled her eyes, she continued, "But really, Sam, you can do better." I wasn't surprised by Molly's answer. She had told Sam he could do better with each of his girlfriends she would meet, from Alice, to Sandy, and now Tiffany.

When Sam looked at me for an answer, I knew Molly's answer didn't matter as much as mine. Sam wanted mine, so I couldn't help it. I had to be honest and I said, "She's a hoot!"

Sam laughed and said, "Well, don't worry; I don't see wedding bells in our future. But what I see is a girl who didn't get a lot of guidance as a child, and just maybe I can help her out. She's really sweet."

I replied, "That's you, Sam, always helping someone out. Plus I know the right girl will come your way as it did for Will."

Sam would say, as he got up from the table, "Well, you take care, girls, and have fun at the cottage. I hope the fish will be biting."

I said, "Thanks, Sam, will do." He winked at me, and it was the same wink Dad would give me, and another thought came to me. Sam has to be Dad's son because somehow, God just told me.

That's when Will and Susan would stand and announce a big "Thank you to everyone for being here for us on our wedding day, and our first breakfast as man and wife." We all said our good-byes and nice-to-meet-yous in the parking lot of the hotel. John Walters would get his small suitcase and his fishing pole to put in our car; right away he looked at Molly and I and said, "I call window seat." Molly rolled her eyes and I knew she was thinking the same as me. Here we go, a whole week of a boy that was nine years old, and was so full of energy and curiosities; we were in for it.

Will and Susan would make their way to Niagara Falls for their honeymoon. I do believe I saw fishing poles in their backseat. Uncle Sam and Aunt Sara would drive Grandpa and Grandma home. Maybe without John Walter around, they would have a second honeymoon. Sam and Tiffany left with Big Bill and Nana, and I could only imagine the conversations they would have on their drive back to Traverse City. We headed towards the Mackinac Bridge to take us to the U.P. and on towards Drummond Island.

My mom would let John Walter have her front window seat, and she would sit next to Dad. I watched them smile and talk, like they were on their own honeymoon. I knew they were so in love, and felt they have always been in that love. That's the thing that was hard to understand about what I heard Mom and Uncle Sam talk about. How could they have let something so wrong happen; and did they think they could keep this secret from my dad and Aunt Sara to their graves? What about all the times both Dad and Mom would tell us about being honest and having integrity? How, if you do something bad and try to hide it, that it would somehow always come forth? To own up to it right away, deal with it. Then, I thought, maybe Dad knew everything, as well as Aunt Sara and the four of them had already dealt with it. That's what I would think when the secret would weigh heavy on my mind, usually in the quiet of the night.

The Right Catch

When we reached our destination, our little home away from home, it was close to noon. After a quick lunch of pickled bologna sandwiches—without the mustard—we would get busy unpacking and helping Dad get the boats in the water from where we stored them in the boat shed.

We kept our big boat up here now, along with a small boat with a little three-and-a-half horsepower motor for getting around in Scott's Bay. We had another boat that we kept at the house. Dad said it just made more sense to not have to hull a boat up here each trip.

John Walter had been here before with his dad and mine, so he knew the rules, and I knew he wouldn't be that much trouble. He pretty much did what any nine-year-old boy did: kept busy.

This was Molly's first time to our cottage. She said, "Faith, it's just like you have described it. I love, love it!" I thought to myself, *It has grown to be a very happy place.* A place where Mom and Dad would more than likely retire to someday, and us kids would bring their grandchildren for a vacation of fishing and sunrises and sunsets.

Dad and Uncle Sam had built a wood deck off the front since the last time I was here, and that was great now for us girls so we could get some sun without worrying about snakes in the grass. Mom's perennials were all in bloom. She sure knew what to plant and where to plant as to have such a pretty landscape. I would think to myself, *Someday I need to pay attention to how she makes her gardens grow, because it was an art, an art she had mastered.*

Mom would hang a hummingbird feeder, and it wouldn't be long before one would visit, like they had been up in the trees waiting for Mom. Dad would say, "Why I believe they are the same hummers from home, and they followed your mother's pretty smile up here." He winked at Mom.

Dad and I knew how much Mom liked birds, not just hummingbirds— why, she could name every species of birds. Mom's favorite was the bald eagle.

The only one Mom had seen in the wild was up here, and she was always looking towards the sky for another sighting. Both Mom and Will were saddened by the bald eagle's decline because of pesticides PCB and DDT, and were delighted when it was band in the '70s. They were advocates on bringing back the eagles, and Will would keep Mom informed on any new nest.

Around two o'clock, Molly and I were in our bathing suits. I just had gotten a new, bright yellow two-piece suit, and Molly's was royal blue, of course. We wanted to work on our tans, and maybe pull in a few fish for supper, so we took off in the little boat. Mom would make us some lemonade, and Dad gave us a few crawlers for bait.

"Good luck," Dad said, as he pushed the boat from the dock.

John Walter said, "Sure you don't need my help?"

"No, we're fine, but thanks anyways," Molly said as she waved. I motored around the bay and stopped just beyond the weed beds where there was just enough drift to make a worm look tasty bouncing around the lake's bottom.

After our poles were set and lines in the water, Molly began again telling me about how someday Mark would take over his dad's gas station or maybe open his own, and they would marry. She would become a teacher, and they would have lots of babies, and so on and so forth. I, on the other hand, wanted all that stuff, and was happy for Molly and Mark, but I also wanted to travel, and see the whole big wide world. Well, and having lots of kids—I don't think I wanted that. I wanted a family, but a small family would be fine.

I was putting a small amount of baby oil on my already tan arms when a jerk of my fishing pole made me take notice. "Holy crap!" Molly said, as I grabbed my pole before it left the boat. I held on the pole and whatever it was, it was taking my line and running with it.

As I stopped the line from running, I said, "I don't know what it is, but it's big and it's a fighter."

Molly yelled, "Don't let it get away, Faith, hold tight!" We were both now standing in the little boat, balancing our weight as not to tip. The fish had surfaced, but too far from the boat to tell what it was. Molly was laughing and said, "Maybe it's a descendant of Moby Dick!"

I said, "Too funny, Molly, whatever it is. I'm not letting it get away; get the net ready."

We must have been making quite the ruckus because I looked to my side and saw the tip of another boat come up alongside us. I didn't see the person, but I heard them say, "Do you need some help?"

Molly did the talking, and said, "No, thanks, us girls know how to fish. We'll have this monster under control and in the boat in no time."

I heard the voice laughing, and saying. "Really, I think you're going to need a bigger boat."

Molly replied, "Ha-ha."

I had the fish by the boat and was remembering all the tips that Dad and my brothers had given me over the years. Let the fish get tired. Keep the rod tip up, don't give it any slack. Don't pull a big fish straight up, it could break the line. Net from underneath.

As the fish now lay on the small boat's bottom, I would see the master of the voice from the other small boat, a very good-looking master. Then I looked at the monster fish. It had to be the ugliest, water-breathing, cold-blooded, cartilaginous fish ever. I said to Molly, "What kind of fish is this? If it didn't have fins, gills, and scales, I wouldn't believe it was a fish."

That's when the handsome young man would be now holding on to our boat and leaning over the catch. He said, "You girls have impressed me with your fishing skills, and that there has to be the biggest dogfish I've ever seen."

Molly said, "Dogfish! What the heck?"

As I took the pliers out of the small red tackle box to remove the hook and release the big fish, I said, "It's got to be at least ten pounds."

The young man then said quickly, "Be careful, they can bite."

I hesitated, and said, "You're kidding, right?"

Molly said, "It sure is ugly."

The fish wiggled and jumped. I held it down with one hand, took the hook out with the pliers, and picked it up and threw it back into the water. As it splashed away, the young man said, "Again, I'm impressed by your skills." He held out his hand to me and said, "Nice to meet you. I'm Christopher, but of course, you may call me Chris, Chris Sutton."

I leaned over and rubbed my slimy hands together in the cool water and dried them on a hand towel in the boat. I took Chris's hand and said, "Nice to meet you. I'm Faith."

Molly leaned toward Chris, took his hand and with a nod, and said, "Molly here," then both us girls proceeded to put our T-shirts on over our bathing suits. I would think it's kind of late; I'm sure Chris has seen enough skin from us girls already.

As I sat back down, I said, "So Chris Sutton, have you ever caught a dogfish before?"

Chris said, smiling, "Yes, but not that one," as he looked out towards where the fish took off.

Molly said, as she rolled her eyes, "Funny." Then I noticed Chris's sky blue eyes as the light from the sun made them go so perfectly well with his sandy blonde hair, and big, white, perfectly straight teeth. He too must have been working on his golden tan as he had no shirt on his perfectly muscled arms and chest. Okay, okay, he was quite striking, and even if his nose might have been on the large side, it was still fitting. I notice he was taking in my looks as well, which made me more interested in him.

As he broke our gaze at each other, Chris said, "So, Faith, let me ask you, do you live on the island, or are you a visitor?"

By now Molly was drinking lemonade and asked, "Who wants lemonade?"

Chris said, still looking at me, "No thanks, Molly."

I took a cup of lemonade from Molly and said, "Thanks, Molly. And yes on the visitor part, although my family has a cottage right over there." I pointed down the shoreline and said, "You can just see the white cottage with green shutters, and deck out front."

Chris looked and said, "Yes, I see, not far from where we are renting."

I said, "So you're on vacation?"

He replied, "Yes, spending time with the folks before going on to college."

Molly said, "You going to be a doctor?"

Chris said, "No, a lawyer."

"Interesting," I said.

Chris let go of our boat, and said, "Well, I hope to see you two again. How long are you here on the island?"

Molly piped in, "Until Saturday. You can come to our bonfire on the beach some night. If I know Faith's dad, we will more than likely have one every night, starting tonight."

Chris looked at me, his sky blue eyes sparkling, and said, "Would that be okay, Faith? Because I would like that."

I said, "Sure, that's a good idea." By now I was thinking, how did I get so lucky to have such a handsome, pleasing young man want to see more of me? Thank you, God.

Chris pulled the chock out on his boat motor, pulled the cord for it to start, and as he slowly motored away, he said, "Well, Faith and Molly, have fun catching some fish. I just hope they're not dogfish. I'll be looking for a fire." He smiled and waved as he hit the gas, and the boat made its wake.

I was thinking about all the questions I wanted to ask him, that I wish I had been more talkative, and then I said to Molly, "Good going on the asking about coming to a bonfire. You are always thinking."

Molly said, as she took her T-shirt off again, "Well, I certainly couldn't let that catch get away, why, I've never seen you so star struck."

I said, laughing, "He is handsome, someone I would like to get to know."

Molly said, "Yeah, yeah, now back to that fish. Why, could you believe how big and ugly it was?"

I said, "Yes, I would like to have had someone taking a movie of us getting it in the boat. We must have looked funny to have Chris come see. I bet he thought we would tip the boat, or at least fall in."

Molly said, "No, you heard him, we are skilled fisherwomen." We were both laughing then.

Back at the cottage, as we would dock the boat and tie it, Dad and John Walter would help us gather our things.

Dad said, "Did you catch us supper?"

Molly said, "No, but Faith might have caught and released the biggest dogfish there ever was."

As we walked up to the deck, Dad said, "Those bowfins, or dogfish, can put up a good fight. Surprised it didn't pull you out of the boat."

John Walter said, "How big was it, Faith?"

As I sat down in one of the chairs the deck held and put my hand out as if I was going to hug a very large person, I said, "Why, that monster fish had to be twenty pounds."

Molly laughed, "Oh, Faith, now you are telling a fish story."

Molly said to Dad, "Are we having a bonfire on the beach tonight, Mr. Bakker?"

Dad said, "Yes, I think we can manage that, but sometime this week we are going to have to go out and gather some more wood."

Molly said, "Will do, I love it here. It's so nice to be outdoors, and on the water. Thanks for having me come with you this week."

Mom was on the deck by now and she said, "You are welcome, Molly, we love having you here."

That night, we did have a bonfire on our beach, but Chris didn't show up. I was happy Molly didn't tell Mom or Dad about meeting Chris. When Molly and I got ready for bed, Molly said, "Don't worry, Faith, he probably had some family thing going on. I'm sure he will be back around."

I said, as not to sound disappointed, "I'm not worried; like Dad says, if it's meant to be, then it will be."

As I climbed to the top bunk in the small room, I said, "Goodnight, Molly."

Molly answered, "Night, Faith."

Then I talked to God: "Thank you for this day and all the good that came. May you bless my family and friends near and far. As always please forgive my sins, and help me to be better, do better. May peace come to those who seek it, and all will know of your love. God, please bless my new friend, Christopher. Amen."

I would fall to sleep thinking of the new face I had met today, remembering its every detail. Then, my last though was Grandma Mary, how I was forgetting some of her face. My thoughts were maybe we were only allowed so many faces to remember. Then I reached over and took the picture of Grandma Mary and me when I was a few years old. I kept the picture in my purse that was hanging on the post of the bunk bed. Grandma had a big smile on her face as she was knelt down next to me. I was holding a fish on a string; we were both wearing blue dresses. The other picture I carried in my purse was the one of Mom and I that Lily had taken. Mom didn't even know that I had that picture, but as I looked at the black-and-white picture, it would trouble me that for the life of me, I couldn't remember what colors we wore that day. Why was that? I always remembered the clothes I wore.

Morning Brings Sunshine

The next morning, I got up and looked at the round, gold, wind-up alarm clock that sat on the dresser of the small room. 8:30. *Wow, I bet Dad has already gone fishing with John Walter.* As I climbed down from the bunk, I looked at the bottom bunk which held Molly in sleep; I smiled thinking how happy I was to have my best friend with me this week.

I put my pink summer robe on over my long mint-green T-shirt that I wore to bed, and made my way to the bathroom. I brushed my teeth, combed my blonde hair, and I looked in the oval wood-framed mirror that was hung in this bathroom the first year we came here.

The small bathroom had no mirror, and Mom found one at a second-hand store that summer. I can remember her saying as Dad hung it, "We need a mirror to look at ourselves each day, to look at the image that it gives you, and no matter what you think of what is looking back, you are to thank God for its existence, and then tell that image that you will do your best in the new day that you have been given because God loves what you see." I know how some people would probably think how arrogant that is, but I know the fact is, if you can love yourself as God does, you are going to be able to love another the way God has intended. "Love thyself, be true."

As I came out from the bathroom, I heard the voices at the kitchen table along with the smell of bacon. I could have stopped and listened before entering the room, but that wasn't my style anymore. I just entered.

My mouth opened but nothing came from it. Dad said, "Good morning, sunshine. Chris here tells me that he was impressed with your fishing skills yesterday." Dad winked, got up, and pulled a chair out, then said, "Come sit down and eat."

Chris was sitting at our wooden kitchen table, another one of Dad's creations. With a plate of scrambled eggs, bacon, and orange juice, I sat next to John Walter that would put me right across from Chris, who said, "Good morning, Faith. I had just docked my boat at your dock when you're Dad and John Walter were getting ready to go fishing." Chris took the time to chew and swallow his mouth of eggs, and then said, "I was telling your dad that I felt bad about not making it over to the bonfire. But my dad challenged me to a game or cribbage, which went from one to another and on into the evening. I couldn't say no to Dad. One of the reasons for this trip is to spend time with him." Chris smiled at me.

Mom put a plate of eggs and toast in front of me and pulled my long hair back, something she always did when she put food in front of me. She said, "The waters have turned rough out there over night. I was telling your dad he better hold off on fishing."

Chris said, "It's rough. I had all I could do to keep my little boat in line."

Dad said, "Winds out of the North West, hopefully it changes again soon so we can get some fishing in."

John Walter then said, "What are we going to do today if we can't fish?"

Dad replied, "There is plenty to do John; we could go hiking, or take in nature on horseback. This island offers a lot. What do you think, Chris?"

Chris said, "It's going to be a warm day, highs in the nineties, but it's windy."

As I looked around from Dad, Chris, and John Walter—and even Mom as she stood at the sink—I was thinking, does anyone care that I haven't even gotten to say one word yet? Just how do you think I feel about all this? Why do they know that I really don't even know much about this Chris fellow, let alone have him hang around with us?

Just then, Molly entered the room, saying, "Hey! Good morning, everyone! Oh, hi, Chris Sutton. I see you have found us without a fire."

I laughed and said, "Molly, you are so bad. He did have a good reason." Molly pulled up a chair to sit. I was thinking, *I need to tell Molly to look in the mirror first thing in the morning.* Although she was still beautiful with her hair sticking out everywhere, a comb would have been nice. Molly said, "Sorry, Chris that probably wasn't very nice."

Chris said, "Sorry accepted. But the fact that you look out for your friend, it shows respect, support, and all good stuff." As he smiled at me, I would smile back as to say, *that's right, mister. Molly's my friend, through thick and thin.*

Mom would put the cereal box in front of Molly with the red and white carton of milk, and she would say to me, "Chris here tells us his family is from the Lansing area, Faith. That's where your great Aunt Peg lives."

John Walter said, "Hey, that's our state capitol."

Dad and Chris said yes at the same time. I was thinking how far Lansing, Michigan, was from my home in Hudsonville, Michigan. Molly would look toward me and say, "About eighty or so miles, Faith."

I was not surprised that she knew what I was thinking. "Thanks, Molly," I said.

Chris said, "Again, I am impressed, you two must have been joined at the hips at one time."

Molly said, as she poured her milk, "No, we're joined through God." I smiled, and my dad did, too.

It got quiet, so I thought I would make it easy on everyone and said, "How about a picnic on the other side of the island, where maybe it won't be so rough and we can all get in a swim? The beach is better over there anyway."

Dad said, "I like that," as he looked toward Mom, who I knew already had thoughts of fried chicken.

I said, "Chris, will you join us?"

Chris said smiling, "Why, yes, Faith, I would like that."

John Walter would say, "So be it," and jumped up from his chair as if we were going that instant.

We would have a great day. The weather did reach hot, and the cool waters were just right for a swim. The light breeze was keeping the fiery sun bearable. When we ate lunch, Chris noticed that Molly didn't touch the fried chicken, but loved the three bean salad and homemade rolls she helped Mom make.

Chris asked, "I notice, Molly, you didn't eat meat at breakfast or now. Are you a vegetarian?"

Molly and I looked at each other, and Molly said, "Now I am impressed, Chris Sutton, you should be a detective, not a lawyer."

Chris said, "A good lawyer is a detective."

Yes, Molly had given up the eating of animals ever since Mark took her to a county fair last summer. The pigs they had there were for auction, and well, Molly fell in love with those pigs. When she found out they were going to be slaughtered for meat, she told me something just clicked in her, and she no longer had any desire for meat.

Molly told Chris, "I guess I am not a complete vegetarian, because I still want to eat Miss Patty's fish; something in the way she prepares them and cooks them." Chris would find out about the fish at a dinner with us later in the week. My dad, Chris, his dad Roger, and John Walter would fish one early morning catching their limit in walleyes.

As for Molly, she did become a complete vegetarian years later. She would still catch fish, but all her fish were catch and release. My family and I have always supported Molly's stance and have enjoyed many meatless meals with her. Chris and I talked a lot that week. We were learning about each other, about our families, friends, what we had in common, and what we had different. Chris told me his dad was married before he married his mother, and he had two much older stepsisters. Then Chris told me that his mother, who was much younger than his dad, was killed in a car crash when he was five.

Chris said, "Dad married his secretary, Diana, when I was seven. She is also much younger than Dad. Diana has been a good stepmother. I get along with her quite well, and my stepsisters have always been there for me." He added, "They don't get along with Dad, but they do like Diana, who keeps the peace among them."

I asked Chris, "Do you remember your mother?"

He replied, "A few bits and pieces, but mostly it's the pictures I keep of her and I. That keeps the memories alive. I think if I didn't look at the pictures from time to time, I would forget her face."

I said, "I know what you mean."

Chris's dad, Roger, and stepmother, Diana, would come to our bonfire the last night before we were to head home. Chris sure was right about his dad being older. Roger Sutton had just retired as a lawyer, and I dare say Diana was younger than my mother. Roger, or Mr. Sutton, looked every bit like the grandpa he was. He had gray hair, but the same blue eyes, and big but fitting nose, as Chris did. His skin was white like it hadn't seen the sun much, ever, but it somehow looked old just the same. Diana's look was pretty. Her thick, dark hair and green, friendly eyes fit perfectly on her physically fit body. Chris had told me she had taught yoga for years and meditation is very important to her, but with everybody doing the aerobics thing, her studio closed and now she does it just for herself. I found everything about Chris and his family so interesting, so different from ours, yet just as functional.

Chris and I held hands as we took a walk that last night on the island to a full moon. He would tell me he really liked me, and wanted to keep in touch. He had my phone number as well as my address, and I had his. He would kiss me sweetly on my parted lips, and I liked it very much. I thought I could put any book down for this kind of kiss.

That night, as Molly and I would crawl into our bunks, she would tell me again how she missed Mark, and couldn't wait to see him again. Earlier this week, I thought she was being silly, but tonight I knew just how she felt. Then, I talked to God: "Dear God, thank you for the day and the many blessings. May we have a safe trip home tomorrow as well as Chris and his family next week. Thank you for all the fish you gave us, and the beautiful waters that hold their lives. Amen."

Sometimes, my prayers would go on and on into the night, thanking God for every hair on my head to thanking God for the moon, stars, sun, earth, and the whole wide universe.

Getting to Know You . . .
and Who Am I?

I would start my senior year of high school, and Chris would be a freshman at Michigan State. We wrote letters back and forth to each other. Chris called me every Saturday evening without fail. We never ran out of things to say or words to write. It was autumn of 1975.

Will and Susan announced their pregnancy at our family Christmas dinner that year. My brother Sam told us about sending resumes to the top airlines. Chris would come to see me during our Christmas break, bringing me a huge, white teddy bear, and my mom and dad a huge fruit basket with nuts, crackers, and cheeses.

We rode Uncle Sam's snowmobiles and drank hot chocolate by the living room fireplace. My dad and mom would tell Chris stories about me growing up with Lady. Talking about Lady was something we hadn't done much of lately. I would become teary-eyed, and Chris told us that he and his mom had a black Lab named Duke. He said, "I remember Duke being very rambunctious and only Mom's calm could settle Duke down. Then Mom would drop me off to school that November morning going on from there with Duke to the veterinary for his yearly shots. That's when she slid through the stop sign and a truck broadsided her little car, killing both her and Duke. She was only twenty-seven."

Chris looked down into his cup or now warm chocolate and said, "It's funny how Dad would always blame Duke on my mother being killed. It never was the slippery roads to blame. Dad would never let Diana or I have a dog after Duke. He would say, 'I have no use for them.'"

The guest room held Chris those nights of his stay, and I so wanted to lie next to him and hold him. To tell him that his dad not wanting another dog was because he couldn't forgive the fact he wasn't able to save his mother from the accident that put her back in the arms of God.

Paul Jr. and Janet got married New Years Day, and had little Paula Jane two weeks later. They lived in a small apartment above a house in town. Molly would spend most weekends helping Janet. I would think how lucky she was because with all the miles between us, and Will and Susan, it will be hard to see their baby as often.

Chris was my date to senior prom. I was so nervous to see him again, excited, but nervous just the same. Aunt Sara offered to make my prom dress, and my girlfriends would want me to go to the mall with them to pick out dresses. But I would turn them all down and would wear the dress Susan had made me for the wedding. Somehow I just felt pretty when I wore it.

That night went fast with Chris being every bit a gentleman. We did do a lot of kissing, and I think we both wanted to do more, but Chris said, "There will come a time for all of that; let's take it slow." He was good to me. He stayed in the guest room again and I would go to the door and touch the glass knob in the middle of the night, wanting so badly to turn the knob and bring myself to Chris, into his arms, and onto his body, but I would let go and return to my bed and hug the white teddy bear I named Christmas.

After breakfast, Chris and I went to Holland State Park where we walked hand in hand down the shoreline of the sandy beach of Lake Michigan and onto the pier where we would talk, laugh, and kiss, in that order. Before Chris headed back to Lansing that late afternoon, he told me that someday he thought we would have a future together. *Wow!* Could this be? And should it be?

After graduation in '76, I worked at a steak house where they did serve beverages containing alcohol, and I was eighteen, the legal age back then. But I didn't have any interest in drinking. I was busy thinking on what I wanted to do next with my life. Nursing would pop in my head, but then it would get mixed up with, *is that what I want to do, or is nursing just something I wanted to do when I was younger?* I wanted to travel, and knew I would need money. Work meant money, so I worked.

Dad would tell me just as he did Will and Sam, "Reach for the stars, your life is your own." Mom would see my anxiety and tell me, "Take your time, Faith, enjoy your life, your passion will come." I know she didn't want me to rush into something that I didn't want to do and be unhappy.

Molly was set to go to the local college that fall to start her teaching degree. She and Mark were planning for a summer wedding the following year. I worked as many hours as the restaurant would allow me until the weekends that Chris would visit, then I would switch with someone or beg someone to take my hours so I could spend time with Chris.

One weekend that summer, Chris brought me to Lansing for a summer picnic to meet his stepsisters and his nieces and nephews. Both his sisters had college degrees, and they were married. Belinda married to a doctor and Samantha a lawyer. They would corner me telling me I should think about a higher level of education. "At least a bachelor's degree," his sister Belinda would tell me. "Girl, you want to have two incomes before the children come, then sock away as much money for getting your hair done and your nails."

Then, turning her head toward Samantha, while holding my hands out, she said, "Samantha, look here, the poor kid, why I bet she never had her nails done professionally, ever." As I would pull my hands back and put them behind me, Samantha would say, "Faith dear, don't worry, you have what most people would call natural beauty, and a loveliness about you. So sweet, we are just thinking we could help you out, put a little glamour in your step."

Now, I have been known to be a little naïve maybe, but I could tell when someone is being crude, and I wasn't about to have those two fake beauties belittle me any longer. I was just about to tell them where they could step. Step off that is, like maybe a high bridge, when Chris would come save the day. He would say as he approached us, "So ladies, by now you can tell why I find Faith so adoring, and not only does she look lovely, she is all real, nothing fake about her. That's what I find most appealing." My hero, Chris, would later tell me that his sisters mean well; it's just that they both have been pampered and spoiled all their lives by their mom, the dad they shared, and now their husbands.

I asked Chris, "How did you turn out so well?"

He replied, "I have Diana to thank for that. She really has filled the role as mother to me."

I asked, "Did your dad and Diana ever want children together?"

Chris said, "I'm not sure. They have never said, and I've never asked."

I stayed two nights in Chris's family home, a big house with too many rooms for such a small family. But I was not to judge. I always thought my family's home was big as I grew up, but now being in this mansion, I felt small and lost. The room I stayed in had its own bathroom and a walk-in closet. I didn't sleep too well those nights. I tossed and turned. Not even talking to God could settle me. I wanted Chris; I think I was in love.

My Fish Would Swim Away

Will and Susan announced the birth of Miles William—eight pounds, four ounces—that late August of 1976. Dad, Mom, and I would travel to Cheboygan, where they bought a home, to meet little Miles a few weeks old. Mom would hold him and say, "He looks just like his Grandpa John." I then thought, if my brother Sam ever has a boy, would Mom hold him and say, "He looks just like his Grandpa Sam" Although I did make the decision that Sam was my dad's, I still wanted Mom to tell me her secret without me asking. I knew it made no sense, but I wanted her to just spill, release the poison. Tell me everything like she was supposed to.

We left Cheboygan with Will now saying his new family would be visiting at Christmas. I told Susan I couldn't wait to babysit.

That same fall, Chris entered his second year of law school. He was very focused on school as he would tell me when he called. I started to get fewer letter and few missed calls. We still saw each other every weekend through October.

I would ask Mom, "Is it normal to love someone that you don't talk to every day and see less of?"

She told me, "I think what you and Christopher have is a good kind of love. Not a needy love, but a love that can withstand time."

Two weeks later, and a week before Christmas, Chris told me in a letter that maybe the distance between us was getting in the way. He was okay with me dating others and maybe some time without each other would be a good thing. I couldn't tell you all the letter said, although I read it at least a hundred times before I tore it into a hundred pieces. I can tell you, I was wearing brown corduroy pants, a black turtleneck sweater, and my short stubby nails were nicely painted satin pink.

I played it off as if it didn't matter much. I would tell Molly, "It's okay; there has been this cute guy at the restaurant that keeps asking me out. Maybe

I'll just tell him yes one of these days." Just after I convinced Molly that it didn't matter about Chris, I received a letter from him. It was the middle of January in 1977 when Mom gave me the letter as I returned from signing up for a nursing course to get my RN's license. Although I was made manager at the steak house and enjoyed the atmosphere, I did think I needed something else to do, or be.

"Thanks, Mom," I said, as I took the letter from her hand. It felt a little heavier than most letters, and I noticed the extra postage.

Mom said, "Maybe he wants to be friends again?"

I said, "Maybe, but I doubt it."

I turned to go to my room. Once in my room, I sat at my desk and I would look over the envelope that contained words on paper of the man I loved. I moved it back and forth between my hands. I even took a smell of it, like if it still contained Chris's scent. Then I tossed it in my purse, but not before I put "Return to Sender" across the front. The next day I would drop it in the big blue U.S. mailbox on my way to work.

About a week later at the supper table with Mom and Dad, the phone rang. Mom got up and answered, "Hello, Bakker residence. Yes, yes, she's here, Chris." As Mom looked my way, I would shake my head no-no. "Well, yes, Chris, we are all fine. Everything is good, and you?" Mom would nod a few times, as if Chris could see her head. She looked at me again.

I told her, "Mom, I don't want to talk. Please tell him I'm sorry, but I just don't want to talk."

Mom would turn and say, "Faith is sorry, but she tells me she doesn't want to talk, Chris."

Mom again turns, looking at me with one hand out and said, "Faith, are you sure?"

I said, "Yes, Mom, I'm sure!"

She turned this time, grabbing the pencil and paper, then she said, "Well, I will sure tell her, Chris. Yes, you take care also. I will, I will, thank you, Chris. Good-bye now." Mom put the handle of the tan phone back on the hook, finished writing something on the paper, and then picked up the silver coffee pot from the stove and poured Dad a cup of coffee. She sat back in her seat at the table.

She took a bite of her now cold sweet potato, chewed, and swallowed. She said, "Chris told me to tell you that if you ever want to talk, call him anytime. He has a new number. I wrote it down." Then Mom looked at Dad. She reached over and rested her hand on top of his and said, "Chris asked me to say hi to you, Johnny." Dad would just smile and nod.

After both would take in another bite of food, I would finally say, "Well, I don't have anything to say to him. If you will excuse me, Mom, Dad, I need to go study."

Dad said, "Yes, Faith, of course. Have a good evening." Dad knew that once in my room, I would be there for the night. I got up with my plate and glass. After scraping the food scraps in the green garbage can with the swinging top, I rinsed my dish and glass and placed them in the sink.

I went to the bathroom and on to my room where I would close the door. In my room, I now had a full-size bed and my very own television set, something I bought with my own money. I also had painted my walls a florescent orange. My bedspread was full of very large yellow flowers on a background of bright green and purple. Yes, my bedroom was cheery, colorful, a happy place where I could watch a show called *Happy Days* on my TV. But as I cried that night on my bed, I was not so happy. Somehow the last few months, I had become just another lost girl with dreams I didn't know how to fill. I had everything that I needed and still couldn't get my happy on.

Something would speak to me in the night. It said, *what's wrong with you, Faith May? You had such a good childhood, good parents, and brothers, friends, and God. Quit feeling sorry for your lost love. Move forward and get out of this rut.*

Some months later after the phone call from Chris, I would go fishing with Dad. In the boat, we would get our lines in the water, and I would kick off my white tennis shoes. With my bare feet out, I would pour me a cup of cold water.

Dad said, "What's going on, sunshine?" I didn't answer right away, and he added, "Is there something you would like to talk about?"

I said, "No, not especially, just busy with managing the restaurant and nursing school."

Then Dad asked the question I wished not to hear: "Faith, are you happy?" I would look across Lake Michigan only to see water and the sky meet. I would think, if one is asked if they are happy, and one doesn't' know if they are, what do you say?

I said, "Yes, Dad, I'm happy. You know I am always happy when I'm fishing."

Dad would say, "How about the rest of the time? What happens then?"

I thought, *Gosh, Dad, really?* Then I said, "Well, I just tell myself, 'Self, you have a lot to be happy about.' I have a family, friends, and God who love me. I am healthy, with two legs, arms, ears, and eyes!" I put my fishing pole down and stood up with my hands on my hips and raised my voice, "What Dad?! What do you want to hear? I just don't care to be happy all the time! Maybe I just want to feel sorry for myself, Dad! Maybe I'm hurting! Just maybe I was in love with Chris, and think I can't be happy without him." I sat back down, grabbed my pole, thinking, *Boy that felt good to say.* Poison released, gut feels better.

It was quiet, just the light splashing off the waves hitting the boat's side, and a seagull flying by looking to see what was going on. I knew my dad was thinking on what to say. I knew it would be something to do with God. I would hear, "Talk to God, Faith May. He will make it better," or something like, "Happy comes from knowing God. People can help make you feel happy, but only God can help you live it." *I so didn't want a sermon right now, please, Dad, don't preach to me right now.*

Then Dad said something I never expected. "I know how you feel, Faith. Love can hurt you so bad, that you think you never can be happy again."

I looked up from my hands, and at my dad. He had tears coming down his cheeks, something I hadn't seen since the day of his mother's funeral.

I said, "Are you okay, Dad?"

He replied, "Yes, Faith, I'm okay."

I said, "Do you want to talk about anything, Dad?"

As he wiped his face with his handkerchief, he said, "I just know that love can hurt, but love can also heal. You will be okay, Faith May. Give it some time and don't give up on love. We all need it, crave it. Love is the best gift God has given."

Just then we started catching some nice perch from good old' Lake Michigan. I said as we pulled in the last fish to get our limit, "Boy oh boy, Mom will be happy she has fish for supper tonight and some nights to follow."

Dad said, "Amen."

I didn't know what made my dad tear up that day. But he made me feel somewhat better. I said to myself that night: "Self, feel better, be better, as God gives you another tomorrow."

Happy Molly, Losing Faith

July 9, 1977 was the day of Molly and Mark's wedding. The church was full of people and flowers that Mom would arrange just so, picked fresh from her garden that early morning. Lilies, foxgloves, cosmos, and Shasta daisies surrounded with Queen Anne's lace. I dare say it was the prettiest wedding I have ever attended. It had everything just so, everything a girl could dream her wedding to be . . . right down to having the right man.

I stood alongside Mark's three sisters: Margie, Mary, and Missy. I would watch as Mr. Paul walked his healthy, beautiful daughter down the aisle. I could only imagine him thanking God for this moment. Mr. Warner had become such a grateful man. I could say, a man of God, but it was more like a man of life. He never preached, but lived a life praising God. A happy man.

Miss June looked pretty that day. She had her dark hair cut short, and she no longer smoked. Her smile with her at all times. That day she wore pearl earrings and a diamond necklace, something Mr. Paul had gotten her for their twentieth anniversary, an anniversary that might not have happened if Molly hadn't gotten hurt. Miss June had become quite the cake maker, making cakes for all occasions, with Molly and Mark's wedding cake being a very special occasion.

An old man and his wife would greet Molly and Mark in the receiving line after the wedding. Mr. and Mrs. Warner would tear up as Molly cried in Dr. Neal's arms. "Thank you for coming, Dr. Neal. I'm so glad to see you again," Molly said.

Then, as I stood next to Molly, a very frail woman with one arm on a cane, and one wrapped in the arms of her son, came and hugged Molly. The last time Molly had seen Helen was at George's funeral seven years earlier.

Molly said, "Thank you, Helen."

Helen replied, "I wouldn't have missed this day for the world." As Molly introduced Mark, I heard Helen say, "Be good to her always, as I know you will, and be a good man." Helen passed a week later.

I knew Mark had been told everything about what happened to Molly so many years back. What I don't think he knew, or many people knew, was how close Molly was to Heaven. How she was a different person than most everyday people you meet. She lived each day as if it were a gift, a gift that you better unwrap with care, because there were no rewraps.

Molly was better than I. She had a clear head, she would always say, "Negative energy is bad stuff, it can ruin a day, or even a life for that matter." Yes, Molly was going to make a wonderful teacher, wife, and mother. There was no doubt in my mind that God gave her a little something special for the hurt that the man in the white car had given her. Molly, sweet Molly, I will make sure to talk to God tonight, to thank God for placing Molly in my life and close to my heart.

Later, I was to sit next to my family at the reception. Will and Susan would come with Miles. Sam and his new girlfriend, Penny, would fly in from Detroit. Sam had just started as a pilot for an airline, and was stationed out of Detroit Metro. Penny was a stewardess, of course. Sam and Penny were only going to be able to stay the night at our house, something about Sam having a grueling schedule to keep. That was okay, a little time is better than no time. I knew now why Mom had picked bouquets for not only the guest room but for the den where Penny would be offered a bed. Yes, a full house at the Bakkers tonight.

Molly whispered in my ear, after talking to Sam and Penny, "I think this Penny girl is much improvement. Sam will get it right one of these days."

I laughed and said, "Molly, you are so bad."

As we all threw rice on Molly and Mark, and watched them drive away in the car with the *Just Married* sign in the back window, I found myself saying, "There goes happy."

I continued my nursing classes and was an RN by the end of 1979. I quit my restaurant job after getting a job at the hospital making rounds with one of the doctors. I would take notes and orders for the patients we would visit that day, and making sure they were followed. My other duties were abundant, and most days I would become so stressed on all the things I had to do. I would come home to Mom and Dad's after work wanting a little something to eat and go to bed.

I started buying a six pack of beer on my way home and sneaking it into my bedroom. I would be drinking and watching television until I fell asleep. I would sneak the empty cans out with me in the morning and drop them in the hospital trash as I arrived.

In 1980, I started dating Greg, who was an intern at the hospital. He was an okay guy, but he had the stress of school, and he also worked some nights at a bar in town as a bartender. I would say I felt bad for him; he was always busy and he would tell me someone has to pay the bills. Our time together was kept low key. I didn't tell Mom or Dad about Greg. He wouldn't have had time to meet them anyway. So when I would drop by his apartment after work, I would call home to tell Mom I was working a double or that I was staying at a friend's place that night because I would have to go into work early. That friend being Shelly, whom I befriended when I would go to the hospital cafeteria to get my fix—a big cup of coffee. I needed caffeine to recover from my hangovers. Shelly was always telling me, "Whatever you are doing the night before is disagreeing with you. Why don't you eat something, you're wasting away."

Shelly would sit with me sometimes while I would drink my hot, black coffee. I started talking to her about things that bother me. Shelly would tell me, "Ah, Faith, you have it easy. Try raising two small children by yourself, and live with a husband that likes to fool around on you." She said things like, "Hell, your life is just beginning, Faith, you still have plenty to learn." And "Don't do what I did, jump into bed with the first man that pays you any attention." Too late for that advice. Greg and I were already doing things that would probably make my Grandma Mary turn over in her grave. I would go to Greg's apartment whenever he would give me the signal as we would pass in the corridor. The signal meant meet him after work where he would make me drinks like Manhattans, Margaritas, Tom Collins, and White Lady's.

Then we would do the unthinkable. I was no longer innocent, free from guilt or sin. Greg would tell me the sex was a stress reliever, and I would think, funny it's not for me. I would think it was love, a fast and fieriest kind of love, but I took it just the same. What did I know about love?

Molly would call me and ask how things were going; I would lie to my best friend, something that will always bother me.

"Hi, Faith, how are you? I miss you!" she would say.

I'd come back with, "I'm great, Moll! I love my job, learning so much. Things couldn't be better."

She would always say, "Faith, we have to get together sometime soon."

I'd say, "Yes, yes, we will." Molly had just started a job as a first-grade teacher and was on cloud nine. I knew when she said she loved her job, she wasn't lying. Molly was happy and I was trying to just live my life.

I would tell myself, "Faith, you are happy! You have a home to go to, with a meal waiting. You have a job, that although it was stressful, you are able to sock away money." I did whatever I wanted to. Dressed in cute white smock dresses for work, and had an array of other clothes to show off my slender body. Then there was the boyfriend that was going to be a doctor. As Tiffany would say, "How cool is that?" But I was miserable, sad. As a matter of fact, I was a twenty-three-year-old mess. I talked to Shelly more than I talked to God.

The only time I would talk to God was when I would ask for my period not to be late. Then I would pray that I wasn't pregnant. I would try to avoid church, by picking up all the Sunday shifts at work. I would say to myself as I would enter the church which I had gone to so many times, "Why they are all hypocrites, staring at me like I have this big wart on my nose. Thinking, poor Mr. and Mrs. Bakker, how did they have two wonderful children and then along came Faith, their lost child? Why she can't even find a nice man and settle down." I wanted to get on my soapbox and tell them all: "Don't judge me, why you should be praying for me. Is that not what a church is to do? Pray for the lost sheep. But no, you all think that me looking bad, acting bad, makes you all look good. Maybe I am just learning that no matter how good you have it, or how bad you make it, you still have to live each day, with or without love. Please tell me again how much God loves us."

The funny thing of this all was my parents. They loved me just the same. Never calling me bad or telling me what I should be doing or not be doing. I would listen to them at the supper table telling funny stories about Will and Susan's twin girls, now just over a year old, smiling, laughing, and being happy. I would be like, "What the heck. I'm dying here. One of you please shake me, and tell me to get my shit together! Tell me I am going to end up pregnant with a child I don't want from a man who has already made it clear he would never marry me! And then there's the drinking and taking of pills to help me sleep. HELLO?! Why this was getting out of hand? I was losing faith, don't you care?"

Then it happened. It was a Saturday, early morning, when Dad and Molly entered my bedroom without knocking. As Molly drew open the shade to let the first of the sun in, Dad said, "Come on, sunshine, there are fish to catch."

Molly would say, "It's a new day that God has given us. Let's enjoy it!"

Molly picked up the six empty beer cans and put them in the brown paper bag. She said as she looked at Dad, "I hope you have lots of black coffee."

Dad said, "We do, and Miss Patty made us some special pickled bologna sandwiches,"—he looked at me as he pulled my covers back—"without the mustard," and he winked.

As I sat up with my head hurting like it always did when I sat up these days, I said, "As much as I would love to go fishing with you two, I think I would rather sleep." My mom now stood in the doorway of my bedroom with the clothes on that she would fish with. I said, "Are you going with us too?!"

She smiled big enough that her top gums showed, and said, "Why, of course, what could be better than fishing with Faith?"

Part Three

We Care, God Cares, Faith Cares

That last Saturday in May 1982, in the boat with Mom, Dad, and my best friend, Molly, I would be reminded and renewed of some valuable lessons, heart-felt lessons. Dad started the conversation after he had motored to one of our favorite fishing holes. He cut the motor to the boat and we all grabbed a pole. "Faith, it's clear to us all here that something is bothering you," Dad said. His eyes were fixed on me when he asked, "What can we do to help? I say this because we care."

I didn't answer right away because I was thinking about jumping out of the boat and swimming to shore so I could avoid this whole confrontation. Let's face it, at no time, in one's life does one want to hear there is something wrong with them. Molly broke the silence by saying, "Faith, why don't you start with telling us what you told me last week? How you are sick and tired of all the sadness of this world?"

I thought back to that conversation on the phone with Molly last week. Greg had stood me up and so I came home to my bedroom, finished a bottle of Boones Farm, strawberry wine, and then called Molly in the night. I was sobbing about my miserable life. Not telling Molly anything that had been troubling me before, I realize now, I must have sounded somewhat scary.

I still didn't answer, and Mom said so sweetly, "Faith, love, do you feel okay? Is this a medical condition?"

I answered quickly, "Yes, Mom, it's medical! I feel like crap!"

I cast out my fishing line onto the still waters. I could tell by the way the clouds were parting from the sun that it would become a nice day. I started taking off my pale yellow spring jacket.

Molly wasn't as nice as Mom or the weather though. Her words were sharp and irritable. "Yeah, Faith, take crap, give crap. That's your disease right now." Molly said. Molly looked at my mom then back at me as she said, "Forgive me, Miss Patty, but you are being too nice. What Faith needs is not medical advice or some kind of magic pill." Molly sat across from me. She put her hands to my knees to make sure our eyes would meet. Molly knew I could not lie to her if I was to look her in the eyes . . . the same eyes I had prayed to be healed so long ago.

Molly said, a little more pleasant, "Faith, you know God is right there in your heart holding your soul in this earth body, so you can experience the life you have been given. But Faith, you have to take in a deep, slow breath of air and feel God's presence. God loves you and wants only the best for you. Why Faith, you and I have had the most wonderful experience of feeling God's grand presence together in that hospital room years back. We were blessed very young with the knowledge that with enough love, faith, and spiritual energy, anything can happen. There are people who live their whole life longing for that same energy. Worrying about all the sadness in this world, and adding to it, your own, is not going to do any good. Why are you trying to separate from God with all this drinking and bad behavior? Faith, you have become unconscious to the fact that at any minute your life on earth can cease. Good or bad, happy or sad, the universe takes and gives each day. Don't make it easier by living in a negative space where God may not be able to enter. Remember, you are here for a reason, just like everyone born. It's your mission to find it in every day that is given to you. Quit messing it up!"

When Molly let go of my knees to catch her breath, I said, "You're right, Molly. I have been taking God out of my life because it makes it easier to accept all the wrongs that happen each day. The drinking and pills help me to keep God from entering my thoughts, the thoughts of how crazy life can be and how I can't seem to fix a damn thing!" I wanted to explain my sadness, my inaccuracies. I said, "How can I sleep in the comfort of my bed with food in my gut when there are children going to bed cold and hungry?" I looked toward Dad for the answer.

Dad said, "You know, I believe God speaks from a space in our heart. That may not mean God wants you and only you to solve world hunger, but it sounds like God wants something of you. Listen with clear thoughts, pray, and it will come to you. I truly believe we are here to serve one another. As you, Faith, have been serving God's sick and hurt at the hospital, are you doing so from the space in your heart? If one just lives for his own needs, one will be bothered and will have no peace."

That made sense. I had been going through each day feeling sorry for myself. I wasn't helping people as to serve God. I was doing it for the paycheck it would provide at the end of each week. I remember when I was a little girl, I wanted to be a nurse because of the love involved. Why, I had somehow started living for my own needs, not for the life God had given me.

Mom had always taught us children to take good care of ourselves first, but she meant it in a different sense. I was thinking of myself first, my ego. But I failed at taking good care of myself. I had become selfish. Maybe, that is why I felt so miserable and would try to drown myself in self-destruction.

There was a good reason Mom was with us on that boat that day, as she explained to me another reason I was going down the path of misery. She said, "Faith, I feel there is something more bothering you besides hungry children, and I think I can help."

Mom had my full attention, not even a fish nibbling on my worm would I react. "What's that?" I asked, thinking she would tell her secret.

"As you know, each day will bring love, joy, and peace. Also, each day can bring hurt, anger, and sadness. It's what you do at the end of each day that can make a difference." Mom said. She continued, "If you can truly forgive the hurt, anger, and sadness of each day, and not bring it into the next, then you are living as God lives, as he wants us all to live. Learn from your hurts, forgive them, and only take the joys of that day with you to the next. Be true to yourself, and come in to the present, Faith. Give your pain to God, release it, forgive it, and then it will become powerless."

It was my awakening, and I said, "I get it! I can better help feed the hungry child if I can forgive the reason the child is hungry in the first place. And, like Dad said, if I don't do it from my heart where God lives, then I am only doing it to serve me, not the hungry child." I continued, "But what about the terrible evils? How do we leave them behind? What bothers me is why Molly had to be hurt. How could one possibly not bring that with them each day? How can anyone forgive a hurt as terrible as losing a child?"

Dad spoke, "When you think of Molly being hurt, you are not in the present moment where Molly is here, healthy and healed. That's why your heart aches, because of the past hurt; your head is telling it. Having the power of awareness is knowing the past is gone and cannot be changed. Things are going to happen, sometimes, really bad things. But if hurts are measured by degree, then so is the degree of forgiveness needed. Ask God for help in relieving you from blaming, to guide you into forgiveness so that you can be healed. If you can remember one thing, it's this: One can never have relief from anything that is broken in their life if they don't forgive it. A heart that is full of forgiveness will not have room for evil to enter."

Mom said, "Faith, you are living your own story and can change it at anytime by writing a happy ending to each day. It takes work, but without the work it just becomes another story."

Molly added, "We all live our life from the story we tell. I could tell my story as the little girl that was taken by an angry soul, beaten and left for dead. I could grow bitter each day, blame God, and not forgive. But then the evil in my story wins, not the good. In all my hurt came the healing of a broken family. I believe that by forgiving all that happened that day, my family was awoken to a new love, God's love. My dad said it best to me. He tells how he was living the Poor Paul Story. He had a bad childhood, drank too much, lost his job, his wife was going to leave, and then when I got hurt, he wasn't going to be poor Paul, his little girl is dead. So he told how he took charge and changed his story. With the help of your dad, he came into the present moment where God lives, and asked for love and faith to heal me. He told me that's when he got his miracle. So, Faith, I think what your dad, mom, and I are telling you is that you control your story. You hold the pencil, being present will better write that story."

When my tears formed and fell while listening to the ones I love, and love me back, I knew then I was on my way to a better day, a new beginning. I was living my past hurts from Grandma leaving, to Molly being hurt, to Mom's secret, and Chris not wanting me anymore. These might not have seemed too bad to others, but they were my hurts, my interference to moving forward. I told myself I had forgiven them, but as I just learned, if I had truly forgiven my hurts of the past, they wouldn't have the power and would no longer be in my present making me feel guilty because they happened. Learn, forgive, and be present. I can do this!

Then Molly said, "Besides, you need to get yourself together, because Mark and I are not letting Auntie Faith babysit if she can't even take care of herself!"

I jumped up. "WHAT?!" I exclaimed.

Molly said, "I found out yesterday!" She stood for a hug, and when she and I hugged, it was an honest-to-God great hug. The kind of hug that was intended to be given when hugs were first invented. Mom's top gums showed with the big smile given as she broke out the fresh coffee and tin of breakfast rolls.

"Congratulations, Molly!" Dad said.

"This is great news," said Mom.

As I sat back down, as not to rock the boat anymore, I said, "I'm so happy. I can't wait to hold him or her!"

Mom said, "Now Faith, slow down! We just talked about enjoying the present moment." We all laughed.

That's when I grabbed up my fishing pole in one hand, and coffee in the other, and said, "Oh, I am here, I care again, and I am happy for this day!"

Dad winked at me as he said, "Good to have you aboard again, Faith."

New Day, Open Heart

The very next morning, I woke up to hear the song birds chirp their songs of praise, something I hadn't heard in a long time, or was it just something I didn't care to hear? No matter, it just made me aware that when in the present, everything can be better, sound better. What I would take from yesterday's past is what I had learned. I was in control of how I wanted my day to start by just the way I started it.

That's when I took a moment to give thanks for all I have, and I realized in that moment, I had everything I needed for just that moment. Learn, forgive, and bring your joys forward.

As bare toes hit the bright orange rug beneath, I would smile with delight, knowing I was loved. The drinking would go away and with it, went my headaches and feeling like crap. There was no need for a pill to help me sleep. I was eating better and feeling great. I was to learn how to tell people that I wasn't going to have time to do all that stressed me.

At work, I carried a whole new self, an attitude more positive. I took a position of doing my best throughout my day instead of doing the most. Somehow, it landed me a new job at the top floor of the hospital. I was put in charge of the other nurses. I was to make sure things were in order, that our patients were getting what they needed. I wasn't just helping our patients physically, but mentally. I would relate to each patient as they meant more than a body to heal, but they were a soul first most. That soul carries their emotional and moral essence. That connection would be the essential part.

With my better self, my job had gotten easier, and I had received a nice-sized raise. I liked what I was doing because I was a service to others. I cared, which made my days more rewarding. It would show up in other parts of my life as well. If I had a moment that was stressed or hard, I would stop, take a deep breath, and come into the present where there is calm.

I started looking in the mirror again, looking into my eyes as deep as I could. They would light up as I told myself I was worthy. That inside this body holds a very important energy that God treasures and loves. I had known this as a child with my mom holding the mirror to my face, but what I had learned is with each new day, you must take time and repeat this ritual, because in each new day, you are a new self.

The past day is dead and gone. Take along the joys and live fully in the peace of the present day. It's so important.

As for Greg, I would tell him straight out that, "I no longer need love with conditions."

His green eyes took on a sadness as he said, "Come on, Faith, we are good for each other."

I came back with, "That kind of good doesn't serve me any longer. I crave more from a relationship, and we both deserve more. Time to move on, end of story."

Greg seemed to move on quite nicely. The new pretty young nurse that took over my old job also took over my old job of relieving Greg's stress. I watched them exchange the same looks as we once did; Greg, giving the sign to meet him later. I would shake my head, thinking, *I once was blind but now I can see.*

A few weeks from my awakening, I told Mom and Dad at the supper table, as the green peas and meatloaf that was seasoned just right was served, that I found an apartment to rent close to work. I had on my green paisley blouse. It was my favorite blouse that year. I told them everything about the apartment, and that I could move in the first of July. They were happy for me. Dad told me that I could have the wood furniture that was held in storage out back.

"Hold on, Dad, it's not that big of a place!" I explained with excitement about taking on a new adventure in my life.

My dad had come to a new era in his own life, as he no longer worked for the furniture factory. The times had changed and the factory had closed its doors, giving away to quick, fast, less expensive furniture. Dad didn't care to be a part of the new way, so he told how he put his trust in God and he started his own business in custom cabinetry for old and new homes. He was happy for the new adventure, and did well with it, as to even have a few young men work for him.

My new home was a one-bedroom apartment above an older home on the west side of Grand Rapids. The widow lady, Mrs. Celia Jones, would hand me the key to my door, telling me, "Now, Faith dear, I try to rent to strong young men so they can help with the heavy work around here. Since Mr. Jones's death, I'm not able to do yard work and protection, why, I feel more protected with a man above me." She said this as her glasses slid down her nose.

I reassured her again by saying, "Now you know, Ms. Jones, I told you I will cut the grass once a week and shovel the walkway this winter. As for your safety, why, I had brothers who taught me self defense!"

She smiled showing where a tooth was missing, saying, "Okay, Faith, we will give this a try. Please call me Ms. Celia, child. Welcome to my home, and please come share a meal sometime with me, why, you are so skinny! I must help put some meat on them there bones. Do you like fried chicken?"

My first week living on my own was great. The second week, I would call Molly to report how lonely I was and that I missed suppertime with Mom and Dad. "Oh how we miss what we once had," she would laugh on the receiver. Then she said, "Its normal, Faith. I did the same thing, and I had Mark here with me. You are just grieving your past environment because you loved it. It's all good."

That's when I accepted Ms. Celia's offer of sharing an evening meal with her on Tuesdays and Thursdays. I found Ms. Celia to be very interesting as she would tell stories of her youth, marriage, a son killed in war, and how her only daughter had died of influenza at the age of six. I practiced being present, looking into Ms. Celia's deep, brown eyes. They seemed mystical as she would talk. I didn't see an old lady before me, but a lively, forgiving, beautiful spirit that had lived a lifetime of past hurts, joys, and much love.

It was another awakening to me, as I would come to believe that no matter what our bodies looked like, color of one's skin, or the beliefs of your extinct, we are each more alike than different.

I had never really talked much to a person of color. Where I had grown up, there were a few. With talking to Ms. Celia, I would learn of a new culture and a strength that comes from years of being told that because you look different you are less.

My dad said it best when I told him I had grown a love for Ms. Celia. He said, as we were fishing one Friday evening, talking and sharing, "Faith, you are doing right to love Ms. Celia. It's amazing how different people are put into our lives at just the right time. And, because both Ms. Celia and you, Faith, live with an open heart, you are both blessed to know that although you are both living different lives, and may have many differences among you, you both have found the one thing God wants us to find in each person that is sent our way: that being their soul."

I told Dad, "I like that. Just think, if everyone looked past our bodies, the faults, the differences, and only saw the soul."

"It can be done, Faith, if you allow it. But, for some, it will come with Heaven, never will it be too late."

I loved listening to my dad. He never judged anyone for being different, and he prayed for the people all that they could find the space in their heart where God lives and know from that space is where the peace of being comes. "If you can live without ego, you can live fully in God's presence, quiet your mind, and go within," I would hear him say.

That summer would move by with pleasures taken. Besides fishing with Dad, I would sit with Mom on the porch swing with lemonade in hand watching hummingbirds enjoy the nectar of Mom's flower gardens. Mom and I would visit Will, Susan, Miles, and the twins, Star Anne and Sky Lee, in

Cheboygan. Susan would tell me that I portrayed happiness and I was a natural when it came to children.

I smiled thinking that being an aunt was great, but a mother, well, that's a whole different story.

The last weekend in August we would all be together again for the reunion in Iowa. I would travel with Mom and Dad by plane. Will, Susan, and the children would make the long trip in their minivan. I thought back to the days when we were a young family and would take long car trips. I remembered all the fun of a family put in close quarters and how crazy we would drive each other. What I wouldn't do to have those days back.

Sam and his new girlfriend, Toni, flew from Detroit to De Moines. I borrowed Uncle Jack's car to pick them up from the airport. Toni worked at the ticket counter at Metro. She was pretty and sweet and talked non-stop all the way back to the farm. I thought how much I wished Molly was here to meet this girl. She would be rolling her eyes non-stop, telling me, "When is Sam going to get it right?"

Then there was Mary Hope, now a young lady of seventeen. She looked a lot like her dad, Uncle Jim, so in turn I would think she looked like a young Grandma Mary. She told me she also wanted to be a nurse. But, she added, she wanted to work with babies and help deliver. I told her she would be great at that and added, "You can be a baby doctor as well." Her eyes lit up at just the thought of it!

Uncle Jim was walking proudly with his new prosthetic leg. Aunt Marion told of the scare with diabetes, and how just losing some of her weight had her feeling better. It was a grand reunion, seeing all my cousins and their growing families, and sharing the joys of our past.

Knowing that you were surrounded with people who knew that life was intended and even though death would come to us each, we knew and felt we each meant something in this universe and beyond.

The prayer before we ate would carry a Bakker family tradition of telling God and our universe that we were grateful for all we have been given and may we carry ourselves each day with love in our hearts and joy in our eyes.

Girl or Boy, Lily, Grandpa

The autumn would bring the many colors of the leaves from trees that would soon shed their shade and shelter to bare their naked self to their faith, that after a cold and harassing winter they would be blessed with a spring of renewal. I would think how lucky a Michigan tree is to have such faith.

Molly came to visit with her belly growing with the miracle of life. We sat next to each other and watched as her abdomen took on odd new forms. We talked about how we both wanted John Walters to be a girl and how they surprised me with Mary Hope's birth. Molly went through a ton of names and told me how wonderful Mark was going to be as a father. We were honest about telling each other we hoped for a girl, and Mark wanted a boy. But we would always add to the statement, "No matter what, we want healthy first."

Molly told me how some of her classroom children were coming to school without breakfast. Be it money or time, I didn't care the reason, I wanted to help, so I started dropping off bags of apples, oranges, bananas, and grapes to the school Monday mornings. The fruit was kept in the school cafeteria, and children were told that if they were needing something to eat before class, they could go there, free of charge, for nourishment. I didn't do this because it made me feel better; I did it because I listened to my heart, and it told me I could do this.

Yes, just as Molly was caring for a new life to begin, an old life would end.

Grandpa Allen was to go to the hospital just after Thanksgiving and pneumonia would take his body to the earth, releasing his soul to his maker. As we all shared a Sunday meal after the Saturday funeral, Mom and Aunt Sara prepared all of Grandpa's favorite things to eat: pot roast, mashed potatoes, asparagus, and pumpkin pie. Grandma Rose broke into tears at the table and said, "If I had known that this last Thanksgiving, at this same table, was my dear Allen's last, I would not have begrudged him that second piece of pumpkin pie."

Poor Grandma, how hard to lose someone you have shared so much past with. How one has to move forward still hanging on to what is no longer available. How her story would still write and Grandpa's book was now shut. It would be put on a shelf to be pulled out at times when one could bear the hurt of him no longer being here.

That's when my brother Sam would lighten things up, always knowing what to say. He said, "Why Grandma, you know, Grandpa is still with you; talk to him as you talk to God. He has the same ears now."

Grandma Rose smiled and answered back, "You're right, Sammy, thank you." Sammy is what Grandma always called Sam. Then she said, "Sammy, tell us about you flying them big planes. I pray for your safety every day."

Sam said, "Thank you, Grandma. I do want to share a story with Mom and Faith." Sam took a drink of his milk and continued, "Mom, do you remember that pretty girl named Lily from Cedar Point that took our pictures with the western ware?"

Mom looked toward Uncle Sam and I watched Uncle Sam put down his fork as to help him hear well. I thought to myself, *Oh no! Here we go; could poison be in the meal today?*

Mom said, "Let me think." There was a short pause, "Oh yes, I do remember them pictures and Lily. Why yes, she was so sweet."

I thought to myself, 'Oh Mom, really?'

As Sam looked at Dad sitting next to him, he said, "Well, Dad, you always said if I was to be a good pilot, I'd need to take time to come out before each flight to meet your passengers, and that it was the proper thing to do. So I always walk the plane to say hi, especially to the children aboard. Well, anyways . . ." Sam looked to Mom and said, "There she was, Lily, right there sitting in first class. She said, 'Sam! Is that you? Look at you going to fly me on this big plane.' Then she asked me how I was."

Uncle Sam said, "She remembered you?"

Sam said, "Can't help it, Uncle Sam. Just have a way with the ladies."

This time I thought out loud, *Oh brother!*

Then Mom said, "So I hope you told her I said hi?"

I thought to myself again, *Oh, Mother, she is so jumbled right now.*

Sam continued to tell us how they had lunch together at the next airport before taking the next flight, Lily toward the west and Sam piloting back to Detroit Metro. He said, "Lily, poor girl. She told me her mom had been sick for quite a while and just before she passed away, her mom told her that the Dad who raised her was not her real father and actually her real father is from around here."

At this point, most of my family was in awe, except Will, Susan, John Walters, and the little ones who knew nothing of Lily. Even Grandma Rose whispered in Aunt Sara's ear, "Is this the same Lily I'm thinking of?"

Aunt Sara put her finger to her lips and whispered, "Yes, ssshhh!"

I was thinking, *oh, please, Sam, don't tell us you are bonking Lily. Why, that would just be so wrong.* Also, I thought, *Way to go, Mom, why, you keeping secrets is going to bite you in the butt now. Hope you're happy.*

Then, to my relief, Sam said, "So we had a nice talk over lunch. Did I mention her boyfriend was with her? A nice fellow. I think his name was Ted, or Ned." As Sam shook his head to help him remember, he said, "They were headed to California because she said some big art studio was interested in her nature photos. I guess it was her mom telling her to do something with her passion of photography that Lily would enter some contest and won. I told her moms are special that way." He looked at Mom, who seemed to be in shock.

Mom said, "Well, Sam, that's a nice story, except for the fact that Lily's mother died." Mom glanced over at Uncle Sam.

I said, "And the fact that she doesn't even know her real dad."

Mom looked at Sam and said, "What a small world we live in. Who knew you would run into a girl we met briefly at an amusement park." Then she looked at me as if I said something wrong.

Uncle Sam asked, "Is Lily planning on coming back to where she lived?"

Sam said, "She said she was going to give California a try, but wanted to come look up her real dad someday."

Uncle Sam took Aunt Sara's hand and replied, "Really?"

My Uncle Sam looked white, pale, like he aged ten years during that meal of pot roast. I, on the other hand, wanted so much to have the whole story come forth. But I was smart enough to know this can of worms would have to wait until another day. This was Grandpa's day.

Sam was going to leave out the next day. He didn't do any harm; he just told a story. I figured that as long as he wasn't dating Lily, all was well. As for Mom, she did say to me, as I was to leave for home that Sunday evening with two pieces of pumpkin pie, one for Ms. Celia and one for me: "Faith, I can tell this Lily story has gotten you upset. Like you are trying to fill in blanks or want me to know something. Someday I can help you and tell you more." She sighed then said as I opened the kitchen door, "I love you, Faith. Be careful going home."

"I love you, too, Mom," I said before the door shut.

I climbed behind the steering wheel of my 1975 Mustang. It had been running because of the cold weather. Will had come outside and started my car and cleared the windshield of frost. As I put it in reverse to make the turn to go down the driveway, I looked towards the big picture window. I saw my family in that window. The waving of hands, big hands, little hands, soft or callused . . . they all meant many things to me, the biggest of those being love.

As I turned onto the road to bring me home, I said out loud, "I do believe Mom will tell me her secret someday; patience, Faith. Trusting in the right time will mean the world."

Christmas Cookies, Cards, Chris

The next weekend, Molly, Miss June, little Paula Jane, and I went to Mom's house early Saturday morning to bake Christmas cookies. Susan and the children were staying at Mom and Dad's through Christmas. Will would go back to work after Grandpa's funeral and would travel back here for Christmas the next week.

As we all gathered in the kitchen, Molly and Susan talked child birth, and Miss June would take charge of getting all the children's hands washed so they could take part. Mom took my arm and guided me to the dining area. She handed me an envelope.

"Here, Faith, this came to you yesterday," she said. As I took it from her hand, I could see that it was a card of some sort. Of course, it was addressed to me here. But the return address on the envelope would have me take on a surprised look.

> Christopher Sutton
> 800 Monroe
> Grand Rapids, Mi 49401

Mom said, "Open it, Faith!" to bring me out of my trance.

I asked, "What could this be about?"

Then I let past hurts come to the present and say kind of snippy, "Maybe it's an invitation to his wedding."

Mom said, shaking her head, "Don't be ridiculous, Faith May, I am thinking a Christmas card."

That made sense, *but why?* I thought as I opened the envelope to produce a sympathy card. I read it out loud for Mom. "With sympathy in your loss. May the memories you cherish bring consolation to your broken heart. Sincere condolences, Chris Sutton." Then I told Mom, "He has a little note written, saying, 'Hi, Faith, I had read your Grandpa Allen's obituary in the Grand

Rapids Press. I know how close you are to your grandparents and just wanted you to know I cared. Would like to talk sometime.' Then he has written down his number."

Mom said, "Very nice."

I said, "Yes, but why now?"

As Molly entered and I put the card in my handbag, she announced, "What are you two doing? Come, let's get to baking, this baby of mine wants a cookie." Her hands were holding her grown middle.

"Me too, me too!" Miles said, grabbing Grandma Patty's hand.

Both twins were clapping and jumping up and down. *What a good day*, I thought, as I scooped up little Star Anne and brushed my hand on Paula Jane's head.

Molly gave birth to little Markus Paul Richards late in the night of January 15, 1983, one day shy of my twenty-fifth birthday. On the morning of my birthday, Mark handed over to me their bundle of joy to hold. I said to Molly, "Really, Mol? You couldn't wait just a few more hours and have him share a birthday with me?"

Molly lay in the hospital bed, this time as a beautiful new mother. She rolled her eyes at me smiling, and said, "Faith, I did the best I could. He was already two weeks late. Besides, I wanted him all cleaned up to meet his aunt, and my best friend!"

I said, "Okay, okay! You did perfect!" as I looked over this new life in my arms, his little red face, and so much dark hair, his tiny, long fingers, a perfect soul born into a new little house. I gave thanks to God and the universe.

That evening was to be my birthday dinner at Mom and Dad's. I asked if Ms. Celia could be my guest. "Of course," Mom would say. Mom and Dad met and talked to Ms. Celia a few times when over to my apartment, but just short and sweet, "How are you?" and "Nice to see you!"

When Ms. Celia handed over her fresh-baked apple pie to Mom as we entered the kitchen, Mom asked as I took her coat, "I do hope you like fish, Mrs. Jones? John and Faith's Uncle Sam caught them fresh through the ice yesterday morning."

Ms. Celia threw her hand up in the air and exclaimed, "Oh for heaven sake, Lord, how I love fish. Why, Mr. Jones or I should say, Ray, would go fishing and we would give many thanks to such tasty food." Ms. Celia took my mom's hand in hers and said, "Please call me Celia, or Ms. Celia, as your dear daughter does."

Mom said, patting her hand, "Of course, Ms. Celia. Welcome to our home."

Before the meal, we talked, sitting in the living area. I showed Mom the picture of little Markus taken from the polarized camera I had gotten from Will and Susan last Christmas. She told me of the outfits Sara had made him, and that they were going to the hospital tomorrow to meet him.

As Mom and Ms. Celia made their way back to the kitchen, chatting like old friends, Mom turned back and said to Dad, "Johnny dear, I almost forgot, will you please give Faith that card that came in the mail yesterday? Thank you!" As she disappeared, Dad said, "Sure."

Dad got up and went to the desk drawer, the same desk that Mom had produced Lily and Sam's picture from years earlier. Dad gave me his wink as he handed me the sky-blue envelope. He said, "Someone knows your favorite color." And then he joined the ladies in the kitchen as to give me some space. *I love my dad!* I thought.

Right away my eyes went to the return address: Chris Sutton, 800 Monroe, Grand Rapids, Mi 49401. *Yes!* I opened it and read:

Happy Birthday to a special someone!
May the New Year bring much happiness!

Then in Chris's handwriting, he wrote: *Happy Birthday, Faith. Hope all is well with you on your 25th birthday! Miss you, Chris*; with the same phone number written and *call me sometime* underlined.

I put the card in my purse and was happy to receive it. I then joined Mom, Dad, and Ms. Celia at the table, "Dad, May I please say the blessing?" I asked.

"I would love that," Dad answered.

I said, "To our God, thank you for the many blessings you have given this year alone. From me learning your presence is where I may find my peace, to good health for all those I love, my new found friendships, for Ms. Celia, the miracle of the birth of little Markus. For cards sent of well wishes, and last but not the least, this fish sitting before us to nourish us as we grow in your love. Amen."

The next few weeks, I came home from the hospital and I would find myself sitting in front of the TV daydreaming of Christopher. I wanted to call him but didn't have the courage. I thought of Lily and her story. How a dying mother would tell her daughter a powerful secret, a secret that could have destroyed her, but instead she would write her story happy, by pursuing her passion for photography. How Lily was taking steps to live her best life even when things like not having a mother any longer, or knowing who her real father was. She had courage to go forth, to live her dreams.

In the calm of that very night, as I lay in the quiet air surrounded by my own thoughts, my inner self spoke. *Courage is within you, just as fear and any other emotion. It is I who has the ability to have what I need. Allow what I desire and accept what I have put forth.*

I was to leave work early that warm, sunny day in March. The snow was melting, leaving muddy puddles on the side of the city streets. I took a different way home, bringing me to the law offices on Monroe where the cards were sent from. I pulled my blue Mustang up to the parking meter and got out and put a few nickels in the meter. *This shouldn't take long*, I thought. I felt brave when I walked through the front door of the big brick building.

I looked up and down the board of attorneys, listened, but of course, there was no Chris Sutton listed. Just as my courage was about to depart and I would turn to go back out the same way I came, an older woman in a pretty yellow dress approached me. She said, "Excuse me, young lady, can I help you find what you are looking for?"

I was taken aback by the kindness of her voice and found my own voice talking without my permission. I said, "Yes, thank you. I am looking for a Christopher Sutton. I believe he may work in this building."

She said, "Oh, Chris! Yes, he does. He's such a nice young man. You want to go to the second floor. He works for Mr. Howard." Her smile somehow familiar, friendly, the kind of smile my own mother would produce when she would help a stranger. Then she said, as she pointed, "The elevator is around the corner to your right. I hope you have a good afternoon, young lady."

I said, "Thank you." As I started to walk where she pointed, I turned back to find she was gone.

As I reached the offices on the second floor, I had second thoughts again. *Maybe Chris is happily married, maybe his wife is going to have a baby.* Then I thought, if I go back through the lobby, the nice lady in the yellow dress will think she didn't give me good directions. I entered.

A young lady greeted me from behind the desk. "How can I help you?" she asked.

I said, "Hi. I was wondering if I could speak to a Chris Sutton?"

She said, "Sure, let me ring him. He just got back from lunch. Who should I say is calling?"

I thought fast and said, "Tell him an old fishing friend."

I sat down in one of the six chairs in Mr. Howard's waiting area. There was no one else waiting. *I guess because most people make appointments*, I thought. I had just picked up the new issue of *Field and Stream* and had turned to the article called *The Best Fishing across Canada*, page 87, when Chris would open the door to the waiting room.

As I stood up, my knees became weak, and my heart was beating faster than it should be allowed.

Chris spoke first. "Faith! When I heard fishing friend, I jumped. I am so happy to see you!" He gave me a hug, but a short hug as to let go so he could look me over just as he did that first time in the boat so many years back.

I mumbled as I put the magazine down, "Hi, Chris." I smiled.

He said, "The only thing that's changed is your beauty. Why now it's even deeper if that's possible."

"Thank you," I said, hoping he meant it.

Chris said, "Come back to my office, we can talk."

I followed Chris down a short hall to a little office. Inside, he shut the door and pulled up a chair to me. He said, "Go ahead, and sit, Faith. Tell me some good things."

I was happy for the chair because my knees wanted to bend. I said, "I received the cards and wanted to say thanks. I could have called but—"

Chris interrupted, "I'm happy you came, this is much better," as he sat, not behind his desk, but pulled up a chair right beside me.

I remember what he wore and what I was thinking at that very moment. *Oh my God. I still love him.* His tweed suit was classy, and the blue in his tie made those blue eyes of his sparkle. Nothing seemed to have changed except his skin was now flawless, his hair was shorter. I wanted to kiss him.

Chris broke my dream of thoughts and said, "You know, Faith, I think of you often. You have to know how many times I have gone over the last time we were together, and how I should have never sent that letter about us moving on."

I said, "It tore me up, you need to know that. I didn't heal very well. It's taken some time to come to grips with it all. I don't want to go back."

Chris said, as he laid a hand on my knee, "I understand and I am sorry, Faith. I am truly sorry."

Then Chris stood and walked to his desk, and from behind, he produced his briefcase. As he was clicking it open, I was scanning the room and desk for pictures of a wife or little children who looked like Chris. All that he had on his desk were pictures I had seen before; one with his mother when he was four years old; one of his dad and Diana taken the year I met Chris on Drummond Island, now both framed in new chestnut wood frames.

As he sat back down by me, he handed me a letter; the same letter that had been sent to me years ago. I recognized my handwriting across the front *Return to Sender.* I said, "What's this? Why would you still have this letter?"

He said, "Faith, I have had this letter with me always with the hope I could give it to you again someday."

"But why?" I asked again.

He said, "Please read it, Faith. It will explain a lot about why we are not together."

I wanted to say it right then and there. *The reason we aren't together is because in another letter you broke up with me!* But I held my tongue and asked, "Should I read it now?"

He replied, "No, take it with you, there is time. I am just thankful it is with the rightful owner."

I opened my handbag and dropped it in. Then Chris asked, "How have you been, Faith?"

I answered, "Actually, pretty good lately."

Chris said, "By the looks of your outfit under that coat, you could be either a nurse or doctor. I am sorry not to have asked if you would like me to take your coat."

As I waved a hand, I said, "Think nothing of it. This coat is lightweight, and yes, you are right. I am a nurse at Butterworth Hospital. You were always a good detective."

He said, "And you've always been caring. I am happy for you."

"So are you a lawyer? And what brings you to Grand Rapids?"

He said, "Just associates right now with Mr. Howard. I hope to be made partner someday. As for Grand Rapids, I guess you could say, I needed a change and it's a growing city. So is there a boyfriend or even a lucky husband? I see no ring."

I shook my head and asked, "How about you?"

He replied, "No boyfriend, or husband." He laughed. "I am single."

I rolled my eyes, and he asked, "By the way, how is Molly? What has she been up to?"

I said, smiling, happy to tell of my best friend, "She married Mark and they just had little Markus. Molly is teaching first grade at an elementary here in Grand Rapids." I added, "She's great!"

Chris said, "Good. How's your family."

I said, "Growing. Will and Susan have twin girls. Mom and Dad are good, and Sam, well Sam is Sam. And your family?"

Chris said, "You will have to read the letter, but all is well."

The phone rang from Chris's desk. He said, "Faith, is it possible to have dinner with you? We could catch up?"

I answered, "Well, I do get hungry, so sure, it's possible."

"How about this Friday?"

The phone stopped ringing, and I stood and said, "I'm not sure; Friday tends to be my late night at the hospital." I started for the door and Chris jumped ahead of me to open it. I said, "I should let you get back to work."

As we both headed out of the waiting room and towards the elevator, Chris said, "Can I call you at your parents? The same number?"

I said, "No, actually, I have my own place now." I smiled at the sound of it. I reached into my purse to get a pen and paper when Chris said, "Go ahead, shoot! I have a great memory."

As I said the number, I watched Chris store it in his head and pressed the down button. When the elevator doors opened, I moved quickly in because I had a feeling if I stayed in Chris's presence any longer I may throw myself at him.

Chris held his thumb on the open door button to the elevator. He said, "Thanks, Faith, for coming to see me. I am happy you did."

I replied, "I am happy I did also."

As Chris told me he would call me, the doors started to close. I looked into his eyes, and I knew I would see him again.

Hand-written Letters

It had been a Tuesday, the day I went to see Chris, and Tuesdays I have dinner with Ms. Celia. So I stopped at the neighborhood *Shop Rite* to pick up a few things to make tossed salads to bring for supper that night. I always tried to bring something to add to the meal, and although Ms. Celia would call my tossed salads rabbit food, I knew very well she enjoyed them.

Back home in my cozy little apartment, I would prepare the salads and put them in the icebox. I took off my work clothes and jumped into the shower. While in the shower, I thought of Chris and the letter in my purse. *What is it I want to read? What could or would be written that would bring us back together? I was not the same person I was seven years ago. Why was my story going back in time?* I lathered my breasts and brought the soap to my belly. I knew that whatever the letter said, I already wanted Chris back in my life. Seeing him, talking to him today only confirmed that I had truly forgiven him and therefore still loved him.

I got dressed in my favorite navy blue sweat suit with navy scrunch socks. I made a cup of tea and sat on the couch with the letter in my hands. With extra postage, because of the heaviness, I tossed it back and forth, side to side between each hand. It had yellowed over the years. I had a moment of, what if it told of something, I would have to forgive Chris all over again. Maybe he was secretly having a sexual affair with another girl while he was romancing me. My next thought was, *so what, Faith? Whatever this letter read, Chris wants you to understand something.* I couldn't wait another minute. I opened the letter and read it out loud:

My dear Faith,

> *I have been a fool and the last letter to you proved it. Please give me a chance to make it right.*
> *When I wrote you last, I had just returned from the hospital where my father was fighting for his life. Faith, I didn't want to share this news with you. I was so*

angry that my dad would no longer be here to share my life with. When I graduate law school, get married, have children, he would not be here, just as my mother never was.

Faith, I knew you would try to comfort me with telling me you and your family will pray for my dad. Your kindness I didn't want to accept. I so didn't want your faith to interfere with my disbeliefs.

I told you my dad blamed the dog Duke for my mother's death, but what I didn't tell you is that my father stopped believing in God the day my mother died. I was five and lost this incredible love. Although my grandparents would tell me that my mom was in Heaven, and she still loved me, my dad would come back with, "there is no such thing." He always said, "You are born, you live, then you die. End of story." When Diana came into our lives, she would try to bring this God back to us. But Father would have nothing to do with it, and although I was curious of this God Diana would tell about, I even went to church a few times with her. I was not to believe, because my father was my hero. I believed as my father did. Faith, what I remember most growing up is a prayer that Diana would often say in mine and Dad's presence. The simple prayer that went like this: "Please God, I pray they will give you a second chance. They will forgive the past and live in your love."

I would almost laugh as Diana would never give up on the prayer. Then, Faith, I experienced a wonder of an answered prayer. As Diana and I sat with my father, who was weak but still conscious in that hospital bed, he asked Diana to pray for his soul. He was emotional as he cried out to God to please forgive him for fighting his love all these years and that he didn't want to make the next journey without him.

Then, my dad said something I'll never forget. He said, "God, I forgive whatever took my dear Christy away from Christopher and I, and I thank you for placing Faith in Chris's life. Just as you have given your love to me through Diana, may Christopher find your love through Faith. Please God, show Chris how wrong I have lived." He kissed Diana's hand and told me he will be in Heaven with Mom watching over me, together again. Then he said he was tired and closed his eyes, never to be opened again.

After Dad's funeral, I asked Diana to tell me again why my dad would marry her, knowing full well she believed in God. What she told me is another reason I'm writing you this letter. She said my father did what most humans do when they are hurt so bad. They blame and don't forgive the hurt. No one wants to forget a hurt because then they are saying that the hurt wasn't real, that it didn't mean anything. Hanging on to our hurts keeps us in a safe place of not moving forward. Then she said, "What your father was telling us before he left is that no matter how hard he tried to hurt God for taking Christy, your mother that God forgave him and still was with him and giving him love throughout his life, by either a hug from me, his children, or a beautiful sunset. God never stops giving love, for God is the love."

I had an awakening that I am so thankful for. I miss my dad and I am here to write that he was a good man. He just didn't know how to handle the hurt he was given. It took a lifetime for him to forgive, but because he did, I can move forward from my hurts.

Faith, I was wanting to give up on our love because I thought I didn't deserve your kindness, sweetness, and I would never understand your faith to this God. What I have learned is that no matter how love leaves us, we will always long for more and sometimes wish we wouldn't have thrown away what we had. Faith, I miss you! I want this love God has given me through you back. I am asking for your forgiveness, for being a fool.

My new number: 555-5683
With Love, Chris

The reason for the extra postage was the magazine picture of a beautiful sunrise somewhere over a lake. I wiped my wet eyes and folded the letter back into the envelope. I got up and put the magazine picture on my refrigerator with a yellow happy face magnet, one for each corner. I grabbed the tossed salads and put them on the tray to carry them down to Ms. Celia's kitchen.

With Ms. Celia sitting across from me at her little Formica-top table and aluminum chairs with red vinyl seat, something I thought was weird, because most all the furniture I grew up with had wood involved. I told Ms. Celia my story. How I was madly in love with Chris. How only after a year of being together, I dreamed we would marry and have this wonderful life together. All the time, not knowing he didn't believe in God.

"How could I have missed the part that he didn't have God in his life?" I asked Ms. Celia. And before she could answer, I asked, "Why didn't he just tell me that he didn't believe in God? We talked about everything. I even peaked at him when he sat at our table and his eyes were closed, his head bowed to the prayer Dad gave."

Ms. Celia tried to speak, but I just kept on rambling, "I know he told me he didn't go to church often. I didn't care. I fell in love with what he was, a kind, hardworking, good-looking young man who made me want to be my best. Isn't that what we are to do, not judge one another? No two people can be exactly the same in what they believe; there are so many beliefs of what God is. Can't we just all come together and trust that God is love?"

Ms. Celia put another scoop of mashed potatoes on my plate. Why, I don't know because she knew I would only eat one scoop. I think it was to calm me. Then, in my calm, I asked, "Now I have too many questions to ask him. I am so confused, Ms. Celia, tell me what to do? I should have never sent back that letter."

She took in a big, deep breath of air and said, "Child, why are you going to go over and over in your head trying to figure out why this has happened? Why, if I was to do that about my life, I would only come to the conclusion that everything happens for a reason. With that being said, when this Christopher fellow comes calling and you both feel the same good feeling as you once had, well then my dear, sweet child, start living the life that you dreamed about with him. As for him and God, that's something he will work out, just as his father did. You have had your faith for a long time, and Christopher is just beginning. How fun it will be for you to show off how wonderful it is to believe in what you are made of."

"You are so right, Ms. Celia. I need to let Chris know what I believe, and I accept what he believes. My dad has always said, 'If we accept the fact that we were all made to be different, then we will love the fact that we are all the same.'"

Ms. Celia shook her head, saying, "Faith, you are wise beyond your years. I can tell you right now you are a thinker and I always said it's the thinkers that have so much to say."

I said, "Thank you, Ms. Celia, I think."

We both started with a laugh that would continue to the end of our meal and throughout washing and drying the dishes.

As I left to go back upstairs, something in my gut told me to tell Ms. Celia that I loved her, but I didn't. I just smiled and told her, "Thanks for sharing your life with me."

She said back, "Same my child," as she smiled with her eyes and shut the kitchen door from the night's cold air.

As I got ready for bed, the phone rang. "Hello?"

"Hello, Chris Sutton here."

"Well, hello, Chris Sutton."

"Just calling to make sure I had the number right and set up our dinner date," Chris said.

"Saturday around six PM will work," I said, smiling as big as I could.

Before long, Chris had my address and my "can't wait to see you." I hung up hitting my forehead, thinking, *did I just do the right thing?* So I called Molly.

Molly and I talked until midnight as I caught her up on the cards and my seeing Chris to reading the letter. As Markus woke up to be fed, she'd tell me she was happy for me and agreed with Ms. Celia, that everything happens for a reason. Then she said she would be over Saturday before my date to help me pick out something to wear. Molly knew, although I had a lot of clothes, that I didn't know how to put an outfit together to save my soul.

That Saturday, Molly sat on my bed breastfeeding Markus as I went through a ton of outfits. I asked, "Why do all my clothes have these stupid shoulder pads sewn into them?"

Molly said, "Faith, it's to make you look—" she took a breath, "well, I'm not sure, either." We both laughed.

"I don't know, Molly. Dress? Dress pants? Brown or black shoes? You know how I hate to dress up. How about my navy blue sweat suit?" I laughed.

"Your designer jeans, with a dressy blouse. Put your black boots under the jeans. This is not a time to wear your Laura Ashley dresses, save them for church." Molly said, changing Markus to her other breast.

I trusted Molly and put my face together with a little blue eye shadow and blue mascara, and sprayed my hair with Aqua Net so it was big and puffy. I think back and laugh at how the '80s controlled fashion.

I gave Molly a hug and kissed little Markus's head good-bye. They were out of sight when the doorbell rang. I opened the door at the bottom of the stairs and Christopher stood there. A well-dressed man, with a pretty mix of a bouquet of flowers from the corner florist. I melted. I didn't take the flower but said, "How pretty, thank you. Please come upstairs and I'll put them in water."

We walked up the twenty-one stairs to bring us to my kitchen, knowing full well Chris was staring at my designer jeans.

"Did you have any trouble finding my place?" I asked.

"No, actually, you gave me great directions," Chris said.

I opened the cupboard door under the sink and grabbed a vase. I had plenty from Mom. I put water in the vase and could feel Chris was close behind me. I turned and reached for the bouquet—and Chris reached for my lips.

I Do, Wedding Day

C hris and I never did go out for dinner that Saturday night of March 1983. Of course, we fell into our feelings we both carried with us all of those years. We both knew that it was not our first time in bed with another person, but we both felt it was our first time we had made love to another soul.

We ordered pizza and ate on a blanket in my living room with candles lit. We talked about everything that happened since we had been apart. We talked about God and I told him of Molly being hurt, and that I could never deny a God who I felt came to us when we needed him most.

Chris held my naked body under the covers of my bed as we fell asleep in the quiet of the night and peace of our being. When we awoke, we made love again.

We spent the whole day Sunday talking, taking a walk, and sharing our meals. When we both got up Monday morning to shower and go to work, we knew we would be together from that day on. That life for us had a new start, a beginning of a new story.

The summer of '83 was complete bliss. How could I explain it any other way? I was in love with another soul, and I could feel love returned. It felt right; it felt good. Top of the world. Chris and I talked of marriage right away; why put it off, we were playing the part. But I was still surprised on a fishing trip down the Muskegon River that September day, a cloudy but warm day. I was wearing my favorite fishing pants made of rayon and my T-shirt that was worn so bad it had to be the most comfortable attire one could own. My love, my Christopher, would hand me a sky blue, gift-wrapped little box.

"I can't wait any longer," he said. "Faith May Bakker, will you marry me?"

I opened the box to produce a diamond encased in a white gold band. As I put it on, I said, "Christopher Roger Sutton, it will be my pleasure to marry you!" I smiled to show my top gums.

Chris was still searching for his own answers about God, faith, religion, and spirituality. I was fine with it. I told him I accept that his faith is his own.

He had gone to church with me and my family, but wasn't comfortable with getting married there. With the help of Mom and Dad, we decided to get married outside in nature.

Grandma Rose said, "I am so disappointed. What's wrong with a big church wedding?"

Mom set her straight as she told Grandma, "This is Faith and Christopher's wedding and their choice, Mother. Besides, God is not held up in some Church. God will be at their wedding no matter where it's held."

But of course, that *where* had to be in Mom's flower haven at my childhood home. We were set for a small ceremony on July 14th of 1984. Mom was going to make sure the purple morning glories would encase the trellis we would stand under.

I was to stress everything to be made simple. Only family and close friends. Miss June was going to make the cake, and Susan and Aunt Sara started my fitting for my dress I was to wear.

In the '80s, wedding dresses were mostly puffy, big, lots of stuff sticking out everywhere, not something I felt I would be comfortable wearing. Although Mom still had her wedding dress and I was small like her, I somehow wanted my own.

I wanted simple with just a little lace around a scooped neck. Susan and Aunt Sara knew exactly what would suit me. The dress I wore in Will and Susan's wedding, only white.

Molly would stand next to me, and Chris asked my brother Sam to be his best man.

"Sure, always the best man, never the groom!" Sam said, laughing.

Ms. Celia would be sad, as Chris and I started looking for a house to buy in the spring of '84. She had grown fond of Chris and kept telling us, "Why there is plenty of room in that apartment upstairs for the two of you to start. Ray and I lived in a one-bedroom house for years." I hugged her and told her I loved her, something that came easy for me then.

Before long, the big day was upon us. The Bakker's home was filled with family and relatives coming to share the day. Ms. Diana would stay with Grandma Rose. Uncle Sam and Aunt Sara took in uncles, aunts, and a few cousins. Of course, Will and his family stayed with Mom and Dad, along with Sam.

Just as I would learn, you can plan for everything to go well; it doesn't always go just right. Mom and Dad's house was so full, so I stayed at my apartment the night before the wedding. I told Mom I would get dressed for the eleven AM wedding when I arrive at eight.

This is how the day went, or should I say, how my day went. My alarm was set for six in the morning. It failed. I opened my eyes to oh my gosh at 7:40 AM.

After a shower, scented lotion applied, drying my hair, and a little make up, it was 8:45, and the phone rang. "Yes, Mom, I'm leaving right now! My alarm clock failed to work!" I said, as I hung up. I climbed behind my steering wheel and turned the key to find that my car battery was dead. Mark told me that I was in need of a new battery the last time my car was repaired. But, of course, I put it off.

I knocked on Ms. Celia's door, "Of course, child, I will drive you. I am not quite ready myself. Give me a few minutes, dear." I waited as patiently as I could, pacing back and forth as if it was going to help.

When she finally appeared, so did the dark clouds overhead. We climbed into her perfectly maintained Buick just as the rain came down in buckets. "Oh no. I can't believe this rain. The weatherman said showers last night and a clear sunny morning." I said, looking out at the dark sky.

"That Lake Michigan can change the weather at any moment," Ms. Celia said, shaking her head.

Because Ms. Celia drove so slowly normally, with the rain coming down so hard, she had the car in crawl mode. I thought for sure we'd never get to Mom and Dad's.

Breathe, Faith! Take deep, slow breaths and come into the presence.

We drove up the long driveway, paved with cars at 10:05. The rain still heavy, my brother Will came with an open umbrella and walked Ms. Celia and I into the house full of guests. Mom and Ms. Diana marched me back to Mom and Dad's bedroom to dress.

"Oh, Mom, this isn't good. Rain, and outdoor weddings, maybe Grandma was right," I said.

Mom pulled my hair back off my shoulders and said, "Faith, it will be fine. We have the big white tent up your dad has prepared. Remember, he's a fisherman, he knows just what to do."

Just then, Molly joined us in the bedroom. "Faith, I have been so sick all this morning. This pregnancy is nothing like my last. Hopefully, I can hold it together for the ceremony." Molly said, then quickly left, holding her hand over her mouth.

"Hopefully, the nearest bathroom is empty," I said.

As Diana helped zip up the back of my dress in front of the long wood-framed mirror in Mom's bedroom, I said, "Oh no! I left my wedding sandals in the backseat of my car. I have no shoes here!"

A knock at the door, Dad stood in the bedroom doorway. "Now honey, don't worry, but Chris just called. He had a flat tire on the Ford Freeway and walked to the nearest gas station. I just sent Sam to fetch him, and then we can fix the tire later this afternoon." He explained.

"Oh, Daddy! What is happening?" I asked.

"Things. Just things. By the way, you look beautiful, Faith May." He winked at me as he shut the bedroom door behind him.

"Mom, maybe it's a sign of some sort," I said, as she hooked the simple string of white pearls that she wore at her wedding around my neck.

"Yes, it's a sign that you're worried. Everything will be fine." Mom reassured me.

Susan entered the bedroom. "I am so sorry, but the twins were out of my sight for a few minutes and they made a mess with their little fingers on the bottom tier of the wedding cake," she said with her hands up in the air.

My laughter turned to tears, and then back to laughter.

At 11:45 AM, I walked with bare feet and my arm tightly around Dad's forearm. The dark clouds had disappeared giving the sun permission to shine. As I walked, I looked at everyone sharing mine and Chris's love. Mom was right, everything would be fine.

As Chris put the wedding ring on my finger, the tears started to flow as I could see the spot where my dear Lady was buried years ago. Somehow I had felt she was with me that day, running around, greeting everyone, wagging her tail. I thought for a moment of the life I had already lived, my childhood. A wonderful, love-filled childhood.

I was starting another new phase of my life and sharing new experiences with a partner, someone who I fell in love with. It was scary, but wanted. I was going to do my best.

The rest of the day brought good food, good conversation, and plenty of stories. Tina, Shelly, aunts, uncles, cousins. Then there was Chris's family, my new family. Chris's sister both told me they loved my barefoot ideal.

"Boy oh boy, Faith, you sure know how to set a fashion. Samantha and I just love your barefoot ideal, so down to earth." Belinda said, with Molly standing next to me.

As she walked away, I told Molly, "I never know if they are just teasing me or giving me a compliment."

"Don't matter, you didn't marry them," Molly said, as she ate cake and was feeling much better.

"Thanks, Moll," I said, giving her a hug.

"No problem. That's what best friends do for each other," she said with an eye roll.

"Love you," I said.

"Love you, too," she replied.

Chris and I left as the bonfire started. We stayed in a motel in Ludington that night, and the next morning we were on our way to Drummond Island for a week at the cottage to fish, and well, you know.

House, Buddy, Mom

C hris and I started our life as husband and wife in my one-bedroom apartment. It made Ms. Celia overjoyed to have us above her. She let us use her basement to store Chris's few things from his apartment. It was still short-lived as we found a home to buy in East Grand Rapids. Although Chris and I had good jobs, in what was a hard economy at the time, I couldn't help thinking that it was way too much to afford.

Chris had to reassure me often, as we moved our things into the large house on the first of October 1984. The house had four bedrooms and three bathrooms. "Chris, I hope you realize that this house is way too big for us," I said. He picked me up off my feet and sat me on the kitchen counter, trying to kiss me. "Well then, Mrs. Sutton, we should get busy and fill it with children."

Chris wanted a big family; he made that clear in our many talks. I, on the other hand, didn't know what to think. I knew babies were a lot of work, and maybe I was just nervous I wouldn't do well. I always felt sad for babies being born to mothers and fathers who didn't plan, or consider the fact that a child needs so much. I am not talking so much as in material things, but taking the responsibility of raising another human being shouldn't be taken so lightly. Let's face it, there are a lot of people too darn messed up to be having babies.

I guess it was just my own mother teaching us children that what we do in our life is our business, but once you have a child, then that business it to take your best care of the gift given. I can still hear her say, "Children may grow like weeds, but they will become the beautiful orchid they were meant to be if they are nourished with much love, attention, and guidance. Make sure you are willing to give your whole self and the rewards will be their love returned."

So Chris and I filled the big house with new furniture, knickknacks, paintings, and a puppy. I talked Chris into waiting for a year or two to have children, with the love of a puppy. My first thought was a cat, as I would think of

Molly's Toby; how it lived with June and Paul after Molly got married, seventeen years before it died of old age. A cat would be much easier with us both working all day. But when we entered the pet store in our local mall, the yellow lab puppy was hard to resist.

We became proud parents of Buddy. We soon found out that this ball of fluff could control your life, picking up all the shoes in his path, and wiping up the many accidents that occurred. I asked my dad, as I took Buddy over there to visit, "I don't remember Lady ever being this much work, what am I doing wrong?"

He said, "Nothing, you were a child and had endless energy. Plus, you had two brothers and Mom and I to help." He laughed. "You will do fine, and this puppy stage will be outgrown," he added.

As Dad tired Buddy out with fetch in the backyard, I sat with Mom on the porch swing. "Mom, you look tired, and you are becoming nothing but skin and bones," I said.

"I'm fine, Faith," she said.

"Sometimes, I think you do too much at them greenhouses. Plus all the work for my wedding—that, by the way, was perfect," I said, as I gave her a one-arm hug.

"Your dad and I are leaving for the cottage this weekend, and will stay the week before we close it up for the winter. I will get plenty of rest up there. Then we come home and have everyone here for Thanksgiving." She said happily.

"Is Sam bringing his new girlfriend, Jessica?" I asked.

"I think so, maybe she will be the one?" Mom smiled.

We all gathered at Mom and Dad's Thanksgiving Day. So many of us, with Will and his family, Uncle Sam, Aunt Sara, John Walters, and Grandma Rose. Then there was Sam who brought Jessica, a sweet girl that we all liked very much. And of course, there was Ms. Celia, who had become family. She was invited to all of our family events.

At the dinner table after giving thanks, and filling up on so much food, Grandma Rose announced she was selling her home and moving into one of those retirement villages. She said her hands just didn't work that well and she would lose her grip from her walker. "All I need is to fall and break a hip," she told Ms. Celia.

"Mother, you will move in with Sam and I, don't be silly!" Aunt Sara said.

"You can live with Chris and me, Grandma," I said, as I looked at Chris, shaking his head ever so slightly *no*.

"Well, to tell you all the truth, I am ready to go home. I want to be with Allen in Heaven. So it will make no difference where I take my last breath of air. I just don't want to become a burden to anyone. Now eat, enough talk about me," said Grandma Rose.

During dishes being washed, my mother became dizzy and went to sit down while Susan, Aunt Sara, and I finished.

"Mom doesn't look well to me. I am going to talk to her about getting a physical soon. Why, I bet she hasn't been to a doctor's office since she took us kids," I told Aunt Sara.

"You are right. I too am worried about her, and for a while now she has not been herself," said Aunt Sara.

That evening brought our good friends, Big Bill and Nana, for dessert and coffee. They were down here from Traverse City to their daughter's home for the holidays. It became late, but before I left, I cornered Mom in the kitchen, as Chris took Buddy outside one more time before we headed home.

"Mom, please let me set up a doctor's appointment for you to have a physical," I said.

"Oh, honey, I'm fine. But if it will make you and Sara happy, okay then, set it up," Mom said.

"Thanks, Mom," I said.

The next week, Mom and Dad received the call from Iowa that Dad's oldest brother, Uncle Joe, had passed. They traveled to Iowa and I made the appointment for the day after they would return home.

I met Mom and Dad at Dr. Leppink's office that Wednesday morning. I had known Dr. Leppink and had confidence he could find whatever was making Mom not feel her best.

After an hour, the nurse called Dad and me back to the doctor's office where Mom sat in one chair and Dr. Leppink sat behind his big wooden desk. "I am going to order more tests, but I have felt a lump in your breast tissues that have caused me concern," the doctor said to Mom.

"Mom, did you know about this lump?" I asked, touching her arm, as I sat next to her.

"Yes, I did, Faith. But years ago, I was told I had what they call fibrous tumors, nothing to worry about," Mom said, looking at Dad.

"Well, I don't want to alarm you, Mrs. Bakker, but the discharge you've been experiencing is not at all normal. Let's get you in for a mammogram. That's a breast X-ray, and we will take it from there," Dr. Leppink said, as he was writing something down.

"Discharge! From your nipples? Oh, Mom!" I said, still holding her forearm.

"Please, Faith, let's not talk about it," Mom said, as if she was embarrassed.

Dad stood up and shook Dr. Leppink's hand. "Thank you, Doctor. When can Patty get this test?" I could see he was upset, scared.

"I would like it done today, as a matter of fact. I am going to pull a few strings and have you at Butterworth radiology this afternoon No need for you to come back into town when you are already here," Dr. Leppink said.

"Do we have time to get lunch? Then I will take them to Mary in radiology. She is working today. Mom will be in good hands," I said, as I stood up and felt sick with the news I had just received, even if nothing was confirmed. I knew this path we were to take on could very well be rocky.

"Perfect, Faith. That will give me time to clear the way. We will have the results back in about three days, and I will call you at home. If need be, we will meet again. I will have your blood work back, too," said the doctor, looking then at Mom.

"Thank you, doctor," she said, as she got up.

"You are welcome, young lady. Please, let's not worry and think positive. I will call you soon," said Dr. Leppink.

It was a week later when the doctor had a meeting with Mom and Dad to discuss the results. I couldn't make the meeting because of my work schedule. But, as work was done, I picked up Buddy and headed directly to Mom and Dad's.

Dad was in the kitchen when I arrived. It was snowing and kind of nasty weather, but I didn't care. I needed to see Mom. I didn't want to hear news over the phone.

As Dad was putting leftovers in pots and pans to warm for their supper, I asked, "Where's Mom?"

"Hi, Faith. She was lying down and now she's in the bathroom. Sit, she'll be out soon," Dad said.

Buddy brought his red ball that he kept there to Dad and dropped it in front of him, waiting for him to toss it as Mom entered.

"Hi, Faith. I had a feeling you would be here after work," she said, as she took a seat at the kitchen table. "How was your day, Faith? Are the roads getting slippery out there? I sure hope you drive safe," Mom said. Then she said, "Johnny dear, will you please grab another plate for Faith?"

"My day was fine, Mom, but what does it matter. I want to know what the doctor said," as I motioned for Buddy to sit.

"Are you hungry? Leftover pot roast," Dad said, standing at the stove.

"Dad! What did Dr. Leppink say?" I asked, as if anything else mattered.

I felt like I had entered another dimension. Dad cooking, Mom sitting, this is not normal. I want normal, I thought. Dad sat down at the table and took Mom's hand, and I could feel the lump form in my throat. This was not good.

"Stage four breast cancer, Faith. That is what Dr. Leppink said. I have stage four. Not just one breast, both!" Mom blurted out, her eyes watery.

"Doctor wants to start chemotherapy right away. Also radiation and a possibility of surgery. He said we were not to waste any more time," Dad said, as he was bringing his hands over his face to try to wipe the sadness from it.

"Breast cancer!" I said. "Why, we will get another opinion. We will search for the best doctor in this field. We will beat this!" I said, knowing Dr. Leppink wasn't wrong.

"Faith, I like Dr. Leppink, and I trust him. We will do as he says. Now let's eat a little something and try to make the best of what is to be," Mom said.

"How could God do this?! Give you this bad news, why would you be given this burden? Why, you are the sweetest, kindest woman to walk this earth. I don't get it, and I am not going to let this take you away from us! We are going to fight, Mama. You hear me?" I said with tears flowing.

"Faith, don't start blaming God. That's just what the enemy wants us to do, to weaken us from our strength. Let's ask God to help us all get through this one day at a time," Dad said.

I knew what stage four breast cancer meant in the times we were in. It very well was to be a death sentence. I went home with Buddy that night and told Chris. He held my crying body in our bed.

"Honey, it will be okay. Should we pray together? How do we ask God for help? Let me help you, Faith, tell me what to do," Chris said while softly crying for Mom.

I turned to Chris and it dawned on me. Of course, he would care so much. He lost his mother and knew the hurt well. God had already been working, putting Christopher back in my life to help me get through what could be the loss of my own mother.

Why, yes, we should get down on our hand and knees and pray. We should give thanks, and we should pray for the bad to go away.

The Way We Were

Christmas at the Bakker home that year was quiet even though everyone would still be there moving about. There were few decorations. The family Christmas tree with the same ornaments from our childhood didn't carry the magic from years past.

Chemotherapy had taken a toll on Mom. She was so sick. "Faith, I don't think this is what I want. I felt better not knowing," she would say.

Her hair that she always kept shoulder length was falling out in chunks. The last of it was shaved with Dad's electric razor, and then we would tie the colorful scarves on her head, exposing her beautiful face.

"Mom, you can beat this. Dr. Leppink has already seen progress," I told her, thinking to myself I have to stay positive.

We were a family trying to be normal when we all knew that there was a malignant evil that took up residency in our happy home. The grandchildren seemed to give Mom the most comfort, as they were told Grandma wasn't feeling well. They would still give their hugs and sit in her now very thin lap; Miles telling Grandma, "Homemade chicken soup always makes me feel better, Grandma."

Sky Lee, who looked like she could be Mom's daughter and would have a love for flowers as Mom, would go through page by page of the flower books that Mom had me wrap for her Christmas gift.

"Grandma, Daddy is going to dig more space in our yard next spring for the flowers Star and I are going to plant. I told Mommy that I want a flower garden just like Grandma Patty's." Sky Lee explained.

Sam was the most quiet that Christmas visit. Not saying anything at the table was so not like him. No girlfriend would travel with him, although he spoke of Jessica. He carried sadness throughout the day and then he cornered me outside as we gathered to make the annual snow family.

"Faith, what happens now? Can Mom beat this? How bad is she?" His sad, wet eyes, wanting someone to fix this emotional gut ache.

"I'm not sure, Sam. Doctor thinks surgery is necessary. That will be the next step, but she has to stay strong and she is so frail," I said, rubbing my thick mittens together.

We would look up to see Mom waving from the dining room window, knowing full well she would be out here baring the cold to help the grand-children pack each ball of snow, and making sure the carrot noses were stuck far enough in each face.

"I can't stand this, Faith. My heart will never heal if something happens to Mom," Sam turned to say, as if Mom could read his lips.

"She will either beat this here on earth, or be whole again in Heaven," I said with an arm around Sam, as if I was the big sister going to have to be strong enough for us both.

It was just after New Year in 1985 when Mom had the surgery that removed both of her breasts. Her weakened body came home to bed rest. She had me make up my old room so she wouldn't disturb Dad's sleep, as if he was sleeping well these days.

I took a few weeks off from work to help with her care. Aunt Sara came in the evening as I would leave for home with Buddy. Ms. Celia drove herself over to Mom and Dad's weather permitting, and she and Grandma Rose would take on small chores around the house. Mostly, they gave comfort of a love that is somehow born to the old. I believe most that live a life of learning can be blessed with this gift of giving themselves. They no longer want or need things. All the things that the young crave are no longer of value. To me, someone who has lived a long time seems to give the lightness to a darkened space. They have made it through, knowing that a life is not measured by what you have inquired through it, but what you have learned from it.

Molly came for a visit, and she and I climbed into bed with Mom, one of us on each side of her. Molly's belly was about to give way to another life. We let Markus—now about to have his second birthday—entertain us with his endless energy and excitement of life.

Mom had a good day as we talked about fishing come spring, flowers come summer, growing families, and love for each new day. We were doing everything right. Keeping this positive, talking about the future, but living in the day.

Mom smiled, saying, "I have to give up the need to know what will happen tomorrow, and take time to live today." Then she added, "What will be, will be; I have so much to be grateful for."

Dad's work slowed down this time of year, as the holidays were not a time where people wanted someone working in their home. I felt bad for his idle time, although he was happy to spend time with Mom. I think he was a little uncomfortable with all the ladies gathering during the daytime hours. You could find him out back in his wood shop, trying to busy his hands, so his sad thoughts of what was happening could be controlled.

"Hi, Dad," I said, as I entered the shop with a mug of hot chocolate for him.

"Thank you, dear," he replied, as he took the mug from my mitten hands.

I sat down on a wood chair that was made by my dad years back.

"How are you doing, Dad?" I asked, looking around the shop that would hold all one would need to make anything of wood.

"I'm fine, Faith," he said, as he found a wooden seat. "I start a job come Monday morning, but I will get breakfast for Mom before I leave," he said, taking a sip of the warm drink.

His eyes were wet as he spoke.

"Doctor feels that she should have a good recovery, that they got all the cancer."

"I just wish she would have gotten this care sooner. How could she not have known something was wrong?" I said.

"Maybe it's my fault. How could I not know that my wife was failing?" Dad said, as he blinked his eyes with tears. "I should have known," he said, shaking his head.

"It's not your fault, Dad. It's life. I deal with it every day at work. People's bodies failing because of sickness or an accident. Mom will be fine; we will make sure of it," I said, not wanting anyone to take the blame for what was happening. "Dad, if you don't mind, I think I'm going to stay home tomorrow and spend Sunday with just Chris. I miss him lately," I said, looking down at my moon boots.

"Of course, Faith, that is a good idea. You have to take a break from all of this. As a matter of fact, I was hoping Mom and I could maybe manage church, and then spend time being together before I start to get busy with some jobs I have been putting off," he said.

"Good, then I will tell Mom now, and then Buddy and I are going to head on home," I said, as I got up.

"Thanks, Faith, for all of your help. You are one heck of a great daughter. I sure do love you," he said with his famous wink.

"Love you, too!" I said with the wave of my hand as I left the shop.

The Secret

Molly was to give birth to Michael Hank Richards a few days into the next week. I was delighted to sit with Mom on her living room couch to tell her everything from Molly's water breaking in the grocery store, to Mark being so excited he left the suitcase of Molly's on top of the car, and that's the way it rode all the way to the hospital.

Mom laughed, "He's lucky it didn't fly off and open, throwing Molly's undies to the wind." We both laughed.

We were alone that day. Dad was working and no one was expected to call. It's just Mom, Buddy, and I.

"I remember when your brother Sam was born. I was a mother of two healthy boys, just like Molly," Mom said. You could tell she would go back and have a picture in her head of that time.

"Tell me, Mom, what were you like back then? You were younger than I am now, and had two children. Were you happy?" I asked.

"You would think what I am dealing with now would be my biggest life challenge, but at the time, when your brother Sam was to be born, well . . ." Mom shook her head, remembering a story.

"Tell me, Mom, I want to know. I can handle it, please," I said, moving closer to her.

"Faith, I would like to tell you more about Lily, about your Uncle Sam. I don't know if I want to tell you this story because I feel it will make me feel better, or because somehow I feel you have known something more about me for a long time," Mom explained.

At that moment, I didn't know what to say. Do I tell Mom what I had heard because of my habit of eavesdropping, the secret I heard about my brother Sam in the conversation she had with Uncle Sam doing dishes? Or do I just let Mom release her poison? I listened, and Mom talked.

"It was Thanksgiving weekend, 1955, when your Uncle Sam went across state to visit little Lily. Uncle Sam's mother was not well, but she encouraged Sam to go see his little girl," Mom said. "Your dad would have to call Sam that Sunday morning to tell him the news of his mother's passing. Of course, Sam traveled back home heartbroken. The pain in his heart must have been so bad that his mind convinced him that some whiskey would ease that very pain."

"But Uncle Sam doesn't drink," I said.

"Not anymore."

"Then what happened?" I asked.

"He arrived that Sunday evening to this here house with an empty bottle in his hand, and a rage your dad and I had never witnessed Sam to have. Sam wanted to take his anger out on something, and I think he felt safe throwing his demon out at John, his best friend. He told your dad how unfair his God was, and asking what did he ever do that God would take everything he loves away. The more your dad tried to reason with your Uncle Sam, the madder he had become," Mom said, as she got up to walk to the living room front window. I could see the softness of tears fall, the kind of tears that are released because of remembering sadness.

Then she said, "When Sam wanted to leave here, your dad wouldn't let him. He told Sam to sleep it off on the couch, that he had too much to drink, and things would be better come morning. I had never heard them argue like that before." Shaking her head, Mom came back and sat down next to me again. Her head that was wrapped in a colorful scarf lay resting on the back of the couch. She continued to tell me what I have wanted to hear for so long, releasing her wall of rock.

Mom continued, "Faith, it was a bad night. I was happy little Will was asleep during that time. Your Uncle Sam was determined to leave, even though he could hardly stand. He swung at your dad's face before passing out and falling to the kitchen floor. We put him on the couch. Your dad took his pants off and I covered him with a blanket. That night I lay there next to your father feeling so bad for Sam and trying to understand. I couldn't sleep. I prayed to God that Sam would just cry, just release all the hurt and give it to God. How could I let Sam know that if he gives up on faith, how does one get through a time of pain?" Mom wept.

I put my arms around my mother, pulling her towards me. I felt I was the mother, and she was the child needing my warmth. I thought how many times my mother held me when I needed her. I was now giving back. Like a new love level we had entered when a child becomes the care taker, roles reversed. It felt right.

As she pulled her head up from my arm, she said, "The next morning, your dad, little Will, and I had breakfast while Sam slept on our couch. Then you dad left for work, telling me to just let Sam sleep it out and he would be back home at noon to get him and help him with his mother's funeral arrangements." Mom paused, wiping her eyes.

"Mom, it's okay if you don't want to tell me everything, I understand," I said.

"No, Faith, I need to tell. Telling this story out loud is good for me. It's a pain I have needed to talk about for a long time," she said.

"Come, Mom, let's make some tea and sit at the table," I said, holding my hand out as she followed me into the kitchen. I turned the gas burner on under the black teapot, and she sat down.

"I had just put Will down for his morning nap when your Uncle Sam started stirring in the living room. I heard him go to the bathroom, and I started to warm the coffee. I sat next to him on the couch with the hot cup of coffee in my hand. His shirt unbuttoned and only in his underpants, I felt a little uncomfortable. I started to stand, and I told him I would get some water and aspirin for his aching head. He took my hand and pulled me back down to sit.

"Faith, he started to cry, bawl, break down, and release. I had to hold him, why he was doing exactly what I prayed for. He cried like a baby, almost scary.

"I go back and think, maybe it was me, being a new mom and Sam no longer having his mother, that I wanted to hold him somehow, making him feel better. We were both weak." Mom started to rub her eyes as the tea pot whistled, and I jumped.

I got up and turned the burner off. I got two cups out, put a tea bag in each cup, poured the hot water, and grabbed a spoon.

"Come, Faith, let's sit in the dining area. I will grab the sugar," she said.

As we both sat down with our hot cups in front of us, Mom put a spoon of sugar with her tea and stirred.

"Faith, I want to explain that up to that very morning, I loved your Uncle Sam like a brother, just as I do now. He would tease me, I would tease him."

I interrupted, "He still does," with a smile.

Mom replied, "Yes, he does. We laughed together, gave each other hugs and kisses on our cheek. We were there for each other at the birth of our children. Sam was not only your dad's friend, he was mine as well." Mom looked down at her feet that were encased in warm socks and pink fuzzy slippers. Since her chemo, she was always cold. Buddy lay next to Mom's feet to bring extra warmth. Then she said, "Sam was holding on to me crying when he started to give me a kiss on the cheek, like he had done so many times before, thanking me for being his friend," Mom wept.

"Faith, it was me! I was the one who turned toward that kiss. That kiss turned into a moment of two people who had trusted that the love they had always shared would never get soiled. It would always be pure. How could something like that happen when we both loved John? Me, as his wife, Sam, as his best friend. We were shamed. Afterwards, we both went to separate bathrooms. When your dad came home at noon, little Will was sitting at the table with Sam, and I made them sandwiches in silence. Your dad and Uncle Sam ate and then left to the funeral parlor. I cleaned the house from top to bottom that day, trying to get rid of the feeling of dirt that I felt I had become." Mom took a sip of her tea and somehow looked different, not perfect, but human.

"What happened after that day?" I asked.

"It was just after Martha's funeral that I cornered Sam and told him we were never to speak of that day that we were to act like it had never happened, because it would never happen again. He agreed. That is when I learned slowly, that forgiveness is a three-step process, and you will never be complete until each step is taken."

"What are the steps, Mom?" I asked, wanting to know if I had forgiven all my hurts, my faults.

She said, "The first step is the easy one, and I did it that very next day. I asked God for forgiveness. I got down on my knees and told how sorry I was. That I needed forgiveness, and because of God's love, I knew I was forgiven. I felt it."

"Next step?" I asked.

Mom said, taking in more tea, "Well, a few weeks would go by and I still had an ache in my heart. So I prayed to God to heal this ache that I wanted to feel like I did before that day with Sam. Well, I got an answer, and it was not an easy answer, but one I had to bear. A week later, I missed my monthly. At first, I thought it was because of how upset I had been. Then, when I got a little touch of morning sickness, as I had with Will, I realized I could be pregnant. A week into the new year it was confirmed, I was with child."

"Is Sam Uncle Sam's son? Does Dad know?" I said, then thinking to myself, *from what I had gathered over the years that my dad had a deep hurt at one time, he had to have known.*

"At first, I was no matter what, I would claim this baby your dad's. Why, it very well could be. I made love to your dad that very next night, and even more often in the next few weeks, as to erase the guilt I was feeling. It wasn't until your dad told your Uncle Sam, in front of me, that he was going to be a dad again, and I watched your Uncle Sam take on a look of terror that I knew that there would have to be more forgiveness. That being forgiveness from the ones you have hurt. God was answering a prayer."

I could see that Mom was getting tired, but I didn't want to stop her.

"I needed to tell your dad everything. By telling the truth, I would be risking everything I had. But I had to tell for my baby's sake, and mine. I told Sam in a phone call that I was going to tell Johnny everything. He wanted to be there and wanted Sara there as well. He loved your Aunt Sara by then and said she should know also. I agreed."

Mom took another sip of tea, as I did, too, then said, "I planned a Friday evening dinner together, and had your grandparents take little Will for the night. I was sick the moment we were all together, even though I had rehearsed everything I was to say over and over in my head. As we all sat down at the table with the food before us, I just wept.

"Of course, there was little eating going on, as both your dad and Aunt Sara asked me what was wrong. When I didn't answer, and just looked at my plate of green beans and piece of chicken softly sobbing, your Uncle Sam took over. He just came right out and told your dad and Sara.

'The reason Pat is crying is because the morning I awoke on your couch, John, I took advantage of Pat's kindness. Instead of just a cup of coffee and a shoulder to cry on, I made love to your wife."

"Oh no! I can't imagine hearing such a thing. Poor Dad. What did he do?" I asked.

Mom continued, "Your Aunt Sara was the first to speak as she said something like, 'What are you talking about?' Then your dad would stand and look at me asking me, 'Patty, is this true? And was force involved?' I somehow found my words and I said, yes, it was true, and of course, there was mutual consent, no force. Then I said I was sorry and it was all my fault. Then, I remember Aunt Sara asking, 'Are you two in love, and is this Sam's baby?"

Mom's tears were flowing down her cheeks as she talked. I gave her more tissues from the box next to the sugar bowl.

Then, Mom said, as she wiped her eyes and nose, "Faith, your father never looked toward Sam. His eyes fixed on me. I had broken him in half, and I remember what he asked me like if he just said it to me now. He said, 'Patty, do you want a life with Sam?' I said, 'No, I love you, Johnny. I love you and Will. I want this baby to be yours and mine!'

"Your dad then asked Sam, while he still looked at me, 'Sam, are you in love with Patty? And, if so, are you willing to take care of her and this baby?' Your Uncle Sam was with tears, and said to your father, 'John, what happened should have never happened. I am in love with Sara and always have been. As for this baby, I want whatever Pat and you decide. I have failed both Pat and your friendship. I truly am sorry. I hope all three of you can forgive me.' That's when your father went over to grab his coat, and walked out the door."

Mom stood up and walked to the dining room window. I followed her with the box of tissues as I was now wiping tears from my face.

Mom continued, "I stood and watched him go to the backyard. There was a lot of snow on the ground, just like today, and a very cold evening. Your dad stood in the same spot where he would bury Lady years later. He was out there for a long time looking towards the sky. I knew he was talking to God. I stared out this window and watched as the darkness incased your dad. Sara and Sam cleaned up the table and kitchen, and Sara made coffee. A little while later, Sam grabbed his coat and went out to join your dad."

"Were you scared they might fight?" I asked.

"No, I know your dad. He thinks things through. Your Aunt Sara voiced her concerns, but after a while, they came in the house together, no bloodshed. Your dad asked us all to sit at the table and Sara poured them coffee, and me warm milk."

Mom went back to the dining room table and we both took our seat back.

"Then what happened? What did Dad say?"

"Faith, your dad is so special. I am so very lucky to have him in my life."

I shook my head yes.

Mom continued, "Before doing anything that could hurt us all even more, your dad, with all the hurt that was handed to him, put that hurt and anger through God first, trusting God to find the answer to what was happening. That's when your dad said, 'Please let me say all I want to say before anyone else speaks.' We all agreed and then he continued. He said, 'The news I have just heard is not any kind of news one wants to hear, but I'm not going to make it worse by adding anger. Not only does this involve us four adults, but also an unborn child. That is the most important element. I know we can all agree that the outcome of what happens should be the best one for the child, so here is what's going to happen.'

"Your dad then said just how we were going to continue our lives from that night forward."

Mom's tears were no longer flowing. She almost looked relieved as she quoted my dad.

"Your dad said, 'First off, this baby is mine and Patty's and will be raised as such. No test, no doubt, no turning back. Second thing to happen is, I would like you, Sam, to remain my friend, and Patty's as well, if she so desires. Sam, I want you to be part of this child's life, and any other children Patty and I may have. Sam, you don't deserve the pain of another child taken from your life. I know you two didn't set out to hurt Sara or I, and what happened might still be locked up inside each of you if Patty wasn't with child. But, as hard as this is to believe, good can come from this hurt if we all let it.'

"Faith, your dad continued to talk like he was a great spiritual teacher, finding just the right words to say. He put calm in our presence. I think we all felt it. Your dad had invited God to sit at the table with us that night. Your dad said that he believes we are born to this life, this earth, to learn. He said what he learned that very night is that no matter how hard you try, or how much you pray, or how good you are, each and every one of us will encounter hurt in our life. It's what we do with the hurt that will make the differences. He said the hardest part of being hurt is forgiving the ones who have hurt you, but you have to give it to God and now the past. If we don't forgive each other, this hurt, it will remain, giving it power; the powers of a wound that will open up each time you are hurt by something else, never to heal and no relief is not how you want to live your life. The memory will only remain hurtful if you don't forgive it and learn from it.

'Just like a hard rain will produce a rainbow, we will get through this hurt, all four of us with the birth and love of a child.' Then he said he wasn't going to say another word about what happened. That he trusted the God in each of us to do the same. 'I forgive you both; I will let love win.'"

Mom was done talking, her eyes dry, and her heart empty. As she told me, she would like to take a warm bath and get some rest before Dad got home. I drew her bath and then helped her get undressed. I wanted to check her incision. As I unwrapped the bandage that covered her chest, I thought it wouldn't bother me, why, I have seen wounds before. I was a nurse. I was just to make sure her incisions were healing. What I saw was not a woman that was missing both of her breasts, a part of her body that had been known to define a female; what I saw was my mother standing before me missing a pair of mammary glands extending from the front of an adult female, altering her shape so that she may live. Also, I saw my mother as someone who had taken half a lifetime to bear a secret and release pain that was held within. She had given me her secret, trusting me to love her even through her imperfections. I would find myself crying as she took my hand for balance and climbed into the tub full of bubbles.

As I knelt down to wash her back, Mom said, "Faith, your dad has never mentioned that time again. He did have a new couch from the furniture factory where he worked, delivered to the house a week from hearing about Sam and me. He donated the other couch to a mission. The only time I had said something about that time is when he dug the hole out back to burry Lady. I asked why he buried her there. He said, 'Because Faith is hurting and I had a pain buried there before, and it worked well for me.'"

I left the house that day as Mom would rest in bed waiting for my dad, her husband, to come home from work. As Buddy and I drove home that late afternoon, I had now known the secret. My brother Sam was made from forgiven love.

Mom started to feel better each day. In fact, she was making a great recovery. We were all starting to go back to normal, and the spring of 1985 would bring renewal. Hummingbirds, flowers, hard rains, and rainbows, life was living around us.

Dad got the boat out and fishing would start. Uncle Jack and Aunt Marion visited from Iowa. I remember a Sunday afternoon with Molly and Mark visiting Mom and Dad. Dad, Uncle Jack, Mark, and Chris would take off fishing, and we ladies sat in the living room telling happy stories.

Aunt Marion and Mom passed little Michael back and forth in their arms. Markus was starting to form words, and I knew it wouldn't be long before Molly would teach him the ABC's. I wore a pink simple dress that day and Aunt Marion said, "Now Faith, I see you having a girl someday, yes, pink suits you just fine."

Why, is it that as soon as a girl gets married, the free-to-have-a-baby sign gets waved in front of our face? Chris wanted to start trying. I, on the other hand, was not there yet. I was twenty seven and almost everyone I knew that was my age had already tackled this thing called motherhood. Why, even Tina had two little girls now. Shelly had remarried and had another little boy. I pondered over my thoughts and considered, *was I being selfish to Chris, to God?*

I looked at Molly. As a mother, she did it so well, and Mark was such a good father, as I knew Chris would be. Starting today, I would no longer use birth control and leave this to God.

It was July that we all took the trip to the cottage on Drummond Island. Mom still tired easily and we all took over the chores. Telling her to relax, this isn't easy for her. Chris was a saint when it came to cleaning up. Why, he did all the dishes and the children just loved my husband. They all wanted to play with Uncle Chris, for he was the new kid on the block.

It was a great week, why yes, it was a little crowded at times, but we were a family being grateful and aware that rough patches may come into our lives, but love will get you through.

Mom's hair had come in a beautiful shade of silver, and with her pretty blue eyes, you couldn't help staring at her. I took a lot of pictures that summer and even considered getting a pixie haircut like Mom's. "Oh, Faith, please put that camera down, not another picture," Mom would say as she waved her hand at me.

"Can't help it, Mom. The camera loves you. Say cheese," I'd say.

Besides Mom's picture, I found I took a lot of pictures of Mom with each of her loved ones. I didn't want these moments to ever go away.

Sam didn't make it until the end of the week because of work schedules. But he came up with cake that he picked upon his way through St. Ignace. It was a one-year anniversary cake for Chris and me.

Chris and I took Buddy swimming, and the whole family was being watched by Mom and Dad from their beach chairs. They held each other's hand and laughed with each grandchild saying, "Look at me, Grandma!" "Watch what I can do, Grandpa!" I found myself thinking as I watched them back, *God, I want that.*

After that week, Mom and Dad extended their vacation with a drive around the Upper Peninsula. Taking in the sights of Pictured Rock and beautiful Lake Superior, they stayed in little motels and quaint little cabins along the way, talking to locals over restaurant coffee and homemade pie. They were living.

Back home, Mom told us of the bald eagles and the black bear they spotted. She got excited to tell of the wildflowers they found along the road.

"God has sure made a beautiful earth for us to vast in," she said with her eyes closed, remembering their trip.

Hello

"Hello, Faith, Dad here," Dad said.

"Hello, Dad," I said. "What's up?" I asked.

"I just got off the phone with Dr. Leppink. Your mother has pain and is not feeling well at all. He wants me to take her to the hospital right now. Will you meet us there?" Dad asked.

"Yes, of course. I am leaving right now." And I hung up the receiver.

I wrote Chris a quick note of where I would be and let Buddy in from outside. "You be a good boy, Buddy," I said, as I shut the door behind me.

The snow was falling as it was the very first of November. I was on my way to the hospital that I had worked at for years, and I had taken the same way to work every day since Chris and I moved into our house in East Grand Rapids. But today, I turned down a different street and then another and another. The snow was not gently falling anymore; it somehow became mixed with the force of a mighty cold wind. I could hardly see out my windshield when I pulled along some side street lined with houses.

I was lost. Somehow I wanted to get lost, never to find the hospital that Mom and Dad would be. I didn't want to hear news about Mom's health. In my mind, if I didn't arrive, I would never know. I started to cry. I cried like I had never cried. The car was running, but the windows would fog with my warm breath bawling out words to God.

"Please God, I don't want to lose my mother. I would do anything for a miracle right now!" I shouted and pounded my cold bare hands on the steering wheel.

I still don't know how the lady saw me. Maybe, she had just heard me, but there came the knock of her padded leather knuckles on my passenger side window. I leaned over and rolled the window down.

"Hello, dear soul in there. Are you okay?" the lady asked.

As I wiped my red eyes and focused on the voice, I could see someone familiar. I believe it to be the lady that had talked to me in the lobby where Chris worked. I remember telling Chris about her and how she changed my mind about leaving, and directed me to the elevator. Chris said he never knew anyone to work in the lobby, like her, and said she must have just been a nice lady.

"Are you lost child? Can I help you?" she asked.

I reached over again, this time opening the door. "Yes, I am," I said, sobbing.

The lady stepped in, shut the car door, and rolled up the window from the windy, cold air.

"It sure is cold out there today. Going to be a harsh winter, she said, as she smiled at me, a smile that I had seen before; not only when she met me in the lobby, but I knew this smile. I just couldn't place it.

She said, "So where is it you need to be?"

I started to cry again, as I explained, "I was on my way to Butterworth Hospital to meet my mom and dad. I work there and have gone there so many times that I can't believe I could get lost." I sobbed my sentences out.

Handing me a soft handkerchief, the lady said, "We all get lost sometimes, especially if we are upset about something. Can you tell me why you are crying?"

"It's my mother. She is sick again. She is trying to beat breast cancer, and I thought she was going to be okay, but . . ." I was bawling. I had not only lost my way; I had lost control.

"Oh dear, that's a hard one. No wonder you are in so much pain. Let me guide you to the hospital where your mother and father need you. Pull yourself together, and as you drive, if you don't mind, I'll talk," she said.

I hit the defrost button, put the car in drive, and the lady talked.

"Now, take a right up at this next street corner that we come to," she continued. "What you are already thinking is how unfair that your mother may not be here much longer. That all this wonderful love is going to disappear, cease. But, if she is sick, child, and her body pains her and her soul aches to move on, what a better time to show someone you love so much your faith. The faith that you know that no matter what happens, or when, that she will be okay."

The lady pointed, "Turn here, up here to the left, and the next street, take a right."

Then she said, "Every one of us born will die, someday, releasing our soul to another dimension. We all know this to be true. We just all feel better if the body lives a very long and healthy life. This doesn't always happen. But you, dear, should be very thankful that you are being blessed with, what I call, 'precious time.' That's where a loved one is sick, and their body may not heal. But it gives you time to care and love them. It means a lot to a soul that is trying to transmission. Some people don't get this time; they lose what they love in an instant.

"The only thing when one is given precious time is sometimes, one starts to grieve right away, like you are doing now. Don't grieve now, child; you will lose this time to show the one who suffers how much you love them. With the faith you will not leave each other, but change forms to one another for now.

Remember, you only think your mother will be okay if she stays in her body for your own needs. Turn left up here."

"I know where I am now," I said.

"Are you saying I'm being selfish?" I asked.

"You don't mean to be. But when one loses somebody, we tend to think that's the end. Nothing to hang on to, nothing to hold. True faith is trust in the love that is released from the body when it dies. Trust that God has already taken care of our death, just as with our birth.

"Pull over here, dear. I will get out here. Thank you," the lady said, pointing.

As I neared the hospital and pulled my car to the curb, I was thinking of Mom, just as I once thought of Molly.

The lady opened the door and as she moved to get out, I could see the yellow dress from under her coat. "Wait, I have more to ask you," I said, my hand reaching for her.

"Be strong, young lady. God loves you," she said, as her feet hit the snowy sidewalk, and she gave me that big smile that had warmed me.

"Wait!" I said. "Who are you?! Where can I find you again?"

She leaned her head into the car, "I am always here. Just talk to me, dear," she replied, as she took a step back and shut the car door.

I hurried to get my door open and get out my side of the car. The cold wind grabbed my breath only to not see where she went. I got back into the car, shut the door, and looked for the handkerchief.

It was gone.

Good-bye

When the doctors would give the news that Mother's cancer had returned in full force, we would all want Mom to stay in the hospital for treatment. She said, "No, I want to be home. Please let me accept what is happening. I am not scared. I want to be home."

I understood. We all took our time sharing the precious time given. Will and Susan stayed the first week while Susan's parents watched the children.

Sam came with Jessica, as Sam couldn't bear this hard time alone. Jessica introduced Mom to healing baths of soothing lavender and Epsom salts. She made her herbal teas and tried to get her to eat earthy salads. Sam would bundle Mom up and take her outside in her borrowed wheelchair. They would sit with hot tea and long talks, sharing, sometimes laughing.

When it came to my time, it was just after Thanksgiving and Mom had taken to bed, too weak to get out. I took her in some soup broth and crawl in bed with her. I found her alert that day, and asked her, "Mom, you never did tell me the third step in forgiveness."

"Oh, yes, the hardest step, and the one so many of us never get to," she said, as she handed me back the cup of broth. She talked, and I listened.

"Of course, you have God's forgiveness the moment you ask. And if you get the forgiveness from the one you hurt, well, then you would think all would be well. Not so, as I would come to find," Mom said.

"What was missing?" I asked.

"Well, after your brother Sam was born and your father named him Sam after your Uncle Sam, I could tell that your Uncle Sam would receive the last step. Forgiving oneself. He felt that Dad still loved him as his best friend and that it didn't matter what happened. It was past hurt, forgiven. I, on the other hand, would come home from the hospital and hold this wonderful little boy and would find myself wondering, worrying that he may grow up to look just like your Uncle Sam, and then I could never forgive myself. Everyone would know that I was unfaithful. I made it about me. I started to hate myself. 'How could I have let this happen?' is what kept me up at night, not little Sam. I felt that when one fails, then sometimes we start failing at more and more in life, that I was destined to doom," Mom said.

"What did you do, Mom?" I asked.

"This is hard for me to tell you. Only God and Grandma Mary know about that time," she said.

"What Mom? Tell me, please."

She continued, "Well, after Sam's birth, I decided I didn't deserve these two wonderful little boys, and my sweet, kind husband. Your Grandma Mary was here visiting to help with the new baby, just as she had done when Will was born. I knew if I was to do anything, I wanted her here for John and the boys."

"Were you going to leave, Mom?" I asked.

"Yes, but not in the way you think. I didn't pack a suitcase or buy a bus ticket; I was going to take a different route of travel," she said.

"What ever do you mean, Mom?"

"Little Sam was just over a week old, and Mrs. Vandyke, Grandma Rose's friend, so wanted to meet him. She was house-bound, so I went to her home with Grandma Rose, for a short visit. As Mrs. Vandyke held Sam, I noticed the bottle of pills at her sink as I got a drink of water. I asked if she was having trouble sleeping. She said yes, but she was not going to take the pills the doctor prescribed, and that she just hadn't taken the time to get rid of them. Faith, I thought that was my answer as to how to leave," Mom said, as tears started to form and fall.

"Mom, what were you thinking? This is so not like you. You are nothing like this person you are describing. What did you do?" I asked, not believing this was my mom.

"I acted like I threw the pills down with the running water when I actually poured them in my dress pocket. I told Mrs. Vandyke I took care of it. Your Grandma Mary was due to go home the coming weekend so I had to act fast. I was going to take the pills that very night." Mom was now crying, and I wished I hadn't brought her back to that time.

"I'm so sorry, Mom. I don't know, but this pain had to be the worst to even think like this," I said, putting my arm around a thin shell that held my mother's soul.

Mom continued her story, "I was taking the red pills one by one out of my pocket and putting them into a cup to be taken at bed time, when your Grandma Mary would come up beside me in the kitchen. Why, she was just in napping with little Will. She scared me. At first I told her they were pills for my headaches. Mama Mary was too smart for that and as we sat down at the kitchen table, I told her my plan to end my life. She grabbed me up and held my painful, crying body. I felt even worse that I had to tell her everything that had led to that dark day."

"I'm sorry, Mom, I can't even imagine." I cried with thoughts of Grandma Mary and how I miss her.

"It's okay, Faith, because that was the best thing that could happen. Your Grandma stopped me from telling her what would lead me to taking all those pills. She said it didn't matter, what was done was done. That all I had to do right at that very moment was to forgive myself. That's what was missing. Nothing could change if I held onto this hurt. She said that if I didn't give this hurt to God, I would cause my children to hurt so much more, that to miss the love I would bring them over the years was interfering with the plan of life I was given," Mom said, her tears starting to stop.

"Grandma Mary was like an angel coming at just the right time," I said.

Mom said, "I forgave myself. It was a new day as Grandma Mary told me my shoulders were broad enough to carry all that had been assigned to me, and I would move forward with love. Faith, she never questioned me about that day, and never told anyone. I learned that day, that true love comes from your heart, your soul. It never questions, never judges, never wants more from you than you can give. Little Sam started to look more and more like me each day. I took it as God thanking me for staying, God's love coming through my baby's face," Mom said.

"I love you, Mama," I said, as I held her close.

"I love you, too, Faith," Mama said.

Mama left two days after Christmas that year. No suitcase, no ticket. She was fifty-one years old.

Spring Grace

That next spring would still bring the beauty that Mama loved. I walked around her flower gardens remembering her telling me she could feel the presence of God surround her, making her feel that with each step she took, she was walking on holy ground. I found by thinking back on all the stories Mama had told me; it was opening wide my heart and mind to receive more and more.

I would not question God why she was to leave, but thank God for her and the precious time we were all given. One thing I did soon after Mom couldn't give her loving touch of moving my hair off my shoulders, the gentle touch as she pulled my hair away from my face. I missed it so, and as the girl was to cut away my hair she asked, "How short do you want to go?"

"Short, please. A pixie will do," I answered.

Within the next few years, more people that I loved would also go to rest, walk the path of peace. Nana and Big Bill would leave us only a few days apart, and Grandma Rose never came out of her sadness after Mama passed.

Aunt Sara would say she just gave in. That no matter what you said, Grandma was determined not to be a burden. Grandma Rose left this earth just as she had lived it. Everything in order, neat and tidy, asleep in a rocking chair.

Just as love would leave us, new love would be born to us. John Walters and his new wife, Melinda, would be blessed with a little girl that they named Rose Lynn. My cousins from Iowa were producing what seemed to be monthly. Yes, life is to go on.

The year was 1989 when I awoke with the feeling of life within. My life was about to take on change. I reached over and took Christopher's hand as he slept and put it to my belly. "Do you feel it, Chris? He or she is moving. I can feel movement!" I said.

As Chris would stir awake, I would describe it to him. "It feels like a butterfly trying to escape the hollows of a hole in which it's held," I said.

Chris would lift his head as his hand held my growing belly. "I am so excited, so happy, Faith. We are going to be great parents," he would tell.

I would read all the books, and ask Molly, Aunt Sara, and even Ms. Celia so many questions. I so wanted to be assured that I was doing everything just right. Molly and Mark were great parents. Markus, then six, and Michael, then four, were children you wanted to be around, happy and well-behaved.

"You will do just fine, Faith! Look at you with child, why, you just glow," Molly said.

"I love everything about it, Molly. I just wish Mom was here. She would just love all that is coming," I said.

"She's around, Faith. She knows," Molly would tell me because she knew it made me feel better.

Molly, sweet Molly. I have said it before; sometimes I swear we share the same heart. That is why she would get the second phone call. Right after I called Chris to come home from the office to take me to the hospital, I called Molly's home, knowing she probably had just gotten home from teaching.

"Hello, Molly!" I said with excitement.

"Hi, Faith. I just knew it. I could feel it the moment I got to school this morning. I just knew I would get this call today. How far are they? The contractions?" Molly asked.

"About five minutes apart, but it feels like seconds." I laughed.

"Chris is on his way home now," I said. "Then we will go."

"Well, don't forget to tell him to put the suitcase in the backseat." She laughed.

"It's four-thirty now. Mark will be home shortly to watch the boys and I will be up after supper. How does that sound?" asked Molly.

"Sounds good! Oh, Molly, I am so excited!" I shouted before hanging up the phone to call my dad.

At eleven in the evening, Molly would head on home. Having to go teach in the morning, I understood. I was in full labor, no turning back. But this baby was in no hurry, as I would walk the halls with Chris to try to stay awake.

At 1:05 AM, September 19, 1989, I was to give the last push to give way to the most precious gift I have ever been given. Grace Christine May Sutton was put into my arms, and I would fall instantly into a new kind of love.

"Can this be true? Look at her, why she is the most beautiful baby I have ever seen?" I would hear myself say, as if no other mother had ever said that before.

I am here to say that sometimes in one's life, you have moments that just seem to slip away; like it was one big long day, and one very long sleepless night that you know you lived but can't—for the life of you—remember how.

Now, I have a great memory of most everything. But that first year of Gracie's life, all I could say is the words busy, sleepless, sweatpants, spit up, and messy. Then I would add the words joyful, grateful, fun, and still sweatpants.

I didn't go back to work. Chris and I decided that we had enough money coming in, and so what if we would have to be careful of our spending. What better than to have me home for Gracie.

So I became a full-time mother, just as my mother did. Why, I was going to do everything right. The caring of my baby girl, how lucky I was to be with her, protect her day, and rock her to sleep at night. Be there for all her needs, with a babysitter on rare occasions, and I was sure everything would fall just right. I mean, how could it fail?

When Gracie was about to turn three years old, it is when I realized I had failed. My child was a complete and total brat! Why, she was so ill-behaved that I could feel that no one wanted to be around her. Not even Buddy would stay in the same room with her. She would tell me "NO"—her first word—and scream with kicks if she didn't get her way.

I said to Chris, "How could I be this inadequate as a mom? Why, I had the best mom there was!"

"Maybe it's because you never give her a crack on the bottom!" Chris would shout back.

"Oh, you would love that. I don't believe in spanking. I was never spanked!" I yelled back.

"Faith, a spanking is done with an open hand on the buttocks. I am not asking that you pull her pants down and beat our child. But let's face it. You giving her everything is not working. When you are not around, she is fine for me. Gracie just knows you are weak with her love, and therefore you don't show her that bad behavior will not be tolerated," he would say, trying to put calm back in the conversation.

Maybe Chris was right. Maybe I was trying to reenact my childhood because it had worked so well; when really, it involved different souls, at a different time in life. I must come to realize what worked before may not work again. Yes, Chris and I would disagree in the raising of little Gracie. Matter of fact, Chris and I were disagreeing about a lot of things lately. I wanted to move to the country; he was happy in the city. I wanted to take car trips for our vacations; he wanted to fly to Florida and sit on the beach. Somehow, being new parents put pressures and responsibilities on us that would make us a little edgy.

I had never really witnessed my own parents feeling this tenseness, but the way Gracie would act, I wondered if she could feel the air thick with anxiety at times.

I told my dad on a visit to see him one day come early spring, "Dad, I am a failure as Gracie's mother. Gracie just doesn't respond to my guidance. I don't get it. I love her so, but she is so different than any of her cousins or my friend's children."

"Faith, Gracie is no different than any other child that is healthy and active. I think little Gracie is in search of her calm. Nature can help, and you and I can help," Dad said.

"How so?" I asked.

"What I think is, we need to go fishing with Gracie. It's time," Dad said.

"Oh, I don't know Dad; she can't stay still for a minute. Why, putting her in a boat could be a real challenge," I said, smiling, picturing the boat rocking, not from the waves.

"I'm up for it. How about this Saturday? The weather is supposed to be nice. I would love to spend some time with my girls," Dad would say.

"Okay, we will be here early. I'll bring sandwiches, no mustard," I said, my hand in the air smiling, thinking this might be fun.

That Saturday was the first of many that I would pack Gracie up and we went fishing with Dad, Gracie's Grandpa. Gracie was a natural, cool as a cucumber. She loved everything about being in the boat with my "Faith May" fishing pole in her hand.

Dad told Gracie about my first fishing trip on the very same lake. How she was just like me and that some day, she too would steer the boat. I would marvel at how being in the boat brought such a calm to my little girl, and therefore to me. We could become the mother and daughter we were meant to be.

"Thank you, Dad," I told him again when I helped him put the boat away that late fall.

"Gracie and I have come a long ways this summer. Thanks to fishing," I said.

"Everything you think is a problem, there is an answer. Sometimes we just question too much and blame, push buttons; repeat, trying to fix it in different ways. When to fix something that is emotional is to use the greatest emotion, that being love." Dad would smile and wink.

Gracie became a new child. She was caring and thoughtful, saying please and thank you. Chris and I would tuck her in at night with a story book. And after giving her dad a kiss goodnight, she would ask me to stay with her as she talked to God. Buddy slept at the foot of her bed with her new calm.

Gracie was also quite the talker. More than you can imagine. She talked early. She told me at four years of age, "Mother, I am here for a reason. I am not sure what I have to do, but I know that our bodies are just our house for out guts." She told me one night.

When I told her of God, she told me, "God is all the good guts we are born with."

I asked, "What about the bad guts, where do they come from?"

"That's easy, Mother. We are born with bad guts, too, but if you only use your good guts, then you will have no need to use your bad guts," she said.

"Perfectly said, Gracie." I told her.

"Thank you, Mother."

She called me Mother, and I laughed because I called my own mother, Mama, all those young years. I would often wonder, if she grows out of calling me Mother, who would I become?

Dreams and Reality

I t was Fourth of July the year Gracie was to turn five. We Suttons had plans with the Richards, just like we had done on other Fourth of Julys. We would meet at the park for a picnic and then leave out on our speed boat with the kids for a day on Lake Michigan, then end our day with the celebration of fireworks at the local park.

I talked to Molly the night before about what we would bring: food, drinks, etc. We were happy that the skies were to be clear and the weather warm.

"Don't forget your swimsuit, Moll," I said into the phone, as I walked around the house picking up toys and things Gracie would leave behind.

"Yea, Faith, me in a swimsuit, gone are the days of the bikini. Time to break out the one piece," laughing as she talked.

"Oh, you still have it, Mrs. Richards. It's me who carries the little pouch around the middle," I said, "which reminds me, did you make your famous cupcakes? I am so hungry for them."

"Oh yea, red, white, and blue, and hidden from all the boys around here," Molly said.

"So we will meet you at the boat launch and picnic tables say eleven?" I asked.

"We might be running a little behind. Mark has to finish some work at the shop in the morning; he closes the shop for his employees, but darn if he can't leave work behind. I told him that he needed the whole day off to relax with his family and friends. But you know him; he can't relax if there's work to be done," Molly explained.

"Well, I am going to have a talk with him about just letting go and enjoying the day," I said.

"Good luck with that, Faith. No matter, I wouldn't change a thing about Mark Richards. Can you believe we are going on seventeen years of marriage? How does that happen?" Molly said.

"This reminds me, we have to make plans for us adults to go out for a dinner to celebrate our anniversaries. Chris and I will be ten years. Time flies," I said.

We ended our happy conversation with, "See you tomorrow and love you."

Gracie was standing by my bed, shaking me awake at 5:55 AM. I remember the time well because I so didn't want to be awake.

"What is it, Gracie? Here, come lie next to me for a while."

"Mother, I had a dream and it woke me up."

"Was it a bad dream, honey?" I asked with my eyes closed.

"No, I don't think so. It was someone leaving and he wanted to say good-bye. He told me that he was going to send a beautiful flower to earth and wanted me to show someone the flower."

I heard every one of the words Gracie was telling, but it was a dream, and who's to say what dreams mean. I said, "That's nice, Gracie. Do you know who is leaving?"

"I don't know, Mother, but he said I would know when I see the flower. I do know he had good guts," Gracie said.

We both fell back to sleep and when we got up for breakfast, I was in a hurry for I had to do packing of picnic baskets and swim gear and pink lemonade to make. I was in the kitchen putting the last of everything together when the phone would ring.

"Hello," I said.

"Hello, Faith. Paul here," Paul said.

"Well, hi, Mr. Warner. How are you? I haven't seen you and Miss June for a while," I said, surprised by the call.

"Faith, can you please come to Molly's home right now?" he asked in a calm voice, but in a voice that wanted to tell so much more.

"What's wrong? We are just getting ready to meet Mark and Molly," I said, confused. I looked at the kitchen clock; it was 10:45.

"Faith, I can't explain it over the phone, and I don't want to. Molly needs her best friend right now!" Paul said.

"Why sure, but you are scaring me. Do I need to bring Chris and Gracie?" I asked.

"Maybe you better not come with Gracie," Paul said, with what sounded like a sob.

"Chris!" I said into the TV room with both of my loves engaged in cartoons. "Mr. Warner just called. Molly needs me. I'll call you as soon as I find out what's up," I said, as I turned and grabbed the car keys and my purse.

My drive to Molly's was always twenty minutes. That day it took fifteen. But fifteen minutes is a long time to go over all the things that possibly could have gone wrong.

"Oh God, please don't let it be one of those boys! Whatever it is, don't you dare take one of Molly's boys home!" I found myself saying out loud, pleading for everything to be okay, because everything that could have gone wrong went through my head except for the one thing that went terribly wrong that summer day.

I pulled up Molly and Mark's driveway to their well-maintained brick ranch to find not only Mr. and Mrs. Warner's car parked there, but at least four others.

"Oh no, the universe has done something awful," I said, as I got out of my car and walked to the front porch.

Miss June opened the door.

"Faith, come in," she grabbed my arm as hers just shook then said, "It's just so bad, Faith!" She cried.

"What has happened?" I asked, looking around the room with an array of Mark's family, two sisters, brother-in-laws, his mother, Marge, and children, but not Markus or Michael. "Where are the children? Where are Markus and Michael?" I pleaded.

Mark's sister walked over and took my hand as she said, "The boys are with Molly, locked in her bedroom," she told, as I looked at her eyes and saw some kind of terrible pain, but also an angry pain.

"What for, where's Mark?"

Mr. Paul put his arm around me and led me to the small kitchen. With Miss June and him holding onto me, they told me the reason.

"Mark was to leave here early this morning to get some work done at his shop. What we now have come to know is that two men must have followed Mark into the shop to rob him. It was very early and when Mark's friend Don drove by the shop on his way home from his night job, he had seen Marks's car and pulled in to tease Mark about working on a holiday. The two men ran out the shop and jumped in a beat-up black truck. Don knew something was wrong and took down their license plate number and got a good look at them as they sped away." Paul was now crying. I had seen this look before on Mr. Paul when Molly lay in the hospital.

"Is Mark okay?" I asked.

"Of course, we don't know exactly what happened. But Don found Mark on the floor next to the cash register." Paul would cry the next sentence out and I didn't want to hear it. I wish he could take it all back. *Don't tell me. No, this can't be!*

"Mark was killed with a gunshot wound to the chest. He never made it to the hospital." Paul was trying too hard not to cry, and as the three of us held each other and cried, I knew I would have to pull myself together and go face Molly and the boys. God, give me strength.

Miss June then said, "Mark's dad and sister are at the funeral home now making arrangements, and Molly took the boys to her bedroom to tell them. She said to give her an hour with the boys then to call you, and said as she shut the bedroom door that she needed Faith." Miss June was so tiny right now, like she just wanted to disappear into the thin air. "Faith, my heart is so broken right now." She cried.

I hugged her again, then broke our embrace and started down the hall towards Molly and Mark's bedroom. *Pull yourself together, Faith*, I told myself. Get into a place of calm, come into the presence, and bring God with you. Molly needs me to be calm. The boys need just love, not anything but God's love.

I knocked and said, "Molly, it's me, can I come in?"

"Faith!" I heard the door click and as I opened it, Molly would return to her neatly made full-size bed and sit between her and Mark's creations, the two boys now eleven and nine, who would somehow have to become men that very day because of violence.

As I went over and knelt down before the broken family, my hand reaching up to Molly's helpless face, I said, "Molly, I was told what happened. I am so sorry." With my tears flowing, there was no need for her to repeat what she knew.

"What can I do for you?" I asked.

"Faith, Mark has left and there is nothing anyone can do. Just be here in our pain for a while. I told the boys that their father is not in pain, but our pain will stay with us for as long as we need it," Molly said.

"Aunt Faith, is it true that my dad is not of his body but is among a place where he is happy?" Markus asked.

I looked in Molly's eyes, "Yes, Markus, your dad is in a good place right now. He is dead to earth, but alive in God," I said.

Michael then said, "My mom said she was where my dad is now, but only for a minute and then she had to return. She said it was the best place she had ever been and when she is called again there, she will be happy to enter." Michael held his mother tight.

"That is true, Michael. I am sure of this place also," I said.

As I looked up at the family that now was missing a limb, I was thinking Molly is so right. The pain will remain for a long time. How unfair because of some other person's pain within, that awful pain they had carried into Mark's shop would now be released over so many, causing more pain.

The two men were apprehended with the forty dollars they had taken for a human life. They now would sit among all the other lost and painful souls waiting for the trials, courts, and legal judgment to decide what will become of their life.

Molly would stress too many of us that she didn't want to bring the two men into our thoughts at Mark's funeral unless we were praying for them.

"We are going to celebrate Mark's life in the next few days. We are not to waste our time deeming the ones who have caused this. I don't want my boys to hate what has happened, but to accept what has happened and move on," Molly was heard to say.

So the next few days, we would do what each family does when they lose a loved one. We would meet with family, friends, and people from the community that would come and pay their respects. We hugged, cried, told stories, and remembered events, and then we hugged and cried some more.

Molly was strong because of faith. Molly was also weak because of love.

I asked Gracie if it was Uncle Mark that was the one in her dream that had to go away. She told me, "I'm not sure, Mother, because the person had no body, only good guts. But I will never forget the beautiful flower."

Heading North

Two days after Mark's funeral and burial was to be Molly and Mark's anniversary. They were to celebrate, but instead, it was a day Molly locked herself in her room and no matter what, was not going to come out. I went to see her and the boys every day. There was so much sadness in the now messy home. Molly had always kept her house neat and tidy. But things change when you are lost in the discomfort of suffering.

Molly told me she was going to sell the shop and was going to quit teaching for a while.

"I understand selling the shop, Molly, but Molly, don't give up on teaching. You love your job!" I said.

"But I don't want to feel joy right now. I just want to totally be here for the boys," she said.

"The boys will be in school, just as you will, during the day," I said, trying to reason with her.

"Faith, I know Mark is okay, but I am not. I can't do this without him. I feel like half a person. And the anger of what has happened has gotten the best of me. I thought I could get pass this anger, but it's eating me alive," Molly said.

I didn't know what to say to help her feel better. At this point, I was also angry at the men who took my best friend's life and turned it sad. I told my dad about how Molly was acting on our fishing day with Gracie.

"Dad, if I don't go over to her house, she calls me asking where I am. She has become short with me the last few days. I don't think she has showered lately, and her hair hasn't seen a comb since the funeral. I do all her shopping, and Miss June has started doing the cooking and cleaning. Mr. Warner is taking care of her finances, and Mark's parents are helping with the boys. Yesterday, I found her back in bed at two in the afternoon," I said.

"Faith, you and the others are starting to enable Molly. It's all right to let her grieve, but she needs to know she must find a new normal for her boys," Dad said. "Maybe a few days away would help."

"No, I have to be there for her."

"Do you want me to talk to her?"

"Yes, could you? I would like that," I said.

"I will call on her tomorrow after church," he said.

That Tuesday, I would receive a visit from Molly and the boys. As I opened the side door to let them in, I smiled with gums showing at a well-groomed Molly; her brown hair neatly combed into a fun ponytail; she was in her tan shorts and a colorful shirt.

"Well, hello, Molly! Look at you!" I said, as I gave her a hug. "Hello, boys. Gracie just went out back to her tire swing. I'll put some drinks together and we will join you soon," I said, as they both headed out back.

"Okay, Aunt Faith, thanks," I heard Michael say, as the screen door shut to the porch.

"So, I am happy to see you, Moll. I am sorry I haven't called. Did my dad come to visit you?" I asked, trying to feel better about not calling.

We both sat down to the table in the kitchen.

"Yes, he did and he suggested I take the boys to the cottage on Drummond for a few days. And I have two weeks before school starts for the boys and me. So I was thinking that Gracie and you should come with us. I love to fish, Faith, but I think you would do much better for the boys, and I'm not sure I can handle your dad's big boat," she said.

"Oh, Molly! I am so happy you are going to teach. Yes, I will talk to Chris tonight and we could leave out this Thursday," I said.

"That works just fine. The boys are going school clothes shopping with Grandma Marge tomorrow, and I can pack then," Molly said, smiling.

"Well, let me grab some Kool-Aid and homemade cookies for the kids and go tell them the good news!" I said, as I got up and pushed my chair under the table.

"Hey, wait a minute, you made cookies?" Molly asked, surprised.

"Yes! I can bake somewhat," I laughed.

That night I told Chris about leaving Thursday and would be home the next Wednesday. I knew he wouldn't be happy. He was already complaining that I have been to Molly's a lot. He would try to understand, but he had wanted another child, as I did, too.

"We have been trying for a while now, Chris honey, what are five nights away going to hurt? I am going no matter; Molly needs me," I said.

After arguing with Chris, I would leave him with Gracie, and I took the guilt I was feeling to Dad's to get the keys to the cottage. I knew the neighbor Frank had a key to the cottage, but I just needed an excuse to get some air and cool off. Also, I knew seeing my dad would be a good calm.

"So what'd you say to Molly, Dad? She seems better and you are right, a few days away will be great," I said.

"Oh, just a little advice. I hope it helped," Dad said. Then he said, "Your brother Sam will be up come Monday, maybe sooner. I told him that Molly and the boys might be up there. He said that would be fine; he will just stay with Frank next door. He will be happy Gracie and you will be there," Dad said.

"Oh, I so hope he will be there sooner! Last time I saw him was at Mark's funeral and it was such a sad time. I don't think we said but a few words to each other," I said.

"Well, I guess he wanted to meet Will and I up there to do some fishing, so I will leave out the following Friday," Dad said.

"I wish I could just stay the next week and fish with you all," I said, as I took the cottage keys from the hook in the kitchen. The same kitchen that still held Mom's essence; I could still smell her Sunday pot roast and apple pie fresh from the oven. I would look around as nothing had changed. Dad still used the same dish towels and pot holders. Then I would see the pretty flower vase placed on the windowsill and I would have to hold back my tears. Because everything had changed . . . the vase was empty.

"That would be great, but I am sure Chris would miss you," Dad said, breaking into my thoughts.

"Yes, I suppose he would," I said, thinking how grateful I should be to have a husband. My best friend did not.

Healing Begins

We were soon on our way and over the Mackinac Bridge to the U.P., then leaving De Tour on the ferry that would take us to an island that has always held special memories for me, from being a young girl with my family, to meeting the love of my life, Chris, to spending precious time with Mom. It also holds Mother Nature at her best. The sunsets are breathtaking, and the waters that surround not only Drummond, but all the smaller islands, have the flow from the movement of the air that sends so much vibration of life. You can't help but feel better.

We settled in late Thursday. Friday, the waters were rough, so I took the boys and Gracie on a nature walk while Molly sat and stared out upon the waters.

At lunch she asked, "How come I never came up here with Mark?"

"I guess time just gets away from us, but didn't Mark, Chris, and Sam come up here fishing one time together?" I asked.

"Yes, I guess they did, just after you two got married, and they stayed here. I remember Mark telling me about the great sunsets, and some big pike he caught," Molly said with a smile.

"Well, we are going to see a beautiful sunset tonight, and we have marshmallows, graham crackers and chocolate," I said, waving my hand at Gracie to come away from the fishing dock, wishing I would have brought Buddy with us because he would have stayed right by Gracie watching her every step.

But Chris said, "Leave me the dog, that's the least you could do." Buddy was getting old and the long trip with a car load probably wasn't the best thing to do, as I would tell Gracie when she cried for us to take him.

That night, Markus and Michael tucked into the same bunks Molly and I slept in years ago. Gracie in my bed, sleeping, was waiting for me to snuggle with her.

Molly and I sat by the camp fire as I opened a bottle of red wine and poured a glass for each of us.

"Cheers, Molly!" I said, as I would tap her glass with mine and we each took a sip.

"What's the occasion?" Molly asked.

"Life," I said.

"Who's life? What life?!" Molly said, as if she had just bit into a sour green apple.

"Well, Moll, it's like this. You know as well as I do, that sometimes life just stinks, and it doesn't seem one bit fair. But that doesn't mean we should just give in. Why, we have a lot to celebrate. Did you happen to notice the looks on our children's happy faces today? The moving abilities of their healthy limbs as they danced among us; I guess I believe that if you are living a life, then you should celebrate that life," I said, taking another sip of wine.

"Faith, do you think people know sometimes when they are going to leave this earth?" Molly asked.

Before I could answer, Molly continued, "Because that night before Mark's death, he held me after we made love and was talking about silly things. You know, Mark wasn't much of a talker. He always said it was because he had three sisters that did all his talking," Molly laughed a little as she got up and threw another log on the fire and sat back down.

"What did he say?" I asked.

"He told me I was a good mother and that I being a teacher was exactly what I was to do because I glowed each time I left for work in the school year. Then he said something that didn't seem strange at that moment, but now it gets turned over and over in my mind as if he felt a shift in his universe. He said, 'Molly, I just want you to know that I feel very lucky and grateful to have had you and the boys in my life.'"

Molly was tearing up, but held herself together and said, "Faith, we, Mark and I, lived our life like that last night together. We would forgive each other for our faults and never sweated the small stuff. We loved the time that was given to us, and we both loved the God that we held in our hearts. We believed in heaven on earth, and we both believed that when our time on earth was done, we would be glorified in a heaven that God holds for us." She stood, hands in the air. "So why then, am I so damn mad?! Who am I mad at more? The man that took Mark from my boys, or the universe for letting it happen, or am I mad most at myself for not turning off that stupid alarm clock that would wake my soul mate and send him on his way?! I told your dad that because of violence to my family, I have such an intense hostility for another human life, and I want to blame God for creating such a human. When I got hurt because of violence, we all could forgive the man because of grace. I am fine, I lived! The man didn't! Well, there is no grace here!" Molly cried, her hands on her face, her body shaking from a cold that no campfire could warm.

I put my drink down and stood. I put my arms around Molly as she kept weeping questions of why.

After she calmed a little, I asked, "What did my dad tell you?"

185

"He told me that losing Mark was not the hardest thing in my life. He said the hardest thing in your life is to forgive the person that has caused this pain. That being the one who pulled the trigger and fired the gun, when I forgive, I will receive my grace," Molly said.

"But how do you forgive someone of this? I don't think I could," I said, thinking maybe my dad wasn't right on this one.

Molly said, "That's just it. He said I don't have to face that man to forgive him, that could come later, but to go within myself and give it to God. He said that each day, take a few minutes and sit in your pain, and tell God that it hurts to forgive, but it hurts more to hang on to this pain, so I am willing to forgive something about the man each day. One day, I will not want to sit in that pain for not even a second because I will receive the relief that will enable me to move forward." Then she said, "I also told your dad that day I locked myself in my bedroom, I prayed to God and Mark's spirit to give me a sign that everything was going to be okay. I know that sounds funny coming from someone who knows they have seen the light of Heaven, but don't I deserve some kind of proof that Mark is with God?"

"What did he say?" I asked.

"He told me, 'Molly, it's your faith that is your proof. Asking for proof is also doubting your faith. The faith in what you and Mark believed.' He told me he talks to God every day, so he never leaves room for doubt, and when Miss Patty went home, he now talks to her in that presence. That sometimes he sees her in a pretty flower, or feels her in a soft breeze to his face. Your dad said he believed that God speaks in stillness, and just maybe that is another form of proof. Then he told me, 'Molly, a love given is never really taken; it only changes form." Molly said as she sat back down.

"I have heard that before," I said.

"I told your dad I didn't think I would see Mark in a flower, but maybe in a car wrench," Molly said with a smile and dry eyes once more.

"It makes sense. I have my best talks to Mom in the presence of calm. Maybe that is where the souls of people we have loved and lost hang out waiting for us to enter," I said, thinking I might be a little deep. I got up and started to kick a little dirt onto the fire when Molly said, "Wait on that, Faith. I think I would like to sit out here a little longer."

"Sounds good, Molly. But I have promised two boys that Aunt Faith would take them fishing in the morning, so I better get some shut eye," I said, as I picked up my empty wine glass.

"Are you still planning on taking Gracie to Harbor Island in the other boat so she can spot a copper hawk or maybe a bald eagle?" I said.

"That's the plan!"

"Well, have a good night sleep, Molly," I said, and turned to walk up to the cottage.

Molly said, "Love you, Faith."

"Love you, right back, Molly," I said, glad we were up here.

Fishing with Faith

I moved a sleeping Gracie to Molly's bed and woke up Markus and Michael. With a bowl of cereal each, coffee in the thermos, sandwiches and lemonade in the cooler of ice, we were soon off in the boat just as the sun was coming through the trees off the island.

It wasn't long before the fish started biting out in the middle ground of Potagannissing Bay. The boys were amazed by the way a fish would fight to not enter the boat.

"Aunt Faith, you are a pro at fishing just like the fishing shows we watch on TV. You know everything on what to do to catch a fish," Michael said.

"Thank you, Michael. Just years of practicing and patience from my dad," I said, thinking maybe I shouldn't have mentioned the word *dad*.

"My dad had a lot of patience. He taught me how to swing a baseball bat, giving me that homerun to win a game two years ago," Markus said proudly.

"That's right, Markus, your dad was great. He sure did love his boys," I said, smiling.

"And my mom, too!" Michael would add.

"Yes, your mom, too, Michael. Are you two okay? Is there anything you want to talk about? I can try to help with any questions you have," I said, a little scared that I might not give the right answers.

"I think I am okay," Michael said. He then added, "Grandpa Paul helped me a lot with all my questions. Even your dad, Grandpa Bakker, told me that I could talk to Dad any time. I felt I needed to. He said my dad listens and still loves me very much."

Markus said, "I am still mad at the man who shot my dad. I told Grandpa Paul that I hated him, but Grandpa said that no matter how much I hated that man, it wasn't going to make me feel any better. That the man is in a place where he must think about what he did every day and hopefully someday, I will forgive him as to make myself feel better. I don't understand that part yet, but

Grandpa said I will someday. Grandpa said it's sad and dangerous to carry hate inside you every day because just like with any emotion, if you have it, you will release it. That man carried hate inside him, and he released it from the gun he held and he killed my dad. Grandpa said that man didn't hate my dad; that the man just hated what was inside him." Markus was not crying as he talked; he was just trying to make sense of why things happen. He had grown up so much this last month. *A good man*, I thought.

"Fish on!" I shouted. "Grab your pole, Markus, hold your pole up, reel, Markus! Good job! Keep the pole up, tire that fish out before he sees the boat," I said as Markus reeled.

"Okay, get the net, Michael! You are going to get this fish in the boat for your brother," I said.

"I don't know, Aunt Faith, what if I can't do it?" Michael would say with doubt.

"Have faith in yourself, Michael, your dad is watching," I said, steering the boat as to make it easier for Markus to reel in.

"I see it, Aunt Faith! It's a walleye!" said Markus. "It's giving a fight!" he added.

"Put the net under the fish, Michael, and scoop up and into the boat," I said calmly just as my dad said to me so many times.

"Oh my GOSH!" said Markus.

"I did it! The fish is in the net!" Michael said with both arms holding the net as if it was his lifeline.

"It's in the boat!" Markus shouted.

"Good job, boys. What teamwork, a nice-sized fish! Way to go!" I said, giving each a high five.

The universe was good to us that day, giving us a good amount of fish. As we reached the shore, Molly and Gracie would greet us at the dock.

"How did it go?" Molly asked.

"Mom! I caught two walleyes and a small mouth bass," Michael said, throwing the rope to his mother.

"It was good, Mom! I think Dad was with us the whole time," Markus said.

"Wow! Sounds like we all had a good day," Molly said, happy to hear her little men in such good spirits.

I was bending over looking for a fish hook I knew I had dropped earlier. I had started saying, "They did well, and now comes the job of cleaning the catch. Not my favorite part; wish my dad was here right now." That's when I would look up and see my brother Sam.

"How about me? Think I could clean those fish for a dinner?" Sam asked.

"Sam!" I said, taking his hand for a lift up on the dock. Giving him a hug, I said, "You came early. I was hoping you would."

Sam grabbed the fish cooler and said, "It just worked out better to come today. I am going to sleep at Frank's, but I'll clean fish for supper."

"Sleep at Frank's, but please spend time with us," I said.

"Hi, Uncle Sam!" Markus said, as he shook his hand and Michael gave Sam a hug. The boys knew Sam well, and called him Uncle Sam. *Everyone should have an Uncle Sam*, I thought. Happy Dad was forgiving, and gave us our Uncle Sam's love.

"Mother, I have seen a Copper's Hawk and Uncle Sam gave me a pony ride," Gracie said.

"He did? Well, you be careful with your Uncle Sam. He's getting to be an old pony, and his back might not take it," I laughed, as we all headed towards the fish cleaning house my dad had built.

"Funny, Faith, I think I can handle it," Sam said, as he brushed his hand on Gracie's head.

"Come on, boys, let's clean us some fish," Sam said.

"I want to watch," Gracie said.

"Fine. Aunt Molly and I will sit. I am tired," I said, turning toward the cottage.

"Now who's getting old?" Sam laughed, walking away, with the children following behind.

Back at the cottage, on the front deck, Molly poured us each a glass of iced tea.

"Thanks, Molly," I said.

"No, thank you, Faith. Sounds like the boys had a good time," Molly said.

"They did great; I think they are going to be just fine. I love them so," I said, taking a big gulp of tea.

"How was your morning? Sounds like you made it to Harbor Island," I said.

"Yes, we just got back and Sam was here. What a wonderful day!" Molly said. I could tell she had something she couldn't wait to tell me. I know my friend well.

"So Molly, what's up?" I said, smiling because she was smiling.

"Oh, Faith! I have such great news. Mark came to me today! He and God let me know that all is good and Gracie is my angel, my messenger!" Molly said as she grabbed my arm.

"How so?" I asked.

"Well, it happened like this. We were walking the trail on Harbor Island. No one else around, not a soul, and we came to this big, open grassy area. Then Gracie says, 'Look, Aunt Molly, a flower out there, all by itself.' Faith, as we walked over to this single orchid, I felt this light breeze that gave me a chill. We both just stared at its beauty, looking at it until we were both kneeling before it in silence. When out of the blue Gracie shouts, 'This is the same flower that was in my dream! This flower was meant for you, Aunt Molly. Now I know Uncle Mark was the good guts and he wanted you to see this flower!" Molly said, pinching the fat of my arm to where it would hurt. "I don't know where she gets good guts from, but she convinced me she knew what she was saying," Molly said, letting go of my now red arm.

My mouth hung open in disbelief. How could this be? How do I tell Molly about Gracie's dream that morning of Mark's death, and that I have just been told of a miracle. What is happening? Does this happen every day to just ordinary people? Was I to call a press conference and tell them that God came through my child? The real live spirit of Mark Richards came to my child so she could deliver a message that is proof that we may die to our body, but we live on, we still exist through dreams, flowers, and gentle breezes. What do I do with all this wonder of information?

"Where is the flower now?" I asked Molly.

"Oh, I could never have disturbed it, Faith. It was magical, mystical. I have been touched again by what we all are to become, God's love," Molly said.

Then we both sat in stillness looking out at the trees, the waters, and surrounding. Listening to birds chirp and children's laughter in the background, I knew—and Molly knew—we were thinking the same thing at that very moment in time. No matter what happens in one's life, you will come through. We all have a choice on what emotions to use, and who we invite on our journeys. We can bottle up hate and be miserable, or we can release love and forgiveness and heal.

Conversations

At the table that evening, we would serve fish, fried potatoes, and corn on the cob—the kids' favorite.

Sam and our neighbor Frank would join us. Frank lived in a big house across the street from the cottage and has been our family friend from the day he introduced himself. Frank was born on the island and was just a little younger than my dad. A very interesting man who was an open book. He would tell you anything you wanted to know about himself and about anyone who lived on the island. Frank would proceed to tell Molly about his life; how he served in the Vietnam War and met a beautiful young lady when the war ended. They were married, and he took her to this island. They bought the house he lives in now. They soon had a son and when the boy turned three, his wife packed up her things and the boy's and left south.

"She never liked the island, couldn't stand the isolation. We never did divorce, and she would send my son up every summer to live with me. I put him through college and he's a fine doctor now. He comes to see me every summer still. Has himself a lovely wife, and I have two grandsons," Frank said, smiling.

At the table, the children told us about their excitements of the day. Gracie told us all the different birds she had spotted. I was amazed on how she had become such a birder, just as her Grandma Patty was.

As everyone ate their dessert of strawberry shortcake, I would go into the living room area of the cottage where an old big trunk sat. Inside I would pull out three new journals and three new pencils. Dad had kept an array of journals in that trunk, and each year would give us kids one with a new pencil. I remember the covers of the journals had pictures of fish, black bear, deer, birds, and flowers. I picked out a bird one for Gracie, and fish would be the cover for the boys.

"Here you go, kids. This is a journal so you can keep track of all your excitements," I said, as I handed them out. "You can keep track of all the birds you come across, Gracie, and you boys can tell about your fishing trip today. Anything you want to write about, it's good to journal," I said, as I sat back down at the table.

"What a good idea," Molly said.

"Thanks, Aunt Faith! Mom, can I be excused right now? I have a lot to write," Markus said.

"Me, too," added Michael.

"Yes, take your dishes to the sink and rinse first," Molly said, as the boys were up before she finished her sentence.

"Mother, how do you spell blue jay?" Gracie would ask.

"Oh, Gracie," I laughed, thinking she is going to be five and knows about words, and can write cat or dog and her name, but she would need help. "I will help you, Gracie. We can do it together," I said.

From the kitchen, Michael would shout, "Come on, Gracie, I will help you for now!"

Gracie got up, took her dishes to the kitchen, came back, gave me a hug, and ran to join the boys with her new journal and new pencil.

"Well, I don't care to write down anything about my day, why that seems silly," Frank said, because Frank always had something to say.

"Why, Frank, of all people, your stories should be written down. They are interesting and I love listening to you. You make me laugh," I said.

"Thanks, maybe I'll give it a try," Frank said.

"I want a journal, Faith," Molly said, pouring us coffee.

"I have the perfect one for you, Molly; it has flowers on the front." I gave her a wink and smiled. "I'll get you one too, Frank," I said.

"I remember those journals. Mom and Dad wrote in theirs each night before they went to bed. I wonder now what they wrote about. Not to say Mom and Dad were boring, but let's face it, they kept things simple and easy," Sam said.

"Oh, I bet there could be some interesting things written. I know I would like to read Mom's someday. I wonder where they are." I asked.

The next morning, Sam would take the boys fishing for pike along the shore. Molly, Gracie, and I put on our summer dresses and made our way to church. We went to the church my parents would go to when vacationing here, so as soon as we entered the front of the church, Esther would greet us.

"Well, look who's here. Frank told me in the general store yesterday that the Bakkers were up here," Esther shouted, as she walked her way through the crowd.

Molly rolled her eyes, and I whispered, "Be nice."

"Hi, Esther. It's Sutton now, as you know," I said, because she knew Chris as well.

"Look here, why Gracie, you are growing up fast. Last time I saw you, your mom was holding onto you the whole time," Esther said, as she gave Gracie a pink peppermint.

"Thanks, nice lady, and my mother still tries to hold me," Gracie would tell Esther as we all laughed.

"Now, is this the young lady Frank told me about? I am so sorry to hear of your loss," Esther said, as she took Molly's hand and patted it.

I was thinking, boy oh boy, that Frank doesn't let any information stay with him. I hope he will start writing and less talking.

"Yes, Esther, this is my best friend, Molly. I know you have met her before. She was up here with the family once or twice," I said, as to save Molly from explaining her loss.

"Why, if I think hard enough I bet I could recall. Well, it's so nice to see you all in church this morning. I heard your dad will be up come Friday, Faith. Tell him I will be bringing him a fruit pie," Esther said. Then as she looked another direction she said, "You will have to excuse me, there's Mrs. Schepler, and I want to chew her ear. She has a new recipe I've wanted to try. Tell Sam to come see me, I know he's up here, too," Esther said, as she turned and waddled toward the lady. Esther was a big lady, and I'm sure that recipe continued something sweet. But you couldn't help but love Esther, for she carried a big heart and loved everyone.

Molly was here for a reason. She wanted to thank God for the gift she received yesterday. Although I was a thank-you-God-every-day kind of girl, and did so in the night before I would wonder into sleep, just as a child, I felt closest to God when I was alone in his presence. Molly told me she needed to be able to be in a home built for God to feel closest to God. She'd tell me it was going to church each week that would refuel her faith and love. So here we were among a group of people hearing the word, giving thanks, praying, and refueling.

Back at the cottage, the boys wrote about the Northern Pike they caught and released with Uncle Sam. Gracie would have me write about the Osprey that would perch in the high tree by us and watch for a fish to scoop up and carry away. She had a grand list of bird species before the day was done.

More Conversations

That Tuesday evening, Sam and I went to the local pub and restaurant to have a few beers and talk before Molly and I would leave out with the children the next morning. As we sat down, Sam said, "I am getting me a big juicy steak to go with my beer. Don't get me wrong, Faith, I love Molly, but I can only go so long eating all that vegetable stuff. At least she allows fish to be eaten among her," he said, and smiled as the waitress handed him and I a menu.

"Oh, it's not that bad, but I do feel for the boys now, because Mark would be the one to make them Hamburg's, bake pork chops, and chicken—who lives without chicken?!" I looked at the waitress and said, "I'll take any kind of light beer, don't matter, you pick, and I will have myself a Hamburg with everything but mustard, and French fries." I gave my menu back with a smile.

As Sam gave back his menu, he said, "As for me, I want a regular Budweiser and the prime rib with a baked potato, no vegetable, no salad. Thank you."

"Thank you," the waitress said. "I'll be back with your beers." She smiled at Sam.

"So speaking of Molly, is she going to be okay? She sounds good," Sam said.

"Yes, I think it will take some time, but she has faith. She was a complete wreck a week or so back," I said, shaking my head of the hair that I had grown back to my shoulders once more. It had turned dark blonde after Gracie was born, so I got it highlighted now and then.

"I can imagine. I still can't believe what happened. I really liked Mark, he was a good shit, and those boys are great. So well-behaved, polite, just nice to be around," Sam said, as he took a drink of his beer, shaking his head.

"How's Chris? Why didn't he come up?" Sam asked.

"He's fine, I guess, and I didn't ask him," I replied.

"You guess? What's up with that? Are you two fine?" Sam asked, taking in more beer.

"Yeah, we are fine. I just think Chris just wishes I was more dependent on him, like his damsel in distress sometimes. But, you know me, always have done my own thing. I do love and appreciate him. He makes a damn good living; I never want for anything, and he's a good father to Gracie. I wish I could give him more children. I know he would love more kids."

"Well, have some then, silly."

"We are trying; it's just not happening."

I went to the restroom, and then we were quiet when I sat back down. I guess we both were thinking when the waitress brought our plates of food. I then bowed my head for a short word of thanks. As I looked up, Sam had already taken a bite of his meat.

"Sorry, Faith, sometimes I forget what I have been taught," Sam said chewing.

"No problem, Sam, I don't judge," I smiled. Then I asked the questions, "How about you, Sam? You break up with Jessica after what? Four or more years. I thought she was the one and now you aren't with—what's her name—Jill? I can't believe there are any more single girls you haven't dated left in the Metro area." I laughed, but was serious.

"I know, I know, as soon as they start nesting, I get restless. It's me, not them. I have issues with settling down," Sam said.

"You think?!" I said, putting a fry in my mouth.

"But I am here to make changes. I am thirty-eight years old, never been married, no children, I know it's time. That's one of the reasons I want to talk to Dad and Will," Sam said, putting a piece of meat in his mouth. "Oh! This is good. Yum yum!" Sam waved his hand for the waitress to bring us each another beer.

"Sam, what do you think makes you fear being with someone for longer than a few years? Why, you have to know you break hearts, and that's not nice," I said with concern.

"Mom explained it to me on one of our talks before she passed. Now, you know I can get emotional when I talk about Mom, but she always made sense of things. She would bring me back to the time when Molly got hurt. Nobody knew it but Mom. Faith, I was so very upset that someone could hurt our Molly. I remember sitting up in the bed Mom made for me in the den because Pauly would take my bed so he wouldn't be alone. I would cry and beg God to make Molly okay. Mom would come in and try to comfort me, but I would tell Mom that I would never forgive someone like that man who hurt Molly. I told Mom I was to never love anyone more than who I love right now at that moment, because it hurts if you lose them, just like when Grandma Mary died," Sam said.

"But Sam, that's crazy! How about your nephews and nieces, I know you love them," I said.

"That's just it, I can, and do love others, but Mom would tell me that I want complete control of my love so I won't be hurt. She said I hold animosity for things I have no control over, like when Molly got hurt," he said, as he opened his wallet to produce the picture of him and Molly at Cedar Point. He took it out and handed it to me.

"Mom gave me this picture on that last talk I had with her," Sam said, as a tear started to fall. "She told me to look at it whenever I was sad about love and be reminded that all my prayers to God were answered when Molly was healed. That here I stood, with Molly, on a happy day and she then said, she wanted me to be happy." Sam wiped his tears on his napkin, took back the picture, and put it back safe in his wallet.

"Sam, I never knew this, but you are in love with Molly, aren't you?" I asked with a look of shock.

"Always have been," Sam said with another drink of beer.

"Mom knew it, didn't she? That's why the picture. Sam, what are you going to do? You can't just step in and take over for Mark. I mean, I know Molly loves you, but not in that way! Oh, Sam, how could I have not known this?" I said, pushing my plate away as not to eat another fry.

"Don't worry, Faith, I'm not going to sweep Molly away. But like I told her last night at the campfire, I wanted to help with the boys. I love those boys, Faith. We have already set up a day this fall for a football game in Detroit. I just want to be Molly's friend like I have always been. Time will have to be our friend. Molly will need time to heal," Sam said. Then he added, "You do know I didn't know Molly was going to be up here until I had already asked Dad and Will to meet me here. Now that's fate, don't you think?"

"What is it you wanted to ask Dad and Will about anyways?" I asked.

"I am thinking about retiring as a commercial pilot," Sam said.

"What? I am so confused right now, you love flying!"

"I don't want to give up flying. I am thinking just flying smaller aircraft. They want to transfer me to Boston, and I just don't feel right about it. I have wanted to get a job up North here for a while now. With Dad going to retire up here soon, and Will and Susan in Cheboygan, I would have family around," Sam said.

"What about me? What am I, chopped liver?" I asked, kind of snippy.

"I bet I'll see more of you when I move up here than I do now," Sam said with a big smile.

"Probably, I do know the time will come when Dad will move here. I am just going to miss him, and selling the house will be sad," I said.

"It's just a house, Faith. We can't sell our memories, and it's time a new family will bring new life. It needs it, hasn't been the same without Mom," Sam said. "Do you want another beer?"

"No, no, two's my limit," I said, and then we both finished our meals.

"Are you happy, Faith?"

"What kind of question is that? Of course, I am." Then I said, "Are you, Sam? Are you happy?"

"For the most part, I'm grateful," he said, as he grabbed up the check and opened his wallet again. He threw a five and some ones down for the tip. "You know, Dad always has said, 'When you seek happiness, you will find it within," Sam said.

"And Mom always said, bring your love to each new day," I said, and I knew we both were thinking how blessed we were to have the parents we had.

"Let's go watch that sunset with Molly and the kids," he said as we both got up.

"Let's!" I said, as I looked at my dear, sweet brother, and he winked at me. At that very moment, he looked more like our Dad than at any other time; he even had the little bit of gray at his temples, as Dad had at his age.

Leaving the island is always bittersweet. There is something in me that wants to hold me here. It tugs at my heart telling me I belong. Maybe because I always feel hope when I'm here. The hope for a better world. A world where everyone could live on an island in peace with nature, as the sun, moon, and stars looked over them. The waters and land bringing them nourishment, and the only thing they would have to do is love and accept each other for who they were made to be. Human.

Epilogue

As the days turn into weeks, the weeks to months, followed by the years, I would have to look back at my journals to figure out how this happens. Dad retired to the cottage in 1999, and our family home would be sold to a young family with children to fill its walls with laughter, tears, and memories. I walked amongst Mama's flower haven for the last time, taking everything in; forgiving time, falling to the ground with tears as I said good-bye to Lady, and Buddy, who was buried next to Lady just after our trip to the island in '94.

Then the year 2000 would bring the wedding of my best friend Molly and Brother Sam. Molly told me how she felt Mark was happy for her. That it was okay to love again. It taught their boys that God doesn't want you to give up on love, ever.

Molly had taken steps to complete forgiveness, as she visited the man that killed Mark. She was in her own prison, a one of hate. But by learning who this man was, and how years of abuse from people who are to love you can destroy you, she said she can no longer blame God for creating this human being. But, maybe, she now blames many humans for letting him grow up with abuse. Sometimes, we all are to blame for not stopping something until it's too late.

She told me my dad was right; forgiving that man of what he had done was the hardest thing she has done. But it was her healing that would come from doing so, and that no one would understand unless they have faced this fear head on. That looking into the eyes of someone who hates and someone you feel hate for. Telling them you forgive them, and will pray for their healing, doesn't mean you no longer hurt; it just means you can allow the rainbow to come after the storm.

As Molly and Mark's boys, then fifteen and seventeen, would proudly walk their mother down the aisle to Sam, I would witness happy again. I secretly told Molly after the wedding, "So I see, Mrs. Sam Bakker that my brother Sam has finally gotten it right."

As she rolled her eyes and we hugged, she'd say in my ear, "I am happy, Faith. God is good to us."

Sam, Molly, and the boys live in Petoskey, Michigan. As Sam acquired a job at the airport there in 1996, Molly was to start a job at an elementary school that fall. The boys were now men, good men.

Will and Susan would see their son, Miles, who would go in the military to serve after high school. After which he came home and married his high school sweetheart, Emily, in 2001. They now live in a little town south of the Mackinaw Bridge where Miles has a fishing charter business, and two children.

Star Anne designs and makes wedding dresses, and Sky Lee works in a florist shop in Cheboygan.

Uncle Sam and Aunt Sara live in the same house, enjoying retirement with grown grandchildren, and now great grandchildren. John Walters and his wife Melinda had six children, and I think how Uncle Sam may have had love taken from him early on, but would be blessed with much more.

As for Chris and I, we would have a rocky marriage. For years we would just ride the waves, drifting apart slowly, not realizing that the distance between us had become overwhelming. I had started working in a doctor's office that year that Gracie was in school all day. We were never blessed with more children. I don't think that was to hurt us. As my dear, sweet Celia would tell me, "Faith, receiving a child is a gift. It's not given to complete you or your partner. It's God giving us a fresh start, giving a new love, trusting us with a very important gift of love. If only we all knew how to care for this gift . . ." she would shake her head.

I tried to visit her often at her much younger sister's home where she now lived. Ms. Celia is going to turn 100 in the year 2014. She would call me her granddaughter, and Gracie called her great-grandmother. Love has no color.

Christopher had a different faith than I, but that wasn't what was different about us. What I have come to know is some people grow up spiritually, and some people just grow up. The year Gracie was to graduate high school in 2008 was also a time that I would come to a new pain. Not so much a loss, but more a pain of failure.

Gracie was to leave to Iowa the week after graduation to stay with Mary Hope, who was now a pediatrician. Gracie was struggling with what she wanted to do next, her next chapter.

Chris would once more come home late. This time, he would bring me a very big bouquet of fresh flowers. Happy to put them in one of Mom's old vases, then I would set them on a living room table. Chris told me to sit, that he had something to tell me. I was blindsided. It hit like a train, his words foggy, as he told me he wasn't happy and hadn't been for a long time. That he was moving out with Stacy, a young girl from his office.

I found my words harass and full of hate as I stood and yelled, "Does happy come in a younger girl?! What about Gracie? How could you do this to us?" I cried.

He answered, "I'm not doing this to Gracie, or to you! I am doing this to me!" He also cried, and I knew he was with pain as he got up and moved to our bedroom and started packing a suitcase.

I tried to calm myself, come into the presence, and soon I was helping him pack like an old friend would do. Somehow, I would think about what Mom had said to me about Dad putting his hurt and anger through God first. I asked, "Why the flowers, Chris?"

He looked me right in the eyes and said with tears, "I have no idea, Faith. I just got this gut feeling I was to buy you the biggest, pretties bouquet of flowers money could buy." He shook his head and said, "I can't explain it," as he threw his dress socks into a bag.

When he left that night, he told me he would tell Gracie. "I love you, Faith, and always will. Please forgive me," as he shut the door behind him.

I sat in a rocking chair that my dad had made me the year Grace Christine May was born. Rocking and staring at the flowers, each bloom different, but I would recognize each as one of my mom's favorites. It hit me as I cried with the deep love of Mama coming through loud and clear. Mama was the gut feeling in Chris that night. She wanted me to have these flowers. She was letting me know that I would be okay. This love is gone; it has changed form. Forgive this and live as God has intended us to.

I did forgive Chris and myself also as I was just as responsible for the dissolution of our marriage. It has taken some time, as I would allow myself to sit in my pain each morning, and give it to God. As I sat with God, I realized that our stories are not only controlled by one's self. Others play important parts in your story, and they can leave your story at any time. Be it by death, by foot or adrift. Others will come and go, human love changes, taking on different forms, different meanings.

I would once again think of Grandma Mary, how just a few years of her love would have much influence on my early years. How important that love was.

Christopher's love was also important, and I would grieve the loss of it, but I would give thanks to it every day. His leaving would wake me up to the fact that my story was becoming dull, sluggish. One could see it in the clothes I was wearing, the weight I was gaining. I started to care for myself again. Taking on cooking healthy, exercising, reading, and new clothes was big for me. Why, I could remember what I wore at eight months, but couldn't tell you what I had on yesterday. It was time for change.

Things are good this year. Chris and I are friends, and Gracie is happy working now at a bird sanctuary in Augusta, Michigan. She would text me to tell me, "Enjoy your trip to Drummond Island, Mother. Tell Grandpa I send my love. Love, Gracie."

Yes, this August, I would take a few weeks off from work and visit my first love, my dad. We would awake early to do what come natural to us: fish. I made sandwiches, and Dad made coffee.

"Don't forget the crawlers, Dad," I would say, as I walked down to the dock with my hands full.

"Thanks, Faith, I need reminders lately," he laughed.

I gave thanks for Dad's health at eighty. He was still strong, and his mind was sharp. He and Frank would look out for each other as old friends do. Esther, who had passed, had a daughter and son-in-law who often came and checked on Dad. They would drop by for coffee and chat.

I wasn't to worry about Dad, with Will and Susan close, and Sam and Molly to visit here often. As my Border Collie named Hope, who I acquired the summer Chris left me, now jumped into the boat to go with us, I told her, "Not today, girl. It's going to get hot; go to the house and lay in the shade." She jumped back out and gave me puppy dog eyes.

"Don't even make me feel bad," I laughed.

As Hope went back up towards the cottage, Dad came down smiling. "It's going to be a good day," he said.

I drove the boat to the middle grounds and got ready to troll. I watched my dad's now worn, thin hands put a crawler on a hook, as he did so many years ago, and tears filled my eyes.

"What's wrong, Faith?" Dad asked.

"Nothing, Dad. That's just it, there is absolutely nothing wrong right now," I smiled, wiping my wet eyes on my bare arm.

We both saw the bald eagle flying in the distance. We said nothing, because we both knew it was Mom, sending her love.

"You're right, what could be wrong when Faith and I are fishing?" Dad said with a wink and a smile, as he cast his fishing line out.

I thought to myself, *It's never been about the fishing.* What I have learned is, it's all about the love for each new day.